CAST OF CHA

Lady Lupin Hastings. Not your average c as she is scatterbrained. But not much esc:

The Rev. Andrew Hastings. Lady Lupin's handsome, older husband, who adores her as much as she does him.

Penelope Stevenson. A lovely, tragic figure who lives her life at second hand, having sacrificed everything for her family.

Dick Stevenson. Penelope's younger brother, who adores her.

Betty Stevenson. "Mrs. Dick," hand-selected for him by Penelope.

Richard Stevenson. A widower, and father to Dick and Penelope.

The Rev. and Mrs. Lancelot Baker. The local vicar and his wife. A hearty sort, he admires Penelope greatly. His wife does not.

Sir Henry and Lady Deering. Old family friends of the Stevensons. They lost their elder son, Henry, in the war.

Agnes Deering. Their daughter-in-law, Henry's widow.

Bob Deering. Their younger son, who worships Penelope.

Col. Charles Graeme. Penelope turned down her chance for great happiness with him, but he has never stopped loving her.

Mrs. Dashwood. A sensible, charming older woman known as "Auntie Boots." She once thought she might marry Penelope's father.

Dorothy Piper. Housemaid at the Limes, who worships Penelope.

Alice Martin. Parlormaid at the Limes, who detests Penelope.

Geraldine and Elaine. Two disagreeable cousins, mother and daughter.

Mr. Borden. A private detective. By now he's accustomed to the way Lupin's mind works and finds her insights extremely useful.

Plus assorted police officers, doctors, nurses, servants and relatives.

Books by Joan Coggin

The Lady Lupin Quartet

Who Killed the Curate? (1944)
The Mystery of Orchard House (1946)
Why Did She Die? (1947)
(U.S. title: *Penelope Passes or Why Did She Die?*)
Dancing with Death (1947)

Girls' Books

Betty of Turner House (1935)
Catherine Goes to School (1945)
Jane Runs Away from School (1946)
Catherine, Head of House (1947)
Audrey, a New Girl (1948)
Three New Girls (1949)

Penelope Passes

or

Why Did She Die?

by
Joan Coggin

Rue Morgue Press
Boulder / Lyons

Penelope Passes or Why Did She Die?

FIRST AMERICAN EDITION

ISBN: 0-915230-61-5

The editors thank William F. Deeck
and Katherine Hall Page
for bringing the Lady Lupin
mysteries to their attention.

PRINTED IN THE UNITED STATES OF AMERICA

About Joan Coggin

In *Who Killed the Curate?* (1944), we were introduced to the lovely Lady Lupin Lorrimer, a 21-year-old earl's daughter who unexpectedly married 43-year-old Andrew Hastings, vicar of St. Mark's parish in Glanville in Sussex. Totally unprepared for the duties incumbent upon a clergyman's wife (she often confused Jews with Jesuits), somehow Lupin managed to soldier on, gladly abandoning her previous life of parties and indolence to be with her soulmate. As scatterbrained as she was, Lupin's tender heart and genuine concern for others won over even those parishioners who thought her too young and too pretty to be a vicar's wife, and her unconventional thought processes still pointed the way to identifying the murderer in this debut mystery.

The Mystery of Orchard House (1946) takes up her story over two years later, again in some indefinite period shortly before World War II. Lupin now has a two-year-old son, Peter, but a recent bout of influenza has forced her to leave him in the care of her husband and her old nanny while she takes a rest cure in the country at the hotel run by her good friend Diana Turner, a children's book writer. There's little rest in store for her, unfortunately, and once again Lupin's peculiar talent for getting at the truth, however circuitous a route she might take, comes in handy when the eccentric guests at Orchard House are plagued by a series of thefts and an attempted murder.

The final two books in the series, *Why Did She Die?* (1947)—reprinted here as *Penelope Passes or Why Did She Die?*—and *Dancing with Death* (1947) are set just after World War II. The first and fourth are the more clearly identifiable as traditional detective stories, although all four fit comfortably in the genre. All were originally published by Hurst & Blackett, a relatively obscure and long-since defunct London publishing house, in what must have been fiendishly small print runs, as they are extraordinarily difficult to find on the used-book market. None was ever published in the United States. *Why Did She Die?* appears to have been written and published in a great hurry, since the original book is filled with typos and two of the characters are given more than one name.

In addition to her four mysteries, Coggin, using the pseudonym Joanna Lloyd, wrote six girls' books set at the imaginary Shaftesbury School and based on Coggin's own school years at Wycombe Abbey. These stories are as charmingly told as Coggin's mysteries, and indeed the young Catherine, who figures in several of these books, bears a remarkable resemblance to Lady Lupin, although unlike Lupin, there's no doubt that Catherine has a first-class mind..

Born in Lemsford, Hertfordshire, in 1898, Coggin was the granddaughter on her mother's side of Edward Lloyd, founder of *Lloyd's Weekly London Newspaper*, which no doubt is why she used Lloyd as a pseudonym for her schoolgirl books. Her mother died when Coggin was eight and the family moved to Eastbourne, one of the easternmost towns in Britain, where she was to make her home for the rest of her life and which was clearly the model for Glanville.

After she was graduated from Wycombe Abbey in 1916 in the middle of World War I, Coggin worked as a nurse at an Eastbourne hospital. Although she suffered from a mild form of epilepsy, Coggin did not let it inhibit her lifestyle. After the war, she returned to those activities expected of a young woman of her class and upbringing—the social round of bridge, tennis, golf and books. She also worked with the blind.

In the 1930s, she turned to writing, producing her first girls' book, *Betty of Turner House*, in 1935. With the exception of that book Coggin's writing career was limited to a five-year period between 1944 and 1949, during which she produced nine books. For the last thirty years of her life she apparently did no more writing. She died in 1980 at the age of 82.

Her contribution to crime fiction was slight but memorable. Lupin, probably the first clergyman's wife to take up crime-solving as a hobby, may remind readers of Gracie Allen of Burns and Allen. She's certainly the spiritual godmother of the Pauline Collins character in the very funny BBC comedy series *No, Honestly* from a few years ago. The Collins character came many years later, of course, and although Coggin may well have been familiar with Gracie Allen's routines, there is little doubt that Lady Lupin sprang fullblown from Coggin's own imagination. She's that rarity in cozy crime fiction—in spite of her many eccentricities she seems more real than most of the people we encounter in real life. Or maybe that's just wishful thinking.

Tom & Enid Schantz
Boulder, Colorado

[From without is heard the voice of
PIPPA, singing—

The year's at the spring
And day's at the morn;
Morning's at seven;
The hill-side's dew-pearled;
The lark's on the wing;
The snail's on the thorn;
God's in his heaven—
All's right with the world!

[PIPPA passes.

The above passage (quoted fondly but quite inaccurately by Lady Lupin) is taken from Robert Browning's 1841 poetic drama, *Pippa Passes*. Late in the gestation of this edition the editors decided that it was the title Joan Coggin would have used for this book had she given it more thought. She certainly laid the groundwork. We know this will cause problems for bibliographers in the future but we can no longer think of this book without referring to it as

Penelope Passes

CHAPTER 1

"MY DEAR, I don't know when I've been so glad to see anyone," said Betty Stevenson, as she greeted her sister-in-law, Penelope. "I am simply terrified."

"It is rather an ordeal, I know. I wish I could have taken them on, but I simply daren't risk upsetting Daddy. If he is agitated it upsets his digestion and then that is likely to upset his heart."

"Oh, naturally you couldn't have them," exclaimed her brother Dick. "But why couldn't the Bakers? After all, they are their pigeons."

"Mrs. Baker said they had no maid, and not much hot water, and that last time they had a visitor she fused the light in the spare room and they had never had it put right."

"I would have gone over and mended the fuse," said Dick.

"I would gladly have gone round and made the beds," added Betty.

"And I could have run in with some hot water in cans," said Penelope.

"Nothing would have been too much trouble," said Dick magnanimously.

"I only hope it won't affect my baby," said Betty.

"If it's a boy it will be a clergyman," groaned Dick.

"And if it's a girl it will be a lady," added his sister.

"And if it's twins, it will be both. I mean one of each," said Betty.

"Well, we are in for it now," said Dick. "That is the worst of living in the country. Things like this don't happen in London."

"I am quite good with clergymen," said Penelope. "But it is no use pretending that I am much good with their wives."

"I shouldn't mind an ordinary wife," said Betty, "but Lady Lupin does sound so very formidable."

"She'll have a face like a horse," said Dick, "and talk about huntin' and shootin' all the time."

"Or she may have turned her attention to good works now she has married a clergyman."

"I expect when she got a bit long in the tooth," added Dick, "she decided to marry the curate and now spends her time huntin' sinners instead of foxes."

"What shall we talk about all the time?"

"Oh, she'll do the talking," said Penelope encouragingly. "We needn't worry about that. We need only listen politely."

"I am glad Bob is coming, because, at any rate, he knows about hunting and that sort of thing."

"You went out three times yourself last winter," pointed out his wife.

"I know, but I was terrified all the time—of doing something wrong, I mean."

"I thought you meant of falling off," said his wife.

"I was terrified of that, too. By the way, it's called 'taking a toss.' "

"Do let's have a drink while we can," implored Betty. "We won't be able to when we've got the Rev. and Lady staying with us."

"Baker likes a glass of beer," said Dick hopefully. "At least, I don't know if he likes it or not, but he comes into the Golden Stirrup and has a glass sometimes, and is 'great chaps together' with everyone."

"There are three kinds of clergymen," explained Penelope. "High, Low and Hearty. Mr. Baker is the hearty type who drinks beer with the working man, but the low church kind are usually teetotallers."

"What about the high?"

"Oh, they are usually knowledgeable about wine. They are allowed to drink, even on fast days, I believe."

"Well, I hope this one will be high, then."

"I don't think he will. Lady Lupin sounds evangelical to me. I'm sure she would think ritual bad form, like shooting a fox."

"My dear, you are wonderful," sighed Betty, bringing her a gin-and-French. "I should never have known all that. I know, of course, that high church means candles and low church the ten commandments, but I should never have guessed which drank and which didn't. But how does one tell at first sight—I mean, whether to proffer lemonade or a cocktail?"

"I can usually tell when I am introduced—it is something to do with the way they shake hands, and their voices are quite distinctive."

Mr. Baker, the vicar of Much Lancing, had elected to ask the Rev. Andrew Hastings to preach for him on Trinity Sunday, and his wife had asked Penelope Stevenson, of the Limes, to put up him and his wife for the weekend. As she was rather afraid of the effect the visit might have on her old father, Penelope had asked her sister-in-law, who lived in a small house in the village, if she would undertake the entertainment of these rather fearsome guests, but she had promised to dine with them to help make things easier, and in the end she had accepted Betty's pressing invitation to sleep at Limes Cottage. Betty kept a room for her there, as she knew it did her good to get right out of her own house occasionally and to feel that she could sleep securely without any likelihood of being disturbed. Penelope hated leaving her father even for a night, but Alice, the parlormaid, was very reliable and, as Dick and Betty pointed out, she owed it to her father to have a rest every now and then, as it would be far worse for him if she were to break down.

"Will you have a rest before dinner, Pen?" asked Betty. "I'm sure you're tired."

"I'm not really, but I think I should like to have a little rest, so as to be fresh for the clergy and aristocracy."

Betty took her up to her room. It was small but very charming, with a western window through which the sun was shining on a bowl of roses. It was a relief to feel that Penelope would be with them during this ordeal. She was always such a standby, but she did look dreadfully tired. Betty glanced at the table by the bed—biscuits, cigarettes, matches, ashtray, they were all there, and a couple of new novels. She loved making Penelope comfortable, for she had a hard life at home. Betty looked at the purple shadows under her eyes and at the white streak in her dark hair and wished that Penelope could live with her and Dick all the time and that they could make up to her a bit for all she had gone through. Not that she wished any harm to Mr. Stevenson. He was really a sweet old man, only just a little bit selfish, like all old people. He did not mean it, she was sure. He had always been charming to her, but he did lead Pen rather a life. There had been a man whom she had loved and whom she had given up for her father's sake. Underneath all her laughter and amusing conversation, Betty always felt the underlying note of sadness. Sorrow had made her very understanding, and Betty felt that there was nothing that she could not say to her. She gave her a hug before she left her and Penelope said, "You are a darling, Betty. It is like heaven coming here and being spoiled."

Betty sighed as she walked downstairs. It seemed such a shame that Penelope was not always spoiled. They had met first during the war when Betty had been stationed at an A.T.S. camp not very far from Much Lancing. Once, when she had missed the last omnibus home, Penelope, who drove for the W.V.S., had given her a lift. They had become friendly at once and Penelope had asked Betty to come over to the Limes whenever she liked. That was how she had met Dick. It had all been like a fairy tale, because so often when people were married, they had to get to know their in-laws afterward, and very likely did not get on any too well with them, but Betty was marrying the brother of her greatest friend. Penelope was ten years older than Dick and had always been more like a mother than a sister to him, but, far from being jealous, she was delighted to welcome Betty into the family, and they were all three ideally happy together.

Dick, an electrical engineer, was soon demobilized after the war and went back to his old job. He and Betty took a flat in London and had the most wonderful time. They were just like a couple of children playing at housekeeping. Everything was fun. Betty quite enjoyed standing in queues, as it made her feel so grown-up and like a real housewife. She loved talking to the other women about her husband and whether he preferred cod or haddock. How she and Dick laughed in the evenings when she told him about her experiences, while they cooked their supper together and ate it at the kitchen table.

Then Limes Cottage had fallen vacant and Penelope had written to suggest that they should come and live in it. It would be just as easy for Dick to get to his work, as the factory was on the road between London and Much Lancing, and he would not be any further from it than he was in Kensington. Betty was rather sorry to leave the flat, but the country would be lovely, and it would be nice for Dick if he could get some hunting and shooting at the weekends. She was sure they would be just as happy in the cottage as in the flat, and there would be Penelope, too. Dick liked the idea, as it would be so nice for Betty to have Penelope with whom to run round while he was at work, and it would be equally nice for Penelope to have them both there. It would make her less lonely, and they would be able to share the responsibility of Mr. Stevenson with her.

They had been there for nine months now and had been very happy. Penelope had had the cottage all ready for them and had engaged a nice maid. Betty sometimes looked back regretfully to the days at the flat and the meals in the kitchen. But, of course, it was nice to have a maid, and it was nice to have Penelope to help with the housekeeping, since she was so good at it and she knew so well what Dick liked and what he didn't like. For instance, Betty had never known that he didn't like liver and had often given it to him in London and he had pretended to enjoy it, but now she knew what things to avoid and what things to give him. To crown everything she was expecting her first baby in November, so the world appeared to her a very delightful place, in spite of having to entertain a clergyman and an earl's daughter.

"Which clergyman do we ask to say grace?" she said, as she walked into the sitting room.

"What?" asked Dick, who was doing the crossword puzzle in the *Daily Telegraph.*

"Well, there will be two clergymen at dinner, and we must ask one of them to say grace."

"Can't they say it together as a duet?" suggested Dick.

Betty giggled. "I wish I'd asked Pen. I'll have to whisper it to her as she comes in, and it will be so awkward."

"I'd ask the home side to do it," said Dick.

"All right," replied Betty doubtfully, "if you don't think it would be a compliment to the visiting team. Oh, there's their car. Do you think we should go to the door and say, 'Welcome to our humble home,' or sit in state while they are announced?"

"As Annie will probably leave them standing on the doorstep while she comes to tell us they are there, I should think it would be better to go ourselves."

"I wish Pen were with us. I shouldn't feel so frightened."

"Cheer up, the rest will do her good. I thought she looked a bit done up."

"I know, poor darling! Come on, I'm perspiring from every pore, but we can't very well back out now."

"Ditto," and they walked to the front door just as a small car drove up.

"It's not them after all," thought Betty as a pretty girl got out of the car, and she felt rather as she had done when she had thought she was killed by a bomb and had climbed out from under the debris, feeling that she would have to go through it all over again.

The girl had no hat and the sun shone on her golden hair. She beamed at Betty. "Mrs. Stevenson?" she asked, surprised at finding her hostess so young and charming. People who put up clergymen and their wives were often so quiet and dull, even if they weren't terrifying. "It is good of you to have me as well as Andrew," she went on, as Betty nodded and held out her hand.

Could this really be Lady Lupin? The man following her was certainly a clergyman, as he had on a round collar. He was middle-aged, but very good-looking, with attractively grizzled hair. "I wonder if he is high or low?" wondered Betty. "I'm sure he's not hearty, he's not at all like Mr. Baker." Pen would have been able to tell at once which he was by his voice, but then she was so awfully clever. "Would you like a glass of sherry?" she asked Lupin diffidently as they walked in together, leaving Dick and the clergyman to bring the luggage. After all, there was something very respectable about sherry, and even a low church clergyman's wife couldn't be very shocked at being offered it, not that Lady Lupin looked like a clergyman's wife at all—high, low or medium.

"I'd love some. What a gorgeous place this is!"

"It is rather nice, isn't it? I say, I suppose you wouldn't rather have a gin-and-French ?"

"Well, I think I should, really, if you are sure you have plenty of gin."

"It is nice occasionally being able to offer people a drink again, isn't it? I am afraid I didn't often when it was so frightfully short."

"Nor did I. If ever I got hold of a bottle of whisky or gin I locked all the doors and put up the blackout. Of course, Andrew wanted to share it with others. He is so good—it comes from being a clergyman, I suppose—so I just used to give him a glass at a time and never let him know there was a bottle in the house."

"He isn't low church, then?"

"No, I don't think so. Did you think he would be?"

"Well, my sister-in-law said if you were low church you would be teetotallers."

"And you hoped we should be, so that you could save your gin. How too sickening for you! Hullo, Andrew, Mrs. Stevenson was hoping we should be low church, so that she wouldn't have to give us gin. Isn't it a nuisance for her?"

CHAPTER 2

BOB DEERING was the first of the guests to arrive. He was a young man of about twenty-eight or nine and had been a close friend of Dick's all his life. They had fallen out of the same apple tree and been chased by the same farmer when they were boys. They had seen very little of each other during the war years, as Dick had been in the army and Bob on a minesweeper. But since their demobilization they had picked up their old friendship where they had left it, and he was a constant visitor at Limes Cottage and indeed at the Limes itself, for his father and mother were very intimate with Mr. Stevenson and Penelope. As for the latter, Bob thought she was the most wonderful woman who had ever lived. He had admired her ever since he could remember. She was ten years older than he and Dick, and he had always put her on a pedestal—she was so beautiful and so unselfish. He looked at her now as she sat in an armchair in Betty's little sitting room. Lady Lupin Hastings was an exceptionally pretty woman and Betty was very attractive with her schoolgirl complexion, happy expression and bright brown eyes, but to Bob, Penelope was as far superior to them both in looks as they were to Mrs. Baker, the Vicar's wife, who entered the room soon after him.

She was a small anxious woman who thought her husband was the most wonderful person in the world, and who had an unfortunate habit of coming out with the wrong remark on most occasions. "It is good of you," she said fervently to Betty, as she hurried into the room several paces ahead of Annie, the maid, who was trying to announce her. "I simply don't know how to thank you."

This extreme thankfulness for not having to entertain the Hastings was not calculated to put anyone at their ease, and while Betty racked her brain for a tactful answer, she avoided Bob's eye. But Mrs. Baker was seldom silent for long enough to allow of any answer, let alone a tactful one. She now turned to Penelope. "It was good of you to persuade your sister-in-law to help us out," she said. "Of course I realized it would be quite impossible for you with your poor father."

"This is Lady Lupin Hastings, Mrs. Baker," said Betty desperately, remembering too late that she should have introduced them the other way round. Still, she felt sure Lupin wouldn't mind.

"Oh, how do you do?" said Mrs. Baker. "I was just saying how sorry I was I couldn't ask you and your husband to stay with us, but I really have no help now except a Mrs. Jones, whose husband drinks, so I am sure you will understand."

"Absolutely," replied Lupin, "and I do think it was nice of your husband to ask mine to preach and to persuade Mrs. Stevenson to have us both to stay."

"Oh, she really needed no persuading, she is always so good-natured. I'll never forget how good she was when one of the Sunday school children was sick—their mothers will give them sweets and oranges at odd times, you know, so what can you expect ? Of course it was the Harvest Festival, so I grant that the atmosphere was a little overpowering; fruit and vegetables, you know, and not always as fresh as they might be. But it made it specially awkward as the bishop was preaching."

"Things always do seem to happen when bishops are preaching, don't they?" agreed Lupin sympathetically. "It was too awful the first time my Peter saw ours in his mitre—he burst into shrieks of laughter."

"I don't see any harm in a mitre," said Mrs. Baker, "but then, my husband is very broadminded."

Lupin found herself sitting between Dick and Bob at dinner, and she found them both congenial companions, but their conversation was slightly disjointed, as Mr. Baker had a habit of taking the whole of the dinner-table into his confidence, and the others had to stop their own conversations in order to laugh in the right places. He was telling Penelope about what fun he had had the night before at the darts match in the 'local,' and every now and then he collected the eyes of the rest of the party before coming out with one of his more witty remarks. Lupin and Bob had been talking about a play that they had both enjoyed and joined in the laughter a shade too late, so, anxious to make up for lost time they roared loudly, only to find that now they had left the 'local' and that all the chaps had gone into church for a short service, then hurriedly composed their faces, and Lupin came out with a sympathetic murmur just as they were all returning to the public house for one more 'swig of beer.' Mrs. Baker seldom took her bright eyes off her husband's face. She led the laughter and intimated with a sigh the moment when fun left off and seriousness crept in.

In spite of the Bakers, Lupin was enjoying herself. As a matter of fact she always did enjoy herself if it were in any way possible to do so. She had taken a great fancy to Dick and Betty at first sight, they were so cheerful and amusing and obviously devoted to each other. As for the sister-in-law, she admired her immensely. She wondered why she had never married. Like most happily married people she always felt rather sorry for spinsters, and Penelope was so very attractive, with the dark hair waved back from the smooth forehead, and just that one intriguing streak of white. Her large hazel eyes were set wide apart, and though there were purple shadows below them, denoting weariness, there were little lines of humor at their corners. She was listening to Andrew with a smile on her intelligent face, and Lupin felt that she must be an interesting personality. She looked fragile with an underlying hint of sorrow beneath her smile, and yet she seemed to rise above it and to present a brave front to the world. Her conversation was amusing, and she had a gay, infectious laugh. Lupin guessed that there had been a sad love affair in her life. What a waste it was, and what a wonderful wife she would have made for a clergyman, intelligent and understanding without being either frumpy or managing!

Betty could not see Penelope, as she was sitting the other side of Andrew, but she could hear her voice and she felt very proud of her. She was so perfectly at home in all circumstances and with all manner of people.

This is a nice party, thought Dick to himself, as he turned to Mrs. Baker and listened courteously to her description of the jam-making competition organized by the Mothers' Union. He could hear Lupin and Bob laughing together and looked forward to the moment when he could turn once again to his other neighbor. To think that we were dreading her coming! he laughed to himself, as he made some remark about bramble jelly. She is one of the nicest girls I have ever met. Then he looked across the table at his sister and was filled with pride. We are lucky to have her with us, he thought. She always makes a party go well. I am glad we came down here, it is much nicer than living in London, and it makes all the difference to Betty. It was a wonderful scheme of Pen's.

That is an intelligent woman, thought Andrew Hastings, and an attractive one, too, as Betty caught Lupin's eye and Penelope rose and left the room.

The four women settled down in Betty's sitting room. Mrs. Baker took the chair proffered her and prepared to keep the ball rolling. "It is so nice of your husband to come and preach for us, Lady Lupin. Lancelot says it is a good thing to have a fresh preacher now and then, though last time we had one, S.P.C.K. it was, one of my mothers said to me, 'It doesn't seem like Sunday without the vicar's sermon.' In fact, I think they are all disappointed when anyone else preaches, but my husband won't believe it, he is so modest."

Lupin gave a queer gurgling sound ending in a hiccup, and Betty blew her nose. Penelope bent down to pick up her ball of wool. She was some time in finding it, and when she emerged her face was rather red. "You are a great knitter, aren't you, Mrs. Baker?" she inquired.

"Oh yes, I am usually knitting, whenever I have a minute to spare that is, which isn't often, but I knit all Lancelot's socks. A clergyman's wife has so many demands on her time, hasn't she?" she said to Lupin.

"Absolutely," agreed Lupin. "I can't think how you find time to knit your husband's socks. I did knit some things for my babies, but they didn't fit very well, it's no good pretending they did."

"I hope this will fit mine," said Betty, looking affectionately at the minute vest which she was knitting.

"Well, if you have any things over that don't fit, I shall always be glad of them," said Mrs. Baker. "The number of babies in this village is enormous, many of them illegitimate, you know."

"Still, I think they would want vests that fitted, even then," said Lupin. "I mean, it's not altogether their fault."

"Poor Lancelot! He's in despair about it, sometimes."

"How nice of him to take an interest," said Lupin, picturing Mr. Baker going round in his hearty way, trying vests on illegitimate children.

"My dear, he is the vicar of the parish. He often tells me that he feels responsible for all the illegitimate babies in the village."

"I'm so sorry," gasped Betty. "It is my hay fever."

"I expect it worries your husband very much too, Lady Lupin," went on Mrs. Baker. "I sometimes think it will be the death of Lancelot."

"Oh dear! Andrew is more worried by colds in the winter."

"Lancelot never thinks of himself," announced Mrs. Baker proudly. "If he gets a cold he never gives it a thought."

"Doesn't he?" replied Lupin wonderingly. "It is so difficult to ignore a cold. I mean, it does sort of obtrude itself, doesn't it?"

At this moment, to her relief, the men came into the room, and she looked forward to continuing her conversation with Dick and Bob. Her relief was short-lived, as Mr. Baker came and seated himself beside her. She tried to feel grateful, as she could tell by his expression that he would rather have sat by Penelope and was sacrificing himself for politeness' sake.

"Mrs. Baker has just been telling me how badly you suffer from hay fever," she remarked.

"Hay fever!" he exclaimed. "I have never had such a thing in my life."

"I am so glad," she replied. How funny, she thought, not to know if one's husband gets hay fever or not. I'm sure she said that he had nearly died of it, too.

"What a splendid person your husband is," said Mr. Baker. "It is very good of him to come and preach for us. He is just the sort of person we want."

"I am glad." Lupin felt on firm ground here. She could understand everyone wanting Andrew. How lucky she was to have him for her husband!

"It is so fortunate that you should have Miss Stevenson for your hostess on your first visit. It will give you a good impression of our parish."

"It is awfully nice of Mrs. Stevenson to have us," replied Lupin.

"Mrs. Stevenson! Oh, of course, this is really her house, isn't it? How lucky she is to have her sister-in-law to help her with everything. I don't know what any of us would do if it weren't for Miss Stevenson. When you know us a little better, Lady Lupin, you will get some idea of what Miss Stevenson stands for in this parish," and he turned his eyes admiringly toward the object of his admiration. "I expect yours is a very jolly parish," he went on, turning reluctantly back to Lupin. "Plenty of activity, I'm sure."

"Well, yes, there does seem to be something going on most of the time," sighed Lupin.

"I am sure there is, and I can guess what a help you are to your husband. You must be wizard with the girls. I don't think you would easily be shocked."

Lupin wondered what he meant and hoped that he wasn't going to tell her a rude story. No, of course he wouldn't, he was a clergyman. Still, you never quite knew where you were with these hearty ones.

"No," he went on. "Being shocked doesn't help. The great thing is to set an example of purity for others to follow. What is more beautiful than a good wife and mother, living a pure life in her own home?"

Lupin did not know the answer to this one. As a matter of fact she was rather sleepy after her drive, and she let Mr. Baker talk on. Luckily, he did not seem to need much in the way of responses. At last, to her relief, Mrs. Baker said that they ought to be going home.

"Yes, indeed!" agreed Mr. Baker. "I expect Mr. Hastings and Lady Lupin will be glad to turn in. It will be a long day for them tomorrow."

"Oh dear," murmured Lupin to Betty, while Mr. Baker was being 'boys together' over a very mild whisky-and-soda. "I don't know what we have been talking about, but it sounded rather rude."

CHAPTER 3

THERE was dew on the grass the next morning when Dick and Betty accompanied their guests to the early service. The air was exhilarating and the lark overhead shared their feelings of pleasure. "Isn't this lovely?" said Betty. "I can't think why we don't always come."

"Yes, isn't it nice? But I am glad you persuaded Pen not to get up," replied Dick.

"So am I. She wanted to, but I said I wasn't going to call her, and with any luck she is sleeping on."

Lupin stood outside the little church after the service, waiting for Andrew and watching Dick and Betty as they walked across the field hand in hand. It was queer to think she had met them for the first time yesterday. She felt fond of them already. They were so happy, and she did hope nothing would ever happen to spoil their happiness. But why on earth should it? she asked herself. I expect I want my breakfast. What was that thing we learned at school?

The lark's on the wing
The snail's on the something
Morning's at seven,
The hillside's (whatever was it?)
God's somewhere
All's right with the world.

"Oh yes, that's it, rather nice!" Lupin said out loud. "Thank goodness, Andrew—I thought you were never coming."

"I should have come sooner, but Mr. Baker had a good deal to say. It seems that the verger is very good at comic songs, and I think it was one of the sidesmen who always played with a straight bat, or it may, of course, have been the organist. I hope you are not starving."

" 'Dew pearl'd' !" exclaimed Lupin.

"What, dear?"

" 'The hillside is dew pearl'd,' that is what it was. I don't know what it means, but it rhymes with world."

"So it does," said Andrew.

"I expect it means there was dew on the hillside," said Lupin thoughtfully.

"I shouldn't be surprised. But don't you think it would be better if we were to walk on? The Stevensons may be waiting breakfast for us, and we could say our pieces to each other at some other time."

"So we could, but it is such a nuisance when one can't remember things when one knows them quite well all the time."

They all went to church at eleven and back to the Limes for luncheon. Dick had gone round to fetch his father and met the others in the porch.

Lupin liked the look of Mr. Stevenson. He was such an upright old man, and his white hair was so very clean and his pink cheeks so very fresh. What a pity he was so selfish! For she had already gathered from chance remarks of Betty's that he led Penelope a very hard life.

The Deerings were also in church, and they all forgathered after the service. Mr. Stevenson and Sir Henry were old friends, and Lady Deering was very fond of Penelope. "I don't know what we should have done without her during the war," she confided to Lupin, after they had been introduced. "She was perfectly wonderful. Of course if she had been free she would have liked to have joined one of the women's services, but naturally she could not leave her father."

"Of course not," agreed Lupin.

"She is a wonderful daughter, but every minute she could spare she was doing war work of some kind or another. I was supposed to be the head of the W.V.S., but I was only a figurehead—Penelope did it all."

"Nonsense," said Penelope, coming up at this moment and hearing Lady Deering's words. "I am sure I hardly did anything."

Mrs. Baker hurried up. "Well, this is nice," she said, "to see everyone gathered together like this. It is just what Lancelot likes, for everyone to feel at home."

Everyone at once made excuses to get away, and to move on to their Sunday luncheons. The Limes was a big square house opening on to the village street, with about two or three acres of garden behind it. There was an air of comfort and spaciousness about it. Lupin sat next to Mr. Stevenson at luncheon, who regarded her with twinkling blue eyes. "Betty was frightened to death at the thought of having you to stay," he told her.

"Nothing like as frightened as I was, I'm sure, at the thought of staying with her. I thought she would be one of those women who are the mainstay of a parish."

Mr. Stevenson laughed. "And when you saw her you knew she couldn't be, I suppose."

"Well, she may be—in fact, Mrs. Baker said she had a wonderful way with children when they were sick in Sunday school—but she doesn't look a mainstay, does she? She hasn't the teeth for it, for one thing."

"No, I don't think she looks like it," and he glanced affectionately at Betty. "If you don't mind an old man being a little personal, you don't look very much like the wife of a clergyman."

"I know. Isn't it awful? But I really am, you know, and I'm sure no one believes it."

Dick stayed on with his father and the others went back to the cottage. Penelope went upstairs to rest, and Andrew retired to think about his evening sermon. Lupin and Betty sat together in the little garden, talking. Betty told Lupin how she had first met Penelope, and how good she had always been to her and how she had given up the man she loved for the sake of Dick and his father.

"Do you think she was right?" asked Lupin.

Betty looked at her out of puzzled brown eyes. "I suppose so. She said she felt that it was her duty. I don't think I could have done it if it had been Dick, but I suppose she felt that she would never have been happy with Charles if she had sacrificed Daddy. Anyhow, he married someone else, though I believe he has been in love with Penelope all the time. But men are funny like that, aren't they? I wonder if Dick would have married someone else if I had refused him?"

They had tea in the garden, and Penelope entertained them with the conversation she had had with Mrs. Baker that morning. " 'It is so good of you to help us with the Sunday school treat, Miss Stevenson. As Lancelot always says, "Suffer the little children to come unto me"—such a beautiful idea, isn't it?' I agreed, though I hadn't realized that the idea was Lancelot's. She then told me that he had said that the children of today would be the grown-ups of tomorrow. That was profound, wasn't it? Anyhow, the upshot is that I have agreed to judge the darning and hat-trimming competition, not that I know much about it. I am not a good needlewoman."

"I do wish that you wouldn't keep undertaking more jobs, Pen," said Dick anxiously.

"Have *you* got roped in, Betty?" asked Lupin.

"Yes, I am doing the infants' tea. I hope they won't be sick."

"But you are so good with children when they are sick, darling," said Penelope.

"It will be rather a business getting the food together, won't it?" asked Lupin.

"It will, rather."

"The last time I judged a competition," went on Penelope, "it was table decorations, and I unfortunately awarded the prize to Mary Browne, whose mother is one of the most regular members of the congregation. Mrs. Baker was very disappointed, as she said it was a waste of a prize. If only I had given it to Peggy Wood, whose mother is very uncertain, it might have fixed that family. So you see, there are a lot of wheels within wheels."

"You had better get Mrs. Baker to tip you the wink as to whom to give it to this time," suggested Lupin.

"It would really save time and trouble if she did it herself," pointed out Betty.

"I wish to goodness she would," exclaimed Dick. "Pen is always being dragged into things, and she has quite enough to do already."

"Oh well, one likes to do what one can," said Penelope, "and Mrs. Baker is quite a decent little thing, though she does think her husband the most wonderful person in the world."

"Very proper," said Dick.

"I suppose most of us do," pondered Lupin, "unless, of course, one is unhappily married or something of that sort."

A rather sad expression crossed Penelope's face, and Lupin wished that she hadn't mentioned marriage. There was a slightly awkward pause, then Penelope announced her intention of going to evensong as she wanted to hear Andrew preach once more. Lupin had intended to take the evening off, but she now felt that the least she could do was to accompany Penelope, so they started off together across the sunny fields.

The little church was warm and Lupin felt comfortably sleepy. She always enjoyed listening to Andrew's sermons, but somehow this evening her mind wandered a little. She did like Betty, but why did she feel a sort of foreboding about her? She seemed happy enough. Was it just because she was so happy that she felt frightened for her? Happiness was such a precarious thing. Lupin gave herself a little shake; she had not a morbid nature as a rule. What was that poem called, the one that she had been trying to remember this morning? Something about somewhere being dew-pearled, whatever that meant! "God's on the hillside, the lark's on the wing, the lark's in the swing," she thought sleepily and she dozed a little. Then she opened her eyes with a start. Of course the poem was "Penelope Passes," that was what it was called, and she closed her eyes again. She awoke to find everyone scrambling to their feet as the organ started the strains of "Abide with me." "Pippa Passes," she told herself.

Whatever made me think of "Penelope Passes?" And she joined in the hymn.

She and Penelope came out of the church into the evening sunshine. They did not wait for Andrew. "He will be having fun and games with Mr. Baker," said Lupin.

"Yes, there is always a lot of 'chaps together' after evening service," replied Penelope. "A hearty service, a glass of beer and some good clean fun, what more could anyone want?" But she spoke rather absently.

"I'm afraid Andrew isn't frightfully clever at good clean fun," admitted Lupin. "But I am sure he will do his best."

It was a beautiful June evening, and there were wild roses on the hedge that bordered the field. "I love them," said Lupin, waving her hand toward them. "I never seem to get used to them, somehow. I don't know what it is about them, but they seem too good to be true."

"I think it is because they last such a short time," said Penelope. "There is just one brief moment of June when the trees are in all their fresh green and everything is on tiptoe, the wild roses come out on the hedgerows and then they are gone. The longest day comes and goes, the flowers fade, the trees get dusty and summer is over."

"Oh dear," sighed Lupin. Although she had been married to a clergyman for ten years she was still inclined to feel thoughtful at evening service, and now all this talk of dying flowers and dark evenings, just as she was beginning to cheer up, was rather trying. She wished she had stayed at home with Dick and Betty. Still, poor Miss Stevenson had had a very sad life, she knew that from what Betty had told her, and probably she got a bit depressed at times, now that she was getting on. Not that she could be more than forty, if that. Still they had just been singing "Change and decay in all around I see," and it had probably made her think a bit.

"But you know," went on Penelope in her charming voice, "when the roses go, the hips come to take their place. A hedge studded with hips and haws is a very beautiful thing. Autumn has a charm of its own."

"Absolutely," agreed Lupin. "We learned a poem about autumn when I was at school. It was something about waiting by a cider press with patient look. I don't think I should stand very long by a cider press. I mean, it is so inclined to give one hicccups, isn't it?"

Penelope laughed and Lupin hoped that she had got over her Sunday evening, autumnal, middle-aged blues. "No," she agreed, "I shouldn't wait long for cider. All the same I do love that ode:

> " 'While harried clouds bloom the soft-dying day,
> And touch the stubble-plains with rosy hue.' "

"Absolutely," repeated Lupin, wishing she could think of something more original to say.

"There was a time," went on Penelope dreamily, "when I could not bear to look at a wild rose."

"Oh, was there? I was like that about buttercups once."

"Were you? Then you have known sorrow, too."

"Oh no," disclaimed Lupin hastily. "It was only jaundice."

Penelope began to laugh again. "You are a lovely person," she said. "I believe you always say whatever comes into your head."

"I am afraid I do. It is rather a mistake for a vicar's wife."

"You are not a bit like a vicar's wife. You are rather like I was when I was young. I don't mean that I was ever as pretty as you are, but I enjoyed life frightfully."

"You are not much older than I am now. I have been married ten years, you know."

"Not in years, perhaps, but in experience of life. But that's enough of my troubles. The roses gave me a sort of nostalgic feeling, but you have quite banished it. I do hate people who talk about themselves, don't you?"

CHAPTER 4

ONE Friday, about a month later, Lupin was expecting the Stevensons for a weekend visit. It was a lovely day and she hoped the weather would hold up until Monday. So often, when one asked people to spend a few days by the sea, it turned arctic at once, and the visitors were naturally aggrieved while the hostess felt as if it were her fault. Lupin was particularly anxious that this should be a successful visit, as Penelope had actually managed to get away from home for a few days, and the sea air would do her good.

Lupin had just been to see the verger's wife's mother's legs, which were "something chronic," as the proud daughter had announced when issuing the invitation to the private view. On her way home the fishmonger waylaid her to say that he had some fresh plaice just in. She weakly said that she would love some and started home with it. She had not gone many steps before she realized that the fishmonger had made a mistake—at least, she hoped it was a mistake.

Walking into her husband's study, she put down the plaice on a pile of sermon paper and said, "Andrew, have you seen Mrs. Poolton's legs?"

"No, dear, are they worth seeing?"

"They are dreadful, but I did not like putting off going any longer, though I was rather afraid that I should be late for the Stevensons. It is so difficult to get away from some houses!"

"I say, darling, do you notice anything funny about this room?"

Lupin looked round vaguely. "What sort of thing?" she asked. "Something new?"

"A smell," explained Andrew. "No, not new, I should think!"

Lupin sniffed. "Yes, I do smell something," she said. "I hope it's not the drains. I wish it hadn't had to happen today. I mean, I feel that Penelope won't care for bad drains."

"I don't care much for them myself," responded Andrew.

"Perhaps it's only rats," said Lupin hopefully. "No, it's all right, it's the fish I brought back for dinner. There it is, on your table. I always said I ought to be a detective."

"Is that my Sunday sermon on which it is lying?"

"I am afraid so, but you don't take it in to church with you, do you? I'll take the fish to Cook."

"Don't you think that you would be wiser to bury it in the garden?"

"Perhaps you are right. Do you know, I sometimes wonder if I am not frightfully hot at housekeeping. Oh, there they are!" And Lupin rushed out to greet her friends, followed by two children and a dog, while Andrew stayed behind to bury the fish.

Chaos reigned for a few minutes, but eventually the visitors found themselves in the vicarage with most of their belongings. The children were dispatched to the nursery, Andrew joined the party and they all sat down to tea.

"What about bathing?" asked Lupin. "I mean, it may be snowing tomorrow. I am afraid we shall have to go some way out, because if one bathes near home one meets so many parishioners festooned round rocks and breakwaters, but the further one goes the nicer it smells. There are not so many old socks or dead crabs or remains of chewing gum. Oh, and talking of parishioners, Andrew, Miss Gibson wants me to take a Sunday school class on Sunday—at least she said Miss Tudor was ill, and she did not know whom to approach, so I suppose that is what she meant—so I weakly said I would think about it, but I needn't, need I? After all, I have got guests!"

Penelope looked at Andrew. "I wonder if I could do anything about it," she said.

Dick frowned. "No, Pen, you've come away for a holiday. You really mustn't start taking Sunday school classes."

"No, of course you mustn't," agreed Lupin. "You must behave like a proper visitor, though it is angelic of you to suggest it. What about you, Betty? As regards bathing, I mean."

"No, I don't think I'll bathe, not that it would hurt Christopher Mary, but a bathing dress doesn't seem to suit me frightfully well just at present. But I should like to come and watch the rest of you and smell the sea."

They drove about three miles out of Glanville to a bare little beach. There were just white cliffs, blue sea and golden sands, and Betty lay in a patch of sunshine on the cushions which Andrew had arranged for her, while the others hurried into the water. She enjoyed the peace and solitude, for she was very tired. It was silly to get so tired! She rather wondered that Dick had not arranged her cushions for her, but naturally he wanted to get into the sea as quickly as possible, and she would have hated him to be one of those fussy husbands. After all, having a baby was a very natural thing; one did not want to be treated as if one were an invalid. She closed her eyes, and voices came to her as from a great distance. How happy she was! She fell asleep.

"Pen, you had better go out," said Dick. "You will be getting cold."

"You pig, Dick," replied his sister. "You never like me to enjoy myself."

Andrew followed her out of the sea. She lay down in a sunny patch at some distance from Betty and he sat beside her.

"This is heaven!" exclaimed Penelope. "I feel as if I had washed it all off in that lovely clean sea."

Andrew smiled sympathetically, and his eyes wandered back to Lupin as she raced with Dick through the clear blue water. To think that they had been married for ten years! To him, she did not look a day older than she had at their first meeting. All the same, he could not imagine what it would be like not to be married to her. The years before he met her seemed like a dream dreamed long ago. He had, in the course of his profession, accustomed himself to looking interested in other people's conversations while pursuing his own thoughts, and Penelope thought how charming he was and she wondered whether he sometimes found his wife a little shallow and superficial.

"Dick is so good to me," she said. "He is always fussing about me and wondering whether I am too tired or too cold. Sometimes I tell him that he is like an old hen."

Andrew laughed politely. "I am sure you have been a wonderful sister to him," he said gravely.

"Oh, I don't know. I have tried to make up to him for not having a mother, and I don't think he has missed her. She said to me, a few hours before she died, 'Look after Dick.' I promised that I would and I think that I have kept my promise."

"I am sure you have." Of course, masses of people swam far better than Lupin. It was just his imagination that she was so much more graceful in the water than anyone else. But he loved watching her.

"Sometimes I think it was a heavy load to lay upon a child. Perhaps she did not realize how seriously I should take my promise," and Penelope gazed out at the far horizon.

After a pause Andrew remarked that it was nice for her to have her brother and his wife living so near her at home.

"Yes, it is lovely to feel that they are there, though of course I do not see a great deal of them. I seldom leave my father. After all, he is my first duty."

"Yes, of course." Lupin and Dick had come out of the sea and were racing toward them along the strip of sand. Lupin's fair skin was sunburned to the color of honey. No one, to watch her running, would guess that she was over thirty and the mother of two children. "I am very glad you were able to get away for this weekend," Andrew continued to Penelope in his courteous voice.

"So am I. It was rather difficult, but I did so want to come. You and Lupin were so sweet when you stayed with Dick and Betty. Besides, I had another reason. I do feel that Betty rather wants another woman with her just now. She is naturally a little highly strung at this time and Dick might not quite understand if I were not here to explain. I am able to smooth things out and to prevent little disputes from turning into big ones."

Lupin and Dick threw themselves down beside them. "Are you sure you are not cold, Pen?" asked Dick.

"Where is Betty?" asked Lupin.

They drove home through the summer evening. The sun shone on the golden cornfields and on one blazing with scarlet poppies. Betty and Dick appeared to be in the wildest spirits and Lupin was very glad they had come to Glanville. Penelope, too, was making a great effort to join in the fun. But Lupin felt that behind her amusing and rather clever remarks there was a tinge of sadness. Was the beauty of the summer evening bringing back her sorrows as the wild roses had done that evening in June? Did the sight of Betty and Dick, and herself and Andrew, all so happily married, make her feel a little wistful? It was rather bad luck on her. Still, she was not the sort of person to let her troubles intrude on the enjoyment of others and she was obviously trying very hard to be gay.

"There is something rather attractive about sorrow, isn't there?" remarked Lupin to Andrew as she got into bed.

"I don't know," he replied. "I can imagine more attractive things."

"I was thinking about Penelope. That touch of sadness makes her more dignified, I think."

"Well, I hope you won't become dignified if you have got to be sad first."

"But you do admire Penelope, don't you?"

"She is a very attractive woman and I gather that she is an excellent daughter and sister."

"It was awfully decent of her offering to take that Sunday school class."

"If she wants to, I should let her. You can't do it, you have quite enough to do with your own family and visitors."

The weather was kind, and on Saturday they went for a picnic to a little bay some miles away and took the children with them. Jill was sick and Peter's nose bled, but otherwise they had quite an enjoyable time. All the same Lupin felt rather tired in the evening, an unusual experience for her especially when, as she told Andrew, there had been nothing but pleasure all day long. Everyone had appeared to be in good spirits, but they had seemed a trifle forced.

"It was rather like the Sunday school outing," she explained. "You remember that time when Mr. Dawson put on a funny hat and we all roared? Of course," she went on, "one does have one's ups and downs when one is going to have a baby. I mean, one comes all over a bit depressed now and then for no reason whatever, and then one tries to be extra funny and it all comes out rather dreary. I expect Dick is in a stew, too, and doesn't want Betty to know it. I remember you were always wondering whether I were all right, and asking whether I were too hot or too cold or whether I had gone and got corns or something."

"Yes, I was very trying, I know," agreed Andrew. "Of course, Dick may be worrying about Betty, as you say, but he always seems to be more anxious about his sister than his wife."

"Why, she isn't going to have a baby, is she?"

"Not that I know of, but she seems to be a little run down. She does not get much rest at home, I gather."

"No, I don't think she does. Betty says that she never thinks of herself. I must say she is awfully nice. She is insisting on taking that Sunday school class tomorrow. I feel rather awful about it because I am sure Dick is furious. But she says it will be a treat for her because she is so fond of children, and you see Nanny is staying in in the afternoon, so I simply must let her go out in the morning."

"Of course, darling! I think it is a splendid arrangement, and I am sure Penelope will be excellent with the children."

Dick met Lupin with a beaming face the next morning. "We have had a brainwave," he announced. "Betty is going to take the Sunday school class."

CHAPTER 5

Dear Lupin,

If you and Andrew could bear a very quiet visit, will you come and stay with Daddy and me for a few days? I expect the middle of the week would be more convenient for you. Daddy would so much like to see you both again and I will try to get Betty and Dick to come and stay in the house. It will cheer Betty up, these last few weeks are a little trying for her. Any time up till about the middle of November would do for us, so choose your own date. I do hope you will be able to manage it.

Yours affectionately,
Penelope Stevenson

Lupin read the letter through a second time and took some more marmalade. "Penelope Stevenson wants us to go and stay with her and her father," she said.

"Would you like to go?"

"Yes, I should, rather. I liked old Mr. Stevenson, and I should like to see Betty again and Penelope, too, of course."

"You always seem rather doubtful about Penelope."

"Do I?" Lupin took a drink of coffee. "Bother, Miss Gibson's coming in at the gate. It's a funny thing about Penelope. Oh, so is Mr. Dawson, they are standing there having a long conversation—at least I hope it's a long conversation—as it will give us time to finish our breakfast in peace. I do like her—Penelope, I mean, not Miss Gibson—but I never feel absolutely at home with her. She gives me a sort of inferiority complex. I suppose it's because she's so good and unselfish, and it makes me feel self-indulgent and . . .Oh, good morning, Miss Gibson, will you have some coffee?"

Andrew and Lupin chose a date toward the end of October for their visit to Much Lancing. The country through which they drove was looking beautiful. "I see what Penelope meant about hips and haws," remarked Lupin. "She said when the roses went the hips came to take their place. A poetic sort of idea, really! And I believe that hip stuff is supposed to be frightfully good for children. I meant to get some for Jill but I forgot."

"That child will burst if she eats much more," replied Andrew.

"Do you think so? I hope not, but I suppose she is a bit on the fat side. Still, I'd rather have her like that, I never did care for scraggy children. Do you think they will be all right while we are away? I always have an awful kind of feeling that something will happen if I turn my back for a minute, though I know that Nanny is really much more careful and capable than I am and they are much safer with her. All the same, think how awful it would be if the house caught on fire or the children got kidnapped or drowned or something while we were away."

"It would be just as bad really if it happened while we were there. Is that Baker?"

"Oh yes. I'd better wave and we might change hats, then he might think we were having some good clean fun."

"We might, but I don't think we will," and Andrew drove up before the Limes.

Penelope and Betty appeared upon the doorstep and Lupin jumped out and greeted them eagerly. She did not think Betty looked frightfully well, she seemed all eyes, but then one did not feel frightfully well just before one had a baby. She remembered seeing her own face in a glass once and having quite a shock.

"Here we are," she remarked cheerfully.

They walked through the hall, which was looking very delightful with big pots of many-colored dahlias grouped round the bottom of the staircase and branches of beech leaves in earthenware jugs. Mr. Stevenson came out of the library and was very glad to see them. "So you have arrived safely," he said. "It is nice of you to come. How have you been getting on since I saw you last? Have you been delivering the parish magazines and taking soup to the deserving poor?"

"You will see Lupin at teatime, Daddy darling," said Penelope. "She wants to see her room now."

Lupin did not particularly want to see her room but would rather have stayed downstairs talking to Mr. Stevenson. Not that it wasn't a very nice room, because it was, and there was a wonderful view of the autumn woods. The sky was pale primrose, and the sun, a great red ball, was sinking behind the trees.

"You were quite right about the autumn," she said to Penelope. "It is almost lovelier here now than it was in the summer. It was nice of you to ask us to stay."

Dick had arrived back from work by the time they joined the others in the library, and they all had tea. Betty and Dick were both rather quiet, but Lupin had plenty to talk about to Mr. Stevenson, and Penelope and Andrew discussed the new education bill. After tea Penelope suggested a walk and Lupin welcomed the idea of stretching her legs after sitting in the car all day, but she was rather loath to leave Betty. "You'll come, won't you?" she said to Mr. Stevenson.

"No, he has had his walk for the day," said Penelope affectionately.

Mr. Stevenson looked a little disappointed, but he turned to his daughter-in-law. "Betty and I will keep each other company," he said.

"Of course we will," said Betty, brightening up a little.

"Betty must rest, Daddy," said Penelope.

The dusk was falling as the other four started out together. The air was very still and there was a smell of bonfires. Lights were springing up in the windows in the village street as they walked down it. They crossed the field where Lupin had seen the wild roses. As Penelope had prognosticated, the hedge was now ablaze with hips and haws. Lupin's mind went back to Jill and the hip-juice, and she thought about her children for a few moments as they climbed the hill to the woods. The sun had quite disappeared by now, but there was still a soft golden haze over everything.

"This is a nice place," Lupin remarked to Dick, firmly banishing the picture of Peter being attacked by a mad bull in the middle of Glanville High Street, which had just risen unbidden to her mind.

"Yes, I am awfully fond of it."

"There is something about a place where one has always lived, isn't there? That you don't sort of get anywhere else, if you know what I mean. We took our two up to our old home in the summer. It really was rather nice seeing them playing about just like my brother and me."

"Yes, I can understand that. I'm looking forward to that rather, myself," he added shyly. "Of course, we've only been here for one generation. It's not like your home, but I was born here. Father had just bought the place and then my mother died—it was rather rotten luck."

"I am frightfully sorry," said Lupin.

"Yes, of course. I never knew her, but Pen adored her. It was harder on her than anyone. Though she was only a child I don't think she ever really got over it, and then she just took her place and—well, I don't know what Dad and I would have done without her," and he slashed rather angrily at a thistle with his stick. "She's been everything to us. I feel rather a brute about it sometimes because there was a fellow she was fond of and she gave him up for us. Of course I was only a kid at the time, or I'd have done something about it. It makes me feel pretty selfish, all the same."

"Well, it wasn't your fault," replied Lupin, "and you are a very good brother, I think."

"I couldn't very well be anything else. She is so wonderful to Betty, too. You know, she insisted on us shutting up the cottage and living at the Limes for these weeks. Annie had to go home to her mother, so it fitted in beautifully. She said it would make all the difference to Betty to be quite free from housekeeping for a bit. Of course it must make a lot of extra work for her, but she never thinks of that."

"Did Betty like the idea?"

"Well." Dick hesitated and threw a piece of wood over the hedge. "As a matter of fact, Betty hasn't been quite like herself lately. Women aren't, I suppose. Well, of course, you know all about that," and he broke off rather embarrassed.. "Pen says it's quite natural," he went on, "and I mustn't take any notice. It is lucky we've got her with us, or I should have been a bit worried."

"I expect Betty does get rather depressed now and then," said Lupin.

"Yes, and then she got it into her head that she would rather stay in the cottage—she wanted a Mrs. Browne from the village to come in and do for us, she'd got it all fixed up—but as I pointed out she'd have nothing at all to do or think about at the Limes, and she would have Pen with her all the time when I was at work. I suppose she thought the old man would fidget her, but Pen is very careful about that."

Lupin's natural impulse was to blurt out whatever came into her head, but after ten years of being a vicar's wife she did occasionally, though not often, bite it back. She succeeded this time and merely remarked, "One isn't exactly oneself at these times. I remember before Peter was born I went to a missionary meeting one day and heard a tale about some heathen in South Africa, or it may have been South America, and I burst into floods of tears. Andrew was terrified, and I said life was all too sad for words, even in South Africa, and I wished that I were dead."

Dick laughed. "I can't imagine you being depressed," he said. "Then I couldn't have imagined Betty, either, but I am sure Pen is right and that the best thing to do is to pay no attention at all, but to talk about something else."

Penelope walked beside Andrew. "This is my favorite view," he remarked, as they reached the top of the hill and looked down on the village with its lights twinkling through a soft mist.

"It is a charming place," agreed Andrew. "Have you lived here all your life?"

"No," she replied. "I was nearly ten when my father retired and bought the Limes, but I do not remember much of my life before that, except that I had my mother. It is just a happy dream of warmth and love and understanding. Then we came here and Dick was born and she died very soon after, and from being the spoiled child I became the woman of the house, whose duty it was to spoil others." She gazed before her through the autumn dusk. "For nearly thirty years I have lived here now. For thirty springs and for thirty autumns I have looked out on to the village street and away across to those woods. I suppose most people would think mine a very narrow life, but I have tried not let myself get narrow-minded."

"I am sure you haven't. After all, a dull man may travel all round the world and return just as dull as when he started, while a man who is interested in his fellow creatures will find life interesting in a country village or even a London suburb."

"I do so agree with you," said Penelope. "I am always sorry for those well-to-do women one meets in hotels abroad whose only interest is in the food or the beds. One feels they would be just as happy, or as little unhappy, in Wigan or Blackpool."

"Have you been abroad much?"

"Oh no, not very much. I have seldom been away from this village. Before the war Dick used to insist on taking me abroad occasionally. He said that I would grow into a cabbage if I never moved, and that would hardly have been fair to him. Besides, he liked to have me with him—he always said nothing was any fun without me! But it was very difficult to arrange things. Poor Daddy did so hate it. There was an old friend who used to come and stay with him sometimes, but the naughty old thing is never happy unless I am with him. Still it is nice to be wanted, even though it is rather a tie."

"Hell!" exclaimed Dick. "I say, I am frightfully sorry, Lupin, but where on earth has Blackie gone?" And he looked round in vain for his black spaniel puppy.

"How awful of us," replied Lupin. "We were talking so much we forgot all about him. Do go back and look for him. I daresay he is frightened. He is very young to be all alone in this wood with the evening coming on. I'll wait here." As Dick went back, she turned her eyes to the conkers lying at her feet. They still had a fascination for her and she started to open a prickly shell and to take out the glossy chestnut it contained, when to her surprise she saw Dick some way ahead. However did he get there? she wondered, surprised. "Got him?" she called out. Then, as her eye fell to the dog at his heels, she realized that it was not Blackie. Even in the dim light she could see that he was liver-colored, not black.

"Hullo, Bob!" cried Penelope gaily. "Don't forget that you are coming to dinner tomorrow. It will be your own pheasants. He is a perfect angel," she explained to Lupin and Andrew. "He is always bringing me the most delicious things to eat, just when I am wondering what on earth we are going to have for dinner. I thought it would be tinned pilchards and spam for you tomorrow night, but lo and behold, there will be fresh trout and pheasants. Betty loves pheasant, so you can imagine how grateful I am."

Lupin could just see Bob's face now, and she wondered why she had mistaken him for Dick. They were not really at all alike close to, but she could have sworn it was Dick at a distance of twenty yards. Bob was plainer than Dick; he had no pretense of good looks, but the expression on his face was almost beautiful at the moment. Lupin would not have used such a term herself in describing a man's face, but she recognized it for what it was: a look of utter devotion.

Bob had no hope of Penelope ever marrying him. In fact, such an idea had probably never entered his head. He knew that he wasn't clever or handsome, or any of the things that Penelope's husband ought to be. He wasn't even heir to the baronetcy (not that that would have weighed with Penelope) because, though his older brother Henry had been killed at Dunkirk, he had left a son. Besides, he knew that Penelope had been in love once, and with her that would mean forever. No, the idea of marriage with her would have rather shocked him. All he wanted was to serve her, and he wished it might be in some more romantic way than in plying her with food. Lupin read his thoughts as she looked at him, then she turned her eyes away, feeling as if she had trespassed on holy ground.

Dick was approaching now with Blackie at his heels, and except for the dog he might be Bob, thought Lupin. Then he joined the little group and the likeness faded utterly and ridiculously. "They are not a bit alike," she told herself as they walked home and saw the welcome lights of the village twinkling in the dusk.

CHAPTER 6

"YOU REALLY quite enjoy being a clergyman's wife, don't you?" said Penelope, as she and Lupin settled themselves down for a cozy chat after dinner. Betty had gone to bed early and Dick and Andrew were sitting with Mr. Stevenson in the library. Penelope was knitting a vest for the baby and Lupin was struggling with a matinee jacket. She was not really a bad knitter nowadays, but she needed to concentrate on what she was doing and she envied Penelope the ease with which her needles slipped along while she was talking animatedly and appearing to pay no attention to her work.

Lupin put her knitting down for a minute and wrinkled her forehead. "Well, I like being Andrew's wife. I suppose if he had been a doctor I should have liked answering the telephone and booking the appointments. If you like your husband you don't really mind what you do, if you know what I mean. I must say I was pretty surprised at the beginning to find myself a clergyman's wife."

"I expect your parishioners were rather surprised, too?"

Lupin giggled reminiscently. "I wasn't very good," she admitted . "Not that I am now, but they have got used to me. I don't know what will happen if we ever have to go somewhere else and start again."

"When the chief thing in life is right, nothing else matters."

"No, absolutely not, that's what I always said when bombs kept falling about the place and one couldn't get any vinegar or soap flakes. As long as Andrew and I and the children were together one could put up with a lot."

"You are very lucky."

"Yes, I know. I feel quite guilty sometimes. I mean, I don't know why I should have Andrew and the children while other people have husbands they don't like and that sort of thing."

"I think there is one person for everyone, but sometimes they don't meet, or they don't recognize each other when they do meet, and then they choose someone else."

Lupin pondered. "I see what you mean but I don't quite see how there can be a pair for everyone, because there are more women in the world than men."

"That's true, but those who miss each other here may find their pair somewhere else."

"So they may."

"I was one of the lucky ones. I met my pair when I was twenty. We recognized each other at once, and like you I should not have minded if he had been a clergyman or a doctor or a shopkeeper. As a matter of fact he was a soldier."

"Oh, was he?" Lupin was rather sleepy after her drive. Naturally, she would have been very interested in this conversation as she had often wondered about Penelope's sad love affair, and in any case a love affair is always interesting, but tonight she found it difficult to keep her eyes open.

"I had always intended to devote my whole life to my father and Dick, and I had never taken any notice of any other man, but then Charles turned up and my whole life was changed. Everyone else seemed shadowy and unreal. For one summer I walked in fairyland."

"Did you?" Lupin picked up her knitting again. Penelope's story was really very interesting.

"I had agreed to marry him and was prepared to live with him in furnished houses wherever he might be stationed."

Lupin could not help feeling that if the houses had been unfurnished it would have been even nobler, but she did not like to say so.

"I thought I could run home every few weeks to see how things were going on, and if Daddy were all right, and Dick happy at school. Then Charles was ordered to India and the dream was over, as a soap bubble melts into the air it was gone, for I realized what that would mean."

"I see."

"It would have meant that I should have had to leave Daddy for three years and I should probably never have seen him again."

Lupin rather wondered why, as all this had happened at least fifteen years ago and Mr. Stevenson still seemed well and hearty, but she tried to give a sympathetic murmur which unfortunately turned into a yawn.

"Dick, too! He had just gone to school and he needed someone to whom to turn in the holidays, someone to make a home for him. I could never have forgiven myself if I had deserted them. I had to choose and I have never regretted it."

"Haven't you?" Bother, she had done a purl row instead of a plain.

"No. Naturally I get times when I wonder if it were worth it, but I know that it really was."

"Have you seen him again?"

Penelope sighed. "That is the one thing I do regret," she admitted. "Charles was heartbroken when he said goodbye to me, but after he had been in India for a year he married a girl out there. I bear him no grudge, though I couldn't have done it myself, but men are different from women."

"I suppose they are in some ways."

"At the end of three years he came home with his wife and we met."

"Did you?" Lupin wished she could think of a more original comment, but her eyes were very heavy.

"We met at a friend's house and the minute I saw him I knew he was unhappy. We talked about ordinary things, but just before we parted he murmured, 'I must see you,' and we lunched together the next day. I should not have done it but I felt I had to, and it gave him the chance of explaining things to me—it was only fair to him, in a way. He told me how unhappy he had been when he arrived in India and how this girl had been very friendly, and how he could not bear his loneliness and so he had married her for companionship, though they had nothing really in common. He asked my forgiveness and I gave it to him freely.

"He wanted me to run away with him then and there, but it would have broken Daddy's heart and there was his wife to consider, too. I should not have felt justified in ruining her life. But for a fortnight we met daily, even if it were only for a few minutes. It was foolish, perhaps it was wrong, but after three years it did not seem very much to take from life in return for the wasted years. I think it would have been better to have separated forever, but we were young.

"Then one day, when we were walking together in Kensington Gardens, we met some people we knew and we realized that if we were not careful we should get talked about. We did not mind for ourselves, but there was his wife and my father. We did not want to hurt anyone else, but we spent one day together at Hampton Court, one last day before we said goodbye forever. One magic day out of a lifetime. It was February, but such a February—the crocuses were like millions of stars spread out before us, the sky was bluer than any sky I have ever seen, even in Italy, the birds were singing overhead and the trees were all about to burst into leaf. I am glad to have that to remember, even if I have to pay for it, it was such a beautiful ending to our love.

"We said goodbye, and I have never seen him since. I went home the next day and he rejoined his regiment and his wife, but on that day every year—funnily enough it is February the fourteenth, St. Valentine's Day—he sends me violets. It sounds very silly and sentimental, I know, but I suppose I am a sentimental person, though very few people would guess it. Most people think I am hard and cynical, but that is only a mask to hide my feelings."

"Oh, I don't know," replied Lupin, wishing she could think of a more adequate reply.

"One develops a shell, you know."

"Well, I think it is an awfully romantic story."

"Now you know why I love to see other people happy. I have missed happiness myself, but I can recognize it when I see it. I could never be satisfied with the second best."

"No, absolutely. It would be frightfully sickening to be married to someone whom one didn't like, wouldn't it?"

"It is a great joy to me that Dick and Betty are so happy. I was afraid at one time that he would never marry."

"Oh, were you?"

"Yes. You see, we were too much together, and he never seemed to want other girls."

"Oh, I see." She knew this wasn't a very hot reply, and felt it was the opportunity for something really touching, but it just wouldn't come.

"The minute I saw Betty I thought what a wonderful wife she would make for Dick, and I did all I could to bring them together."

"What luck that they took to each other! Usually, if you choose for someone else, they hate the sight of each other."

"It would have been funny if I had made a mistake in choosing for Dick. You see, I know him so well we are almost like one person. I can read him like a book. I knew Betty would make him happy. She is just what he wanted, someone young and amusing and gay. Of course, she does not always understand him, but then he has me for that. He did not need anyone to turn to in the serious moments of life, he just wanted someone with whom to play and enjoy himself."

"It is nice they are so happy."

"It makes all the difference to me. I live life now at second hand."

"Oh, do you?"

"You needn't pity me, for I get plenty of pleasure from other things. To watch you and your husband together is like reading a piece of poetry or looking at a beautiful picture."

"Oh, is it?" replied Lupin, rather embarrassed.

To her great relief Dick came in at this moment, saying, "Alice has taken Dad up to bed and it's time you went too, Pen."

Penelope glanced at her watch. "I'm sure Lupin is tired," she said kindly. "We did not realize it was so late."

"We were having such an interesting conversation," said Lupin, stifling a yawn. As a matter of fact, it had been very interesting to her—if only she hadn't been so sleepy she would have been quite intrigued. It was all so romantic, but she felt at the moment that even if Penelope were to poison her lover's wife and then commit suicide she wouldn't be able to take much notice.

The next morning Dick went off early and Penelope suggested golf. "Shall I ring up Bob and ask him to make a fourth?" she suggested.

"I shouldn't," said her father. "He has got his work to do."

Penelope shrugged her shoulders as much as to say, you see what he is like, always putting difficulties in my way. But she smiled brightly and said, "All work and no play makes Jack a dull boy."

Lupin broke in. "I don't feel frightfully like golf this morning. I'd rather stop and have a gossip with Betty. You and Andrew have a game."

Penelope looked very attractive as she started out in a rust-red skirt and suede jacket and a jaunty little cap. Lupin rather hoped she wouldn't find it necessary to start understanding Andrew and supplying him with the deeper things of life, whatever they were.

Lupin and Betty found a sunny spot in the garden. The Michaelmas daisies were still making a show, although their festival had been over nearly a month. Lupin looked ruefully at her matinee jacket, which she had ruined the night before. "I have made an awful mess of it," she said. "I was so sleepy last night, but I meant it to be such a nice surprise."

"It does look a bit of a surprise," agreed Betty and they both laughed.

Lupin was thankful to find that Betty was more like herself this morning. They chatted about various things for some time, and then Betty suddenly blurted out, "Were you ever rather a pig before your babies were born?"

"Rather! Most of the time. I think most people are. I remember I told Andrew he didn't love me because he was writing his sermon when I wanted to play Picquet and I gave the cook notice because she grilled the fish instead of frying it."

"Did she go?" asked Betty with interest.

"No, she just said, 'You have a nice cup of tea, my lady, and you'll feel better.' "

"Oh well, if you were like it I don't mind so much, because I should think you were awfully good-tempered and levelheaded and all that sort of thing. But I really have been awful. I mean, you know how devoted I am to Pen and what an angel she always is to me. I have actually been horrid about her and jealous sometimes because Dick makes such a fuss of her. I'm dreadfully ashamed of myself because of course it isn't really me—it's as if someone else came and took possession of me."

Lupin did a row of knitting hurriedly and not very well, then she looked up. "I know that nasty woman," she said, "Andrew and I called her Lumpy Loo, she often came to me before the babies were born. I was ready to be jealous of the Sunday school superintendent when Lumpy Loo took charge. I believe all expectant mothers are the same."

"I am glad. I thought it was something extra horrid about me and that Christopher Mary would catch it from being with me. What shall we call my woman?"

"What about Bouncing Betts?" suggested Lupin.

"I do hope that Penelope and Dick understand that it is just old Bouncing Betts and not me, because I haven't been very nice lately. You see, I wanted to stay at the cottage. After all, it is my own home and Mrs. Browne has had seven children and is most understanding, so I thought it would fit in quite well if she were to come to us while Annie was away, but Pen was frightfully anxious for us to come here because she said I shouldn't have anything to think about, but you know in a way I was better when I had plenty to think about. I liked pottering about the cottage, but here I've nothing to do but brood about whether I shall die in childbirth, or whether the child will be an idiot or a freak of some sort."

"Actually, I think I agree with you about being happier pottering about," said Lupin, "but, of course, Penelope hasn't had any children so she couldn't be expected to know that, and I suppose she thought it would be a relief to you not having any housekeeping to do. Unless you've had a baby yourself you can't very well know how a person feels beforehand, but I do think it's a good thing for Dick to have something else to think about. Probably he would have got on your nerves if you had been at the cottage alone with him. Andrew nearly drove me mad, always wondering if I had a headache or a tummyache or an ache in my big toe. Oh, here comes Mr. Stevenson. He loves having you here, so that's one person who's happy. Come and sit down," she called out.

"Are you sure I won't be in the way?"

"Well, of course, you will be rather out of it among us godly matrons."

"I think I'll have to learn to knit. Old women can make themselves useful right up to the end knitting for their grandchildren, but there is nothing much an old man can do."

"Now don't start being morbid," begged Lupin. "Betty is allowed an occasional fit of the blues because she is in an interesting condition, but you haven't got that excuse, or have you?"

Penelope and Andrew found them still sitting in the garden when they arrived back from their game. Betty looked calmer and more relaxed than she had done for some time and Mr. Stevenson was laughing heartily.

"Daddy," said Penelope, "you shouldn't be sitting in the garden. I know the sun is quite hot but it is never safe to sit out of doors so late in the year at your age. You are a naughty old thing, the moment my back is turned you go and do something silly. Your husband beat me," she added to Lupin. "Will you take me on this afternoon? Then if I beat you I shall feel I am all square on the Hastings."

"Oh, I'd love a game," replied Lupin. "But won't two rounds be too much for you ?"

"No, rather not. I'm not as old as all that, and I couldn't feel tired on a day like this. Isn't it perfect? I always feel more energetic in the autumn than at any other time."

She certainly seemed energetic enough that afternoon. As she strode along the fairway you would never have guessed she had played eighteen holes that morning. She was a very good player and she beat Lupin four and three.

It was not until they were back at the Limes that she showed the least sign of being tired. "I suppose I must be getting old," she said, as she stretched out her slim legs toward the fire and accepted a piece of crumpet from Dick. "I usen't to think anything of two rounds of golf."

"Oh, Pen, you didn't play two rounds, did you? Daddy, couldn't you have stopped her? Betty, why did you let her? You know she oughtn't to have done it."

Lupin looked at Betty's white, drawn face and sunken eyes, and at Penelope's, glowing with health and exercise, and she longed to smack Dick. Civilization preventing her, she merely remarked that if Penelope played golf as she had done that afternoon when she was tired she wouldn't care to take her on when she was fresh.

"No one ever knows when she is tired, that is the trouble," said Dick. "She just goes on and on and no one notices and then she knocks herself up. Go and rest now, Pen, there's a good girl. Betty, you will see she does, won't you?"

CHAPTER 7

OH DEAR! thought Lupin. Here's another air raid. I wonder if we need get up.

"I say," said a voice, "could you come? Betty's been taken ill." Lupin leaped out of bed and hurried from the room, putting on a dressing gown as she went.

"Will you stay with her while I ring up the doctor?" said Dick.

Lupin was not very clever, but she had had two children and she had had a good deal of experience of one thing and other since she had been a clergyman's wife. She managed to calm Betty while Dick and Andrew went down to the telephone. Alice the parlormaid looked in to see if she could do anything, and Lupin sent her down to put on as many kettles as possible and bring up a cup of tea for Betty.

Dick mopped his brow. "I know I'm a fool," he said.

"So was I," said Andrew. "I wouldn't think much of any man who wasn't at these times. I'd have a drink before you go up, if I were you. Betty will be all right with Lupin."

"She is a brick," said Dick. "I do hope you didn't mind me fetching her, but I was in such a flap. Betty looked so awful and I'm sure she was in frightful pain. Of course, Pen would have gone to her, but I should hate to wake her up as she is such a bad sleeper, and Lupin having had children and everything herself—" He broke off and took a drink of whisky.

They went upstairs and found Mr. Stevenson standing outside Betty's door in his dressing gown. "Is she all right?" he whispered.

"Yes, sir," replied Andrew. "My wife is with her and the doctor will be here in a few minutes."

Dick put his hand through his father's arm. He felt rather as he had felt when he was a small boy and had liked to hold his father's hand.

"Shall I go down and let the doctor in?" suggested Andrew.

"Please do," said Mr. Stevenson.

Dick peeped into the bedroom where Lupin was sitting beside the bed with her hand behind Betty's head, giving her sips of tea while Alice stood waiting. Dick kissed Betty's forehead and she smiled at him. "It will be all right," she murmured.

"Bless you," muttered Dick, tiptoeing out of the room and down the stairs, where he met the doctor coming up. "Thank goodness you've come," he said, "she is pretty bad."

"I've been trying everywhere to get a nurse," replied the doctor. "I've left a message, but they are very shorthanded just now. Do any of your maids know anything about nursing?"

"Alice does a bit, but I don't know about babies—she and Lady Lupin Hastings are in there now."

"I expect they'll be more trouble than they are worth, but there it is," and he went on his way.

"You will pull her through, won't you?" begged Dick.

"I'll do my best," replied the doctor and Dick went down to the library, where he found his father and Andrew.

"Might I light the fire, sir?" asked Andrew, looking at the black hearth.

"That's a very good idea," said Mr. Stevenson.

"Shall I get the doings?" said Dick. He and Andrew found the housemaid's box standing ready for the morning in the pantry, and they worked away at clearing out the ashes and relighting the fire. They soon had quite a comfortable little blaze and the three of them sat round smoking their pipes and not talking much.

"I am so glad you and your wife were here," said Mr. Stevenson. "It makes a lot of difference to Dick and me."

"Rather," said Dick. Doing the grate and lighting the fire had taken his mind off things a bit, but now there was nothing to do but to sit and think and wait for the doctor to come down and tell them. Tell them what? What was happening to Betty? He would never forget that cry she had given or her face as she had lain moaning, unable to speak.

"A word of eleven letters," said Andrew, who had picked up a crossword puzzle, "beginning with F and the fifth letter A, meaning to brag."

"Let's have a look," said Dick.

Dorothy, the housemaid, came in with three cups of hot soup on a tray. "Please, sir, Cook said she did hope you would drink this. Why, whoever's gone and lit the fire?"

"We did," replied Dick, "and a very good job we have made of it, I consider. You women think you are the only ones who can light fires and make beds, but we men can do it, too, when we are put to it, though we don't usually let on for fear we should be expected to do it every day."

Dorothy giggled. "Lor, sir," she said, "but you didn't ought to have done it. I'd have come at once if I'd known."

Dick grinned as she left the room. "Anyone would think it was me that was having the baby," he said, picking up his bowl of soup.

"I was treated as if I were in delicate health, I remember," said Andrew. "Parishioners kept bringing me bottles of port and whisky to help me keep my strength up."

"How decent of them! I wish I'd got some parishioners." Dick's thoughts went back to Betty, and he wished he were with her. He supposed he would be in the way. How useless and helpless a man felt! He looked at his father. The old man had been through all this—he understood, and this thought warmed him up. Andrew, too. It made one feel less lonely somehow to have him with them, knowing what it was like.

"Fanfaronade," said Mr. Stevenson. Dick stared at him.

"To brag," said his father.

"Bananas! I believe you are right," said Dick, picking up the paper. "Now I know where I get my brains from."

The long night wore on, and the light was beginning to filter through the gaps in the curtains when the front doorbell rang. Dick's heart gave a leap—why, he did not know, as he was not expecting any news from without.

"The nurse, I expect," said Andrew.

"Of course," said Dick, and he got up to go to the door. As he crossed the hall, the doctor was coming down the stairs. "All is well," he said , "a dear little boy."

"What about Betty?" asked Dick.

"She'll be all right," he said kindly. "You can just go and have one peep, but don't wake her up. Well, here you are, Nurse. Better late than never."

"I'm frightfully sorry, Doctor, but I was spending the night with my auntie at Polton Heath and she is not on the telephone. I'd have never got the message at all if it hadn't been that my sister knows Alfred Todger, who has the garage there, and she rang him up and he came round to Auntie's and he took me to the station but of course there wasn't a train till three fifteen, but luckily he knew the station-master's wife and she let me rest on her sofa till it was time to start, but of all the slow trains . . ."

Dick was halfway up the stairs before the nurse had finished her recital, and the doctor turned to Mr. Stevenson, who had come out of the library. "You really think she will be all right?" asked the old man.

"Yes, but she will have to take things very quietly for a bit. Who was that young woman who has been helping me? She seems very capable." Andrew was surprised at this description of his wife, but very proud, and Mr. Stevenson explained the situation.

"I congratulate you," said the doctor. "She and the maid were perfectly wonderful. It is a great thing to deal with people who don't lose their heads. It was awkward about Nurse Burton, but she will be able to relieve them now. She is a good nurse, though rather a talker. I'm glad you've got a fire," he went on. "These autumn nights can be very chilly, and it wouldn't help anyone to have you laid up. Still, it must have been a great comfort to your son to have you with him. These times are very trying, very trying, poor young fellow!"

"I don't think any of us have slept much tonight," said Mr. Stevenson. "I know the maids have all been up, either helping you or looking after us down here, making us soup or something. And our guests, the Hastings, have been invaluable."

"Well, it is all natural enough," said the doctor. "The first baby is always a great event, though I get fairly used to them. I think I'll get home and snatch an hour or two of sleep before starting on my day's work, and I'd go and rest yourself if I were you. I'll be round later on in the morning."

Dick came in. "She knew me," he said.

"You don't say so," chuckled the doctor. "Now, you get yourself and your father to bed. There is nothing more you can do."

"Thanks most awfully for everything. I must just go and tell Cook and Dorothy."

"What about your sister?" asked the doctor. "Isn't she at home?"

Dick hesitated. "Do you think I should wake her to tell her?" he asked. "She sleeps so badly. It seems rather a pity to wake her up before one need, and Betty and the baby are both asleep now."

"Yes, I think I'd wait till she's called," replied Mr. Stevenson. "She will want to be feeling her best to welcome her nephew."

"Won't Miss Penelope be pleased," remarked Cook to Dorothy, after they had congratulated Dick and watched him run up the stairs two steps at a time.

"Yes," agreed Dorothy. "She is so fond of children. It's sad she has never had any of her own."

"I expect there's a story there, if we did but know," replied Cook sentimentally. "She must have been a very pretty young lady."

"She is ever so handsome now," said Dorothy. "And always so nice."

"Yes, she is, indeed. A sweeter mistress I've never had, and I daresay she doesn't find things too easy. She looks terribly sad sometimes."

Alice came into the kitchen and was welcomed as a heroine.

"A lovely boy, he is," she said.

"We were just saying how pleased his auntie would be," said Dorothy.

Alice gave a sniff. "Funny she never came down, she said.

"Well, no one knew it was coming tonight," said Cook. "Mrs. Dick had a room at the nursing home for tomorrow fortnight. I remember her telling me as well as anything, because it was my granny's birthday and we said what a coincidence it was."

"Lady Lupin is a capable one," said Alice. "She may look flighty and be a ladyship, but no one could have been nicer than she was, as homely as anything, and handy, too."

"Well, she has two of her own," said Cook. "She ought to know something about it."

"Fancy the master coming down, poor old gentleman!" said Dorothy.

"Well, I don't see as how any of us could have slept tonight," said Cook, "not once we knew what was happening."

"Miss Penelope could," retorted Alice. The others looked at her in shocked silence.

CHAPTER 8

"I JUST had to come along and congratulate you, Penelope dear," said Lady Deering, arriving with her daughter-in-law Agnes, her son Henry's widow, the next morning.

Penelope and Lupin were sitting in the patch of sunshine where Lupin had sat with Betty the previous morning. Penelope looked up at her visitor with a beautiful smile; her eyes were tired but happy. Lupin, who had had barely two hours' sleep during the previous night, wondered why she could not achieve that weary look.

"Thank you so much, Lady Deering. You know how much it means to us all."

"I do, indeed. I expect your father is very proud."

"Dear Daddy, it has made him very happy. Why, Agnes, how nice to see you. Lupin, may I introduce Mrs. Henry Deering, Lady Lupin Hastings."

"How do you do, and how is Betty?"

Lupin was glad that someone had thought to ask after Betty, and she replied before Penelope had time to do so. "She has had rather a rough crossing, but the doctor thinks she will be all right now."

"Poor little Betty," said Lady Deering, "and poor you," she said to Penelope. "I can guess what you went through."

Lupin caught Agnes's eye, and she had a sudden feeling that they understood each other. Mrs. Henry Deering was a plain, rather attractive woman in well-worn tweeds.

"Mr. and Mrs. Baker," announced Alice, ushering the vicar and his wife into the garden.

"Oh dear," murmured Penelope, closing her eyes for a moment. Then she pulled herself together and went to meet the Bakers.

"Will you please bring the sherry out, Alice? How nice of you both to come," she added. "You know where the garden chairs are, don't you, Mr. Baker? Will you be very kind and bring out two more?"

"Anything I can do for you is a pleasure, as you know," he replied. "I wish you would ask more of me than to fetch chairs." His voice was warm with admiration. "You know how we are rejoicing with you at this time."

"Thank you," she said. "Everyone is so kind."

"And how is Mrs. Stevenson?" asked Mrs. Baker.

"That was just what I was wanting to know," said Mrs. Deering.

"Dear little Betty is going on very well, I am thankful to say," said Penelope.

"I heard she had a very bad time," said Mrs. Baker, and Lupin found herself quite warming to the woman.

"A woman remembers no longer her travail for joy that a man is born into the world," said Mr. Baker gravely.

"How true that is," said Penelope, her eyes shining.

"I wonder how she knows," murmured Lupin, as she offered Agnes a glass of sherry.

"We must make arrangements about the christening," went on Penelope. "It is rather nice to think that Dick's son will be christened from the same font as his father."

"You must let me know just what you want," said Mr. Baker, drawing his chair closer to Penelope.

"Well, of course, I must consult Betty as soon as she is well enough."

"How kind of you to think of her," said Agnes, in a perfectly unemotional voice.

Mrs. Baker gave a short, rather shrill laugh, and Lady Deering remarked placidly, "Dear Penelope is always thinking of others. Why, here is Mr. Stevenson! How do you do? We have all come to congratulate you on your grandson, but we heard that you were resting this morning."

"Daddy dear, I told you not to get up till lunchtime," said Penelope, "and you really mustn't sit down out of doors. I do hope my nephew will be more obedient than you are."

"Well, today is a great day," said Mr. Stevenson. "I have just been up to see little Betty, but she was fast asleep, I am thankful to say. Next time you come I shall hope to show you my grandson," he said to Lady Deering. "He is a bit small but perfectly healthy, so the doctor says. I don't know what we should have done without this child here," he added, stretching out his hand toward Lupin.

"Nonsense, Daddy. I didn't do anything," said Penelope truthfully, as she pulled her father down on the seat beside her, "except perhaps help to keep Betty's spirits up and give her a little courage."

"I think that what you did probably made all the difference to both mother and child," said Mr. Baker admiringly. "Your courage and your kindness make an atmosphere which enables others to be kind and brave, too. There are some people who draw out all that is good from their neighbors and those are the people we want in the world. Good morning, Hastings."

Andrew came up the garden path. He had been for a walk with Dick, who had taken a morning off from the works, and he had just left him outside his wife's room. He shook hands all round and accepted a glass of sherry.

"Where is Dick?" asked Penelope.

"He has gone up to Betty," replied Andrew.

"Oh, I don't think he should have done that," said Penelope in a distressed voice. "He may wake her up. I was going to go up presently and could have let him know how she was."

"He won't wake her up if she is asleep, but if she is awake she will want to see him."

"I think it would have been better if I had gone up first to prepare the way, so to speak."

"I should leave them to it," said her father. "It is only natural for a woman to want to see her husband before anyone else. I know your dear mother did."

"Oh, Daddy dear, does this bring it all back?" and Penelope laid her hand lovingly on the top of her father's.

As Bob came up the garden path he saw Penelope sitting between her father and Mr. Baker, with Andrew standing near, rather as if they were the shepherds, as Lupin confided to Agnes when they were discussing the situation long afterwards. The sun shone full on her sad but lovely face, casting shadows over its delicate modeling, but in spite of her weariness there was a radiance about her, a joy that seemed to emanate from another world. Bob gazed at her and, to the women watching him, his face was that of one who has seen the Madonna.

"Well, we must be off," said Lady Deering, who had noticed nothing about anyone's face. "Goodbye, Penelope, my dear. Don't overdo things. It would be terrible for us all if you were taken ill. I don't know what everyone would do without you. Goodbye, Mr. Stevenson, mind you bring your grandson to see us soon. Goodbye," she added graciously to Lupin and to the Bakers, and she stepped into Bob's car, followed by her daughter-in-law.

The next day Andrew and Lupin went back to Glanville. "You have been angels," said Penelope, as she said goodbye. "I am sorry you should have had such a hectic visit, but at any rate it wasn't dull! Of course you will come to the christening, won't you?"

"You asked me the other day what I thought about Penelope," said Lupin, as they drove along. "And I said I wasn't sure. Well, I am now. I don't really like her."

"I am sorry for her," said Andrew.

"Yes, so am I, of course. It was bad luck having to give up that man but I don't really see why she need have done. I mean, I don't believe either Dick or his father would have wanted her to."

"I wasn't thinking about that. I was thinking that she sees herself as a different person from the one she really is, and one day she will find herself out."

CHAPTER 9

LUPIN and Andrew were down at Much Lancing again, quite soon, for Christopher's christening. It was a very beautiful ceremony, and at the moment that Penelope, as godmother, offered the baby to Mr. Baker, there was scarcely a dry eye in the church. The winter sunlight fell through the stained glass windows on to her pale, beautiful face, as she gazed at the child in her arms and kissed his forehead before relinquishing him to the priest, who appeared so much moved that Lupin was afraid that he would drop Christopher into the font. As one of the members of the Mothers' Union remarked afterwards, "One would have thought that Miss Stevenson was the child's mother, she looked at it so loving!"

Bob Deering was in the proud position of godfather, and he stood in awe and wonder throughout the service. He remembered when he had attended his nephew's christening, he had not realized the solemnity of the occasion. He blushed to recall that he had thought rather in terms of tips, and of giving him a good blowout at the tuck shop when he went to school. Now, looking at Penelope's rapt face, he was ashamed of himself. In the future young Harry, as well as Christopher, would be a sacred charge to him. He and this wonderful woman were fellow godparents, and life would be changed for him from today.

After the christening, Penelope held a little court in the drawing room at the Limes. Mr. Baker volubly, and Bob silently, paid their tribute while Andrew stood by, politely concurring with all that was said. He quite agreed with Mr. Baker's statement that baptism was not a mere pagan superstition. As Lupin remarked afterwards, he gave the impression that the idea was quite new to him.

"Well," her husband had replied, "what Baker said was quite true. There was no need for me to say that it had crossed my mind, even before I had seen Penelope Stevenson as a godmother."

Lupin found Mrs. Baker seated beside her, and she turned to her rather thankfully. The sight of somebody ordinary was a relief.

"I do like christenings, don't you?" she said. "I thought it was an awfully nice idea having the Mothers' Union there. I mean, it is the sort of thing mothers ought to be interested in, isn't it ?"

"Yes, my husband takes a great interest in the Mothers' Union. He often says that if there were no mothers there would be no children and I think he is quite right."

"Absolutely," agreed Lupin.

"I am hoping Mrs. Stevenson will join us. She is a splendid person and will be a great help. After all, the Union is for mothers. There is some idea of having honorary members, but I don't agree with it."

Lupin wondered whether Mr. Baker had suggested making Penelope an honorary member. She looked at Mrs. Baker with a feeling bordering on liking. She might be a fool and make the most inane remarks, but she resented her husband making an exhibition of himself, and she would make a fight for it if necessary. Lupin did not think for a minute that there was anything that was not a hundred percent pure in Mr. Baker's admiration for Penelope, but she felt it would be very annoying to have one's husband gazing at another woman as if she were a vestal virgin. She would almost prefer him to carry on an ordinary common-or-garden flirtation.

"No, I am with you," she said aloud. "Let's close our ranks. Mothers only! will be our battle cry."

"Well, I am glad you agree with me. I little thought, when we first met, that we should have so much in common."

Lupin was feeling just the same. She had looked on Mrs. Baker as a pure figure from comedy at their first meeting; now she realized that there was more to her than that, and that she might even turn into a figure of tragedy, little as she looked the part. She found everyone was beginning to say goodbye, and Mr. Baker came up to her.

"Well, we must be on our way," he said. "I have a darts match this evening. We have some good chaps in our club, and I think we shall have a cheery time. This afternoon has been an inspiration. I shall play darts all the better for it. There are some people whom just to meet for a short time alters one's whole day. I expect you know what I mean, Lady Lupin. Just to be in the presence, for a moment or two, of a rare and beautiful soul makes all the ordinary things of life different."

"I know what you mean," replied Lupin. "Something about a richer crimson on the lapwing's breast, or whatever it is. Betty does give one just that feeling, doesn't she?"

Mrs. Baker flashed her a grateful glance and Andrew's eyes twinkled. He had to go back to Glanville that evening, but Lupin was staying the night and she went upstairs with Betty after seeing her husband off.

"I've simply masses to tell you," said Betty, as she threw herself down in an old-fashioned rocking chair and took her baby on her knee.

"Do tell me," begged Lupin.

"Well, you know I told you about that man, Charles Graeme, who has always been in love with Pen. Well, his wife is dead."

"Oh, you mean the man who always sent her violets on St. Valentine's Day?"

"I never told you that," exclaimed Betty.

"No. She told me herself."

"Did she really? She must like you awfully, because she is usually so frightfully reserved and never talks about herself."

"Doesn't she?"

"Well, anyway, she is dead. The wife I mean," went on Betty. "I know it is too awful to feel pleased about it, and I am dreadfully sorry for her and everything, but it does rather look as if perhaps everything is going to come all right for Penelope after all, doesn't it?"

"Yes, it really does."

"It was some time last spring, I believe. I can't think how we missed seeing it in *The Times,* but you know how one always does if it is someone important and, of course, Penelope never hears from him except for the violets on St. Valentine's Day. Then suddenly Lady Deering came out with it one day. I suppose she thought we knew. Penelope was wonderful, so calm and everything, but Dick and I had awful difficulty in going on as if nothing had happened. Anyhow, we have had the most wonderful idea. You know what Pen is like. She is so frightfully unselfish, she would be quite equal to giving him up all over again if it meant leaving Daddy alone, so we are coming to live here. Then she will be quite free and can feel perfectly happy about getting married. I don't mean that we could ever take her place, but Daddy and I do get on awfully well together, and I don't think he would like her to give up Charles again. It was different when Dick was a little boy. It would have been so dreadful for him without her. But you know, Lupin, I don't believe Daddy is really selfish."

"I am quite sure that he isn't," replied Lupin.

"It is just that Pen is so frightfully unselfish that everyone puts on her without meaning to. I am afraid I was a bit of a pig myself before Christopher was born, but that is over now. When she is married, Dick won't feel so responsible for her, and I shall be happier about her, too. And I am quite sure Daddy won't begrudge her happiness."

"I am sure he won't," agreed Lupin. "It is all like a lovely fairy story, isn't it ? I mean, the prince and princess marrying and living happily ever after."

"Yes, that is what I feel, though I suppose we are getting on rather fast and ought to be thinking more about his poor wife. But it is so difficult to feel very sad about someone one has never seen."

"Absolutely! But won't you mind giving up your own home?"

Betty hesitated. "Well, I shall be sorry in a way, because I really like a small house best, where one can do things oneself, you know, without asking the maids. But when I think of all that I've got, I do want Penelope to have it, too. Of course, we'll just pretend that we really want to come and live here, and that we like it better than the cottage. If we waited till Charles turned up she would guess why we were doing it, and it wouldn't be any good. Anyway, when Christopher's brothers and sisters arrive, the cottage would be a bit small, wouldn't it? This will be a lovely house for children, and, of course, Pen might have some, too. Wouldn't it be wonderful if she did?"

"Wonderful!"

"And then you must come and bring yours, and we will have the house full of children playing hide and seek all over the place. I shall like that most frightfully. Don't gobble so fast, Christopher. You are a greedy thing."

CHAPTER 10

LUPIN heard from Betty and Penelope at Christmas. But she was so busy with all her own and parish affairs at that time that she had not much time to think about them, beyond an occasional hope that Christopher was flourishing and that Penelope would soon be married and living happily ever after. It was halfway through February that she received the following letter from Betty:

Dear Lupin,

Could you possibly have Christopher and me for a little while ? I am afraid it is asking rather a lot of you, but I must go somewhere, and you and Andrew have always been so decent.

Love from
Betty

"What do you make of that?" she asked Andrew.

Andrew read the letter. "I think Betty wants to come and stay with us for a little while," he replied, "and to bring Christopher with her."

"Yes, I can see that much, but why does she want to come? Do you think she has quarreled with Dick and Penelope?"

"I am afraid it looks a little like it. Would you care to have them?"

"Naturally! I mean, in a way, it's a sort of compliment that she wants to come, isn't it? And she may feel better if she gets away for a bit."

"Yes, I should write off at once and ask her to come for as long as she likes."

"You are an angel, Andrew. I am not a bit surprised that everyone else always seems so miserable. It must be horrid not being married to you."

Lupin met Betty at the station. She was carrying Christopher and she did not look well. Lupin made no comment and soon had her home, where she handed Christopher over to Nanny and took Betty into her sitting room. Andrew was out, and she told the parlormaid to tell all callers that she was 'not at home.' After a few commonplaces, while Betty drank her tea and ate her crumpet, she turned to Lupin. "I expect you thought it awfully funny, my writing to you like that all of a sudden," she said.

"I didn't think it was funny," replied Lupin. "I expect you felt you needed a change."

"I did," said Betty. "I want a permanent change. I don't mean that I am going to park myself on you forever, but I won't go back to the Limes."

"What's happened?" asked Lupin, guessing that Betty wanted to get it off her chest.

"Well, you know Dick and I said we'd like to live at the Limes, so that Penelope could marry Charles. Well, we fixed it all up and Daddy was awfully pleased about it, and he let the cottage to some other people. I felt a little sad about that because we had had such lovely times there but I knew that I should be quite happy at the Limes and I was awfully glad to think of Penelope having her chance at last. Well, Charles turned up, and what do you think? He came on St. Valentine's Day. Wasn't it romantic of him? The day they had had their last farewell forever, you know."

"Yes, the day he used to send her violets."

"Well, it was all so suitable and romantic. I saw them going off together across the fields and I was so happy, I really was happy at the thought of Penelope being happy because I was awfully fond of her, and then, and then . . ." Betty's hand trembled, and to Lupin's horror she began to cry.

"Cheer up," said Lupin. "Have some more tea. I can guess what happened. She refused him."

"How did you guess?"

"Well, if she had accepted him you wouldn't be here. You would have stayed behind helping to sew lace on her *crêpe de Chine* step-ins."

"That's true, but why? Oh, why, Lupin? I mean, Daddy really would have been quite happy, but it was no good. I tried to reason with her, but she said that I was only a child and did not understand, and that she had chosen her part in life and would stand by it till the end. She would never forgive herself if she deserted her father now, in his hour of need. She would get all the happiness she wanted in helping to bring up Christopher, and I don't want her to help bring up Christopher. I know I am being selfish and horrible, but he is my baby, and I have given up my home and everything. I can't live at the Limes with Penelope. It's not that I'm not fond of her, but I want my own baby, and my own home and my own husband. Why can't she marry Charles and have a home of her own? He is awfully nice."

"I suppose," said Lupin thoughtfully, "that unselfishness is really a kind of vice, like drink. I mean, once people start they can't stop, even when there is no need for it."

"It is rather bad luck on other people," said Betty. "Well, I shall be awfully grateful if you will keep me here for a bit, until I decide what to do next. One thing I am certain about is that I won't go home until I have got a home to go to."

Two letters arrived in the course of the next week, one to Lupin from Penelope.

Dear Lupin,

It was so sweet of you to ask dear little Betty to stay with you and the change will do her good. We miss her very much, but don't let her hurry back until she is feeling quite strong, if you are sure it is all right for you that is, I know another baby in the house must entail a lot of extra work. Tell Betty not to worry about anything. I have collected her money for the nursing fund, and I took her place at the Mothers' Union the other day as an honorary mother! I explained that I was really only an auntie, but Mr. Baker seemed to think I knew as much about babies as most of the mothers! Please give my love to Betty and a big kiss to my nephew. With love to you and to Andrew, if I may, and many thanks for all your kindness to my family.

Yours affectionately,
Penelope Stevenson

The other was to Betty from Dick.

Darling Betts,

I couldn't make head or tail of your letter, but I suppose as Pen says, you were feeling a bit run down. But what on earth do you mean about wanting a house of your own? It was all your idea that we should stay on at the Limes. I am sorry that Pen didn't accept Charles, but I see her point in a way—the old man might feel it rather after all these years, and after all, we could never take her place. It will be much easier for you, too—if she is at home you won't have to bother about Dad, and she will help you with Christopher. She is so frightfully interested in children and has read a lot of books about bringing them up and all that. Of course, I see it was rather a strain for you, not being able to get a nurse, and it must be very nice having Lupin's old Nanny, but we can't go parking on her indefinitely. Pen is trying her hardest to get you someone. She thinks she has heard of just the person, quite a young woman, who has been through one of those training colleges and she sounds ideal. Let me know when you are coming back.

Masses of love,
Your devoted Dick

"Well, it's no use working yourself up," remarked Lupin. "Your milk will go sour or something, and, anyway, as I've always told you, the man is very devoted to you and he obviously wants you back."

"He probably thinks it will be a help to Pen to have me back, and she wants to have Christopher to bring up. I won't have a young woman who has been to a training college and knows about children's minds. I want a proper old-fashioned nanny like yours."

"I quite agree with you there. I always think that children's bowels are much more important than their minds, but, of course, nannies are very hard to get nowadays. They are nearly extinct, like the dodo, but we will do our best."

"But he doesn't understand at all," wailed Betty.

Lupin soothed her as best she could and went in search of Andrew, who was writing his monthly letter for the parish magazine.

"I suppose we had better have the poor mutt to stay," she said, after explaining to him how the land lay.

"Don't mind me," replied Andrew. "If you like to turn this house into a crêche and lunatic asylum combined, I suppose you must. And now I've begged people to keep a good crêche when I meant Lent." He put down his pen with a resigned air.

"Oh dear, it is all my fault. Everyone said that it would be your ruination marrying me. You used to be so levelheaded and now you are getting as erotic as I am."

"Don't you mean erratic?"

"Didn't I say erratic? Well, the point is, what are we to do?"

"I suppose we must try to affect a reconciliation. It is hardly the thing for a clergyman's household to be used as a refuge for a runaway wife."

"Rot!"

"I quite agree with you that Dick is a singularly idiotic and wooden-headed young man, but we must do our best. You had better write and ask him here for a weekend."

Dick arrived on the following Saturday, and the first evening passed off well. He and Betty were so pleased to be together again that all their grievances were forgotten for the time being, but with the next day came a discussion of plans, and the visit ceased to be a feast of reason and flow of soul. They went off for a long walk in the morning, and as soon as Lupin caught sight of them on their return to the cold beef and pickles that formed the *pièce de résistance* of Sunday luncheon, she knew that the further outlook was unsettled, but she did wish they had not hit on a Sunday on which to be difficult. After all, it wasn't as if Sunday were an easy day to start with, and she did like to relax over her cold beef. She had had to sit with the Sunday school children that morning, and Peter, who had accompanied her, had encouraged the otherwise blameless children to behave badly. Nanny would be going out this afternoon, so she would have her own children to cope with, plus Christopher, and probably Betty and Dick quarreling all over everything. Very likely the Sunday school superintendent would drop in at teatime to wonder why the children had behaved so badly this morning, obviously not wondering at all, but knowing quite well that it was the influence of Lupin's badly brought up offspring.

Andrew ate his cold beef with a somewhat abstracted air. One of the churchwardens had made a somewhat startling suggestion this morning, and although Andrew did not altogether agree with it and felt that it would not be acceptable to the congregation, who were not very go-ahead, he did not like to turn down anyone's suggestion without due consideration. He pondered on the matter as he helped himself to pickles.

Dick felt rather aggrieved. He had been overjoyed at the sight of Betty and was perfectly ready to forgive her for staying away so long, and to let bygones be bygones. But now she seemed to think that *she* had something to forgive, and was trying to make conditions with him. Women were the devil and he wished he were back in the army.

Betty did not want to quarrel with Dick. Now that they were together again she could not imagine how she had ever been able to bring herself to leave him, even for a fortnight. All her instincts were to make it up and to do whatever he wished. On the other hand she knew that she was being forced into an impossible position and that this was the moment to make a stand, if she were ever going to do so.

"Did you have a nice walk?" asked Lupin.

"Yes, it was lovely, but we went rather a long way. I think I shall take it quietly this afternoon if you really don't mind coping with Christopher."

"We didn't go very far," protested Dick. "I think I shall go for a real stretch this afternoon. I suppose you will be taking a service or something, Andrew?"

"That is a good idea," said Lupin. "Peter can come with Christopher and me. I think church once a day is enough for him. In fact, it was a bit too much this morning—at least he was too much for the other children. Will you take Jill, Andrew? Just hand her over to Miss Bray. She will look after her."

"I think I had better put the matter before the parish council," said Andrew, who had been following his own line of thought.

The others looked at him rather anxiously. Dick and Betty had a guilty feeling that perhaps their matrimonial disagreement was going to be made a matter for discussion at the council meeting, and wished that they had not confided it to Andrew. Lupin wondered rather vaguely why he was going to ask the parish council about his children's church attendance. But she replied that it would be a very good idea.

I'll have a really long tramp along by the sea and forget all about women, thought Dick.

I'll lie down with that lovely book and forget all about men, thought Betty.

"For what we have received may the Lord make us truly thankful," said Andrew.

Lupin tucked up Betty. "I hope you'll have a good rest," she said. "I expect you walked for miles. You look rather like death warmed up."

"We did go rather a long way. Dick was very sweet, but now he has got some utterly fantastic idea that Penelope and I shall do the housekeeping between us, I think she is going to order the lunch and me the dinner or the other way round. Anyway, it is all going to be too cooperative for words! But I don't quite see how it is going to work."

"Nor do I, but I should do anything rather than have a real quarrel with Dick. After all, having each other is the great thing."

"If I have got him! But you know what he is like when Pen is there—he doesn't seem to see anyone else."

"I know what you mean, but if you had seen him that night when you were having Christopher you would realize that it is you he really cares about. Penelope is a sort of habit. Lots of men are like that about their mothers."

"Still, a mother is bound to die some day, but a sister. . . Oh dear, am I saying something frightful?"

"Oh well, it is better to say things than to brood on them. One often says things one doesn't really mean, but it clears one's mind. Oh yes, Nanny," and Lupin hurried downstairs, saw Jill off with her father to church and started for her walk with the other two children.

It was pleasant on the sea front. The sun was shining and there were not many people at this time of year. Peter was playing some game of his own, which entailed running on in front and jumping down on to the shingle every few yards. It was not very good for his shoes, but it seemed a small price to pay for peace and quiet. Lupin was very fond of Dick and Betty, but she did wish they could have their matrimonial difficulties somewhere else.

"Hullo, shall I push my own son?" said a voice, and there was Dick.

"I thought you were going for a long walk," said Lupin, rather lamely.

"I meant to, then I got sitting on the beach and chucking stones into the water and thinking about things in general, if you know what I mean. I'm awfully glad I ran into you, because I should rather like to talk things over."

Lupin did not share his gladness nor his wish to talk things over, but she murmured "Oh, do you?" in what she hoped were encouraging tones.

Dick did not seem to notice her reluctance but plunged straight into his subject. "It is awfully difficult to know what the right thing is," he said. "You know how I feel about Penelope. You see, she has done everything for me and given up all chance of happiness for herself, so I do feel I owe her an awful lot."

"Yes, I do see that," said Lupin. "On the other hand, unless you were prepared to put your wife first, you had no right to ask her to marry you."

"But I do put her first, I. . . Well, it's a bit difficult, but Betty knew how things were before we got married. I mean she was Pen's friend first and she was absolutely devoted to her. In away, that is what attracted me at the beginning. I shouldn't have liked to have married anyone who was not fond of Pen, and that is why I am a bit hurt at her changing like this."

"I don't think she has changed. I think she is still fond of Penelope."

"In a way, but I mean she has taken a frightful fancy to you. Please don't think I blame you for it. You have been so awfully decent, and I'll never forget that night. Well, I really am grateful, and it is nice for her to have a friend of her own age."

"I am thirty-one."

"Well, you don't seem like it. Of course, Pen is a bit old for her age in some ways—it is all she has gone through, you know."

Lupin wondered vaguely what it was that Penelope had gone through. She had lived for thirty years in the same quiet spot. Even the war hadn't touched her much. She herself had been married for ten years, had had two children, and had had several years succoring parishioners in one of the worst-bombed towns in England, not that she thought very much about that, but she did wonder why Penelope was supposed to have had so very wide an experience of life.

"I see," she replied.

"It is just that I think Penelope was a bit hurt at Betty switching over like that. I mean, they were absolutely devoted, and then she met you and—"

"Her whole life was blighted," said Lupin.

"You know I don't mean that," said Dick rather crossly, "but you must admit it was a little fickle of Betty, and I shouldn't have thought she would have been fickle."

"My dear, you seem to think that Betty and I are a sort of female David and Jonathan or Damon and Pythagoras, or whoever they were, but we are just the most ordinary women who like our husbands and children and are not at all given to gushing female friendships. Naturally we get on very well because we have a lot in common, but as for its being one of those beautiful and emotional affairs that people have when they cut their hair short, and wear tortoiseshell glasses, and figure in banned books—it's not like that at all."

Dick laughed. "I didn't think it was, but she does seem to have put you rather in Pen's place."

"No, she hasn't. I keep telling you, I am married and I've got children, so naturally she likes talking to me about your digestion and Christopher's wind."

"Um, yes. I suppose that's it. Being married sort of forms a link. The only thing is, I don't want Pen to be hurt. She is so terribly sensitive, and I have always vowed to make her happy, and try to make up a bit."

"You vowed to make Betty happy—at least you vowed to cherish her, which is the same thing."

"I do want to make her happy, naturally, but she wouldn't want to be happy at Penelope's expense, would she?"

"Do you mean that for the rest of your natural life, Betty's happiness has got to depend on Penelope's?"

"It is all so beastly difficult. I can't see why they can't settle down happily together."

"Well, if you can't see it, it's not much good talking about it and anyway, it's time we went home."

After tea Andrew withdrew to his study. He had already taken three services that day and was looking forward to a quiet hour before Evensong. He was glancing through the notes for his sermon when Betty came in. "I do hope I am not disturbing you," she said. "But I felt I must speak to you."

Andrew was fond of Betty and felt very sorry for her. So he banished all feelings of regret at giving up his quiet hour and, laying aside the notes for his sermon, drew up a comfortable chair for his visitor. "Tell me all about it," he said.

"I want you to tell me what I ought to do," she replied.

"Well, you must remember that you did take Dick for better or for worse. It seems rather for worse at the present moment. I do think that it is very bad luck on you that Penelope should be taking this line, but I suppose she has got the right to marry or not as she chooses. After all, she did not ask you to give up your house and go and look after her father. It was very good of you to do it, and it does seem hard that things should have turned out as they have. But I am afraid there is nothing to be done at the moment. Perhaps, if you are patient, Dick may find another house or Penelope may change her mind—anything may happen, but I should not quarrel with Dick. You have got him and your baby. That is a great deal, isn't it?"

"Yes, of course. I do realize that, and anything is better than being separated from Dick. But must I give in to Penelope over everything?"

"Not over your baby. You have every right to choose your own nurse and so on. I should make that quite clear. Just say what you have decided firmly and pleasantly, and I think you will find that Penelope will acquiesce. She did not strike me as at all a quarrelsome person."

"She isn't. I can't imagine her quarrelling with anyone but she does get hurt rather easily, and that is worse, really, because then Dick thinks I have been unkind to her."

"It is all very trying for you, and Lupin and I both sympathize. You are always welcome here whenever you want a change."

"You are a comfortable person, Andrew. You and Lupin do understand. Most people think that I am so lucky to have Penelope to do everything for me, but I will try to make the best of things. After all, as you say, I have got Dick and Christopher."

Dick and Betty both attended the evening service and came back to supper in a softened mood. Lupin was feeling rather tired after an evening of playing with the children, undressing them, putting them to bed, and coaxing them to go to sleep, which Nanny always seemed to do quite easily, but at which she was very bad. She was hoping to get to bed early herself but Betty was in a talkative mood.

"I really think everything is going to be all right," she said. "It is lovely to have made it up with Dick."

"I am so glad."

"After all, so long as we are together that is all that really matters. Nothing else can hurt us. And perhaps Pen will change her mind and marry Charles after all, or something will happen. I feel very hopeful about things."

"I shouldn't be a bit surprised."

"And Dick understands about the nurse. I think I should rather like to have a young girl instead of a regular nanny. I mean, I should really rather do everything for Christopher myself. After all, I shan't have any housekeeping to do."

"That is a very good idea."

"Yes, isn't it?" and Betty ran on happily with her plans for the future.

In the meantime Dick followed Andrew to his study. "I say," he said, "I thought that you would like to know that Betty and I have fixed everything up. She is coming back with me tomorrow."

Andrew hoped that his relief did not show too plainly. "That is splendid," he said, "although we have enjoyed having Betty with us very much."

"You have been awfully decent," replied Dick. "I do hope you don't think me ungrateful or anything. I mean, naturally I want her to come home. She has been away for a fortnight."

"Is it really a fortnight?" enquired Andrew politely.

"Yes. I have taken your advice about the nurse, by the way. I see what you mean about Christopher being Betty's baby but I do hope Pen won't be hurt after all the trouble she's taken."

"I hope she won't, but I am sure she will be the first to recognize that it is Betty's concern."

"Oh yes, I am sure she will. Only, of course, you don't know Pen frightfully well, and she looks on everyone's concerns as her own. She is never happy unless she is doing something for someone else."

Andrew resigned himself to a further eulogy on Penelope's character. The clock was striking eleven when he pulled himself up with a start, hoping that Dick had not noticed that he had lost himself for a few minutes. At that moment Lupin and Betty came in and this rather prolonged the session, as both Dick and Betty had to tell Andrew and Lupin several times how kind they had been. Lupin and Andrew then had to tell Betty and Dick, also several times, and not altogether accurately, how very welcome they were. Then there was some more conversation about the future, and a discussion as to whether they should get a real old-fashioned nanny, or a young girl, or the nurse that Penelope had already engaged, and by the time they had all joined in the chorus of how wonderful Penelope was, it was after midnight.

CHAPTER 11

"IT SEEMS funny to think that we didn't know the Stevensons this time last year, doesn't it?" remarked Lupin, as they drove through the now familiar country to Much Lancing. The countryside was looking very different from the last time they had come this way. The trees were green instead of golden, and they passed orchards full of blossom and meadows full of lambs.

"There are some people one knows all one's life without ever getting to know them any better, and others whom one knows intimately at the first meeting," replied Andrew.

"That's like us. The moment I saw you I couldn't imagine ever not knowing you. But about Betty and Dick—one has a sort of protective feeling about them. I don't quite know why—they are rather like the babes in the wood, aren't they?"

"They do seem to be on the verge of losing their way every now and then," agreed Andrew.

"Well, I do hope we gave them a push in the right direction. I am all against interfering with people on principle, but I always seem to get interference thrust on me. I am sorry about Mr. Stevenson. I know it will really make things much easier all round, but he was a dear."

"I liked him very much and I shall miss him, although I have seen so little of him."

Mr. Stevenson had died very suddenly from a stroke shortly after Dick and Betty's return, and Lupin and Andrew were on their way to Much Lancing for the funeral. The sun was shining when they left Glanville, and although the wind was sharp the drive was quite pleasant, past gardens gay with daffodils and tulips and down lanes white with blackthorn. But as they approached the end of their journey the weather changed, the wind grew colder and more boisterous, the sun disappeared altogether and a disagreeable rain started to fall.

"Well, Penelope was justified in a way. I mean perhaps she had a sort of premonition that her father wouldn't live long, and that is why she wouldn't get married," said Lupin.

"There will be nothing to stop her now, and Betty and Dick will be able to have a home of their own, which will make all the difference to them," replied her husband.

"Yes, it must be rather nice for Penelope to think that she sacrificed herself up to the end, and that now she can marry and live happily ever after with a clear conscience. The only thing I rather blame her for is that she always gave the impression that her father was selfish, and he wasn't a bit, was he?"

"No, I'll never forget him the night that Christopher was born."

"It wasn't his fault that Penelope would keep sacrificing herself over him. He never asked her to and would probably have much rather she hadn't. However, that is all over now, and she will be able to sacrifice herself to her husband."

"I feel rather sorry for him."

"So do I, but I suppose he knows what he is in for."

"Some people may like self-sacrificing wives."

"Lucky for me, you don't."

"Isn't it?"

Betty and Dick met them when they arrived at the Limes. Betty's eyes were red and Dick had a lost look—he had suddenly realized, rather late, that his father had been the one rock on which he relied, the one person who had never failed him.

"Pen is lying down," he explained.

Lupin bit back the words "She would be!" and substituted "Of course" in a sympathetic voice. She followed Betty into the drawing room, and when the men left them after tea she heard the details.

"He was all right at breakfast," Betty said. "Penelope went out with Bob. He had to motor over to Greater Lindfold and thought that she would like the drive. I went up to take Christopher for a walk, then I thought I'd see if Daddy would like to come, too—he did sometimes, and it was a lovely day—so I went to the library and I found him. It was rather dreadful," and she began to cry.

"You poor old thing," said Lupin. "It must have been simply frightful. I know how fond you were of him, and it must have been awful the others being out. I expect it gave you a ghastly shock?"

"Yes, though of course it was much worse for Penelope and Dick because he was their own father, but he was always so sweet to me."

"He was very fond of you. Andrew noticed that the night Christopher came he was really thinking more about you than of his own grandson, if you know what I mean. It was 'How's Betty?' not 'How's the baby?' Anyhow, you were always an angel to him, and he had a very nice end. No long illness or anything, but naturally you will miss him."

"It is awful for Pen."

"Yes, of course. She had devoted herself to him for so long, hadn't she? Still, I suppose she will be getting married soon herself."

"I suppose so. It seems heartless to be making plans for the future already."

"I don't see why. Next time I come we shall be singing 'Oh, Perfect Love.' I think Mr. Stevenson would be pleased if he thought you were all going to be happy."

"Yes, I think he would. He was awfully understanding about things. He said once, 'I expect you would like to be in a home of your own, Betts? But it is a great treat to me to have you here.' Of course he adored Pen, but she would treat him rather as if he were an invalid, and I think he liked it because I ragged him and told him things, as if he were my own age."

"I am sure he did. How has everything been going since I saw you?"

"Oh, not too bad! Pen was awfully nice about the nurse. Dick told her that I wanted to look after Christopher myself, and she said she quite understood and would have been just the same. So I got one of Mrs. Browne's daughters—you know, the woman in the village I told you about—and she comes for a few hours every day. She really is very good, but it is no good pretending that I shan't be glad to have my own home, because I shall. Still, I am awfully glad I came home when I did. I should have felt awful if I had been away. I should have felt that he had been worrying about Dick and me, and that it was all my fault."

Dinner passed quietly. Both Dick and Betty made a great effort to behave normally, and as they were leaving the dining room Penelope sent a message that she would like to see Lupin.

"Poor Miss Penelope, she is heartbroken," explained Dorothy in tones of admiration, as she conducted Lupin to the bedroom.

Penelope lay back against the pillows, looking very white with purple shadows under her eyes. Anyone would have thought she had been sitting up with her father for many nights, but Lupin knew that Mr. Stevenson had had a stroke while Penelope was out with Bob Deering and had died within six hours. She had never kissed Penelope before, but she felt now that it would be the appropriate gesture, so she bent and kissed her forehead before sitting on the chair that Dorothy had drawn up to the bed.

"It is very good of you to come," said Penelope in rather a faint voice.

"If there is anything one can do?" murmured Lupin.

"There is nothing anyone can do," replied Penelope. "But it is a help to feel that one's friends are around one."

"I am glad he didn't suffer," said Lupin.

"Yes, indeed! That I could not have borne. I am not grieving for him. It is a great relief to feel that he is at peace, and that I need not worry about him any more. One of my dreads has always been that I might go first, and that there would be no one left to care for him. No, I am very thankful for his sake—but oh, Lupin, the terrible emptiness! What shall I do tomorrow and all the tomorrows? My whole life was wrapped up in his, my only thought his comfort. I used to wake up in the morning and look out to see what sort of day it was, whether it would be fit for him to go out or not. This morning I woke up and looked out of the window as usual, then I realized that there was nothing to look for any longer."

Lupin had a very sympathetic nature. She had thrown her arms impulsively round Betty as soon as she had seen her, and she had felt terribly sorry for Dick. But, somehow, she did not feel at all sorry for Penelope. She did not know why, and it was very dreadful of her. After all, Penelope had sacrificed her whole life for her father. It was natural that she should miss him. All the same, wasn't there something a little theatrical in lying on her bed and having trays of nourishment brought up to her by admiring maids? Wouldn't it have been far more praiseworthy if she had pulled herself together and helped Dick with the hundred and one things he had to do?

"I am so terribly sorry about it all," she said aloud. "I was very fond of your father, although I had only met him once or twice. He was always very kind to Andrew and me."

"He was kind to everyone. I never knew him say an unkind word. It is the terrible feeling of loneliness to which I cannot accustom myself— the feeling that I have no one to go to in trouble!"

Lupin had always understood that during Mr. Stevenson's life Penelope had spent her whole time in looking after him at great sacrifice to herself. This idea of a father who protected her and solved her troubles was quite a new aspect and, in any case, Dick was always standing there, waiting to solve any problem that his sister might have, and Charles was waiting to marry her and to take all her burdens upon himself at the first opportunity. Lupin had never felt so inadequate as she murmured in unconvincing tones that she quite understood. Then she said she was sure that Penelope ought to have a good night's sleep.

"Sleep! I don't expect that I shall sleep, but as a matter of fact the doctor has left me some tablets. I should like to feel stronger for tomorrow. It will be a terrible day, but I won't shirk it. I know that Dick will want me to stay up here away from everyone but it is my duty to receive the guests and to go to the funeral, if I am able to do so."

"You must see how you are."

"I have rested today. I felt it my duty. Besides, I don't want to be a blight on other people. I find it hard to talk and be natural, but I don't want to make Dick and Betty miserable. After all, why should they be expected to feel it as I do? Of course, Dick was very fond of Daddy in his own way, but it is not the same thing for him as it is for me, and poor little Betty did not know him at all well. He was only her father-in-law. One does not expect her to grieve for him."

"I think she is very much upset," said Lupin.

"She is very young," said Penelope. "Naturally the mere thought of death upsets her. I think she feels for me, too. She has always been so attached to me, poor little thing, and she does not like to see me suffer! I have not been the sister-in-law of fiction. I think I have helped her and Dick through some hard times."

Lupin went downstairs and found the others doing a crossword puzzle. She joined them for some time, although she was not much help. Then she went upstairs with Betty and saw her safely tucked up in bed.

The next day was frightful, as such days always are. To add to the general cheerlessness, it was wet and cold and windy. Penelope appeared at breakfast, although everyone had begged her to stay in bed. She looked pale and haggard and drank several cups of black coffee and toyed with some toast. No one else liked to eat much or talk much for fear of seeming heartless, although at dinner the night before they had all been quite natural.

During the morning, wreaths and crosses kept on arriving in great numbers, and Lupin made a list of them for Penelope. At twelve o'clock the first of the relations arrived, a niece of Mr. Stevenson's and her grown daughter. "Penelope, my dear," she exclaimed, kissing her on both cheeks.

"Dear Geraldine," replied Penelope. "And Elaine, how sweet of you! This is our great friend, Lady Lupin Hastings. Her husband is taking the service."

"Oh, don't!" hissed her cousin.

Lupin felt ashamed. It seemed very lacking in good taste on Andrew's part to take the funeral service. They were really nothing better than murderers, she felt sure, in the cousin's eyes.

"It was such a terrible shock. In your last letter you said that dear Uncle was keeping pretty well."

"He was. He got through the winter quite nicely."

Her cousin put an arm round her. "My poor dear!" she said. "It must have been terrible for you, but we all know what a devoted daughter you have been. How true it is that in the midst of life we are in death."

Lupin could not really feel that at seventy-six one was in the midst of life. If one were, it would mean that one usually lived. . .and she tried to work it out—twice seven was fourteen and carry one. . .in the middle of her mathematical problem Dick came into the room.

"Hullo, Geraldine," he said.

Geraldine advanced a bony cheek, and Dick kissed the air some way away from it. "Poor Dick," she sighed.

"Why, Elaine, you have grown," went on Dick cheerfully. "The last time I saw you, you were in a gym tunic."

Elaine smiled wryly. "The last time I came dear Uncle was here," she replied reprovingly.

"Have some sherry, Geraldine?"

"No, thank you. I couldn't touch anything."

"Elaine?"

"Oh no," said Elaine in shocked tones. "Lupin?"

"Please," and she thankfully took a full glass.

"Here, Pen, drink this," he ordered, and handed a glass to his sister.

Penelope looked doubtful. "Well," she said rather apologetically, "if you insist, Dick, I will have just a little. It does sometimes pull one together."

"You are quite right," said Geraldine encouragingly. "It will do you good."

Penelope sipped the sherry sadly, and Lupin felt a little impatient with her. Surely she need not look as if she were tasting it for the first time and did not know what it was like! After all, when she wasn't drinking sherry it was usually because she was drinking gin-and-French! She turned to the girl at her side and tried to make herself pleasant.

"Have you come far?" she said.

"From Croydon," replied Elaine. "We left home at eight o'clock this morning."

"You poor thing! What sort of journey was it?"

"It was very cold," replied Elaine, "but we didn't notice it much."

"Didn't you? I hate the cold."

"When you are in sorrow you don't notice things like that."

Lupin disagreed with her; she was sure that when you were in sorrow you noticed being cold and hungry more than you did at other times. "I do," she said aloud. "It is when I am happy that I don't notice things. On my honeymoon we had an awful journey. We had to wait at Crewe for half an hour and it was after two so we couldn't get a drink. It was icy cold, and when the train did come in it wasn't a corridor one, which was awkward, if you know what I mean."

It was only too obvious that both Geraldine and Elaine did know what she meant, and they gazed at her with horror. Penelope, who would naturally have laughed, was staring sadly at her empty sherry glass. Dick gave a great shout of laughter and said, "You are a fool, Lupin," and his cousins transferred their horror-struck glance to him.

"Mrs. Dashwood," announced Alice, and a small upright woman with snow-white hair and bright blue eyes advanced into the room. Dick dashed forward and gave her a hug. "Auntie Boots!" he exclaimed. "I am glad to see you."

Penelope got up, both hands outstretched and a welcoming smile on her pale sad face. "Thank you for coming," she said huskily, then she introduced the rest of the party and they all sat down again.

Geraldine said in her sad voice, "We have met before, I think."

"Dozens of times," replied Mrs. Dashwood. "Is this your child? Time does go, doesn't it? Thanks, Dick, just what I wanted," and she drank her glass of sherry with evident enjoyment.

Another uncle and aunt arrived. After what seemed interminable ages they all went in to luncheon.

"You must try to eat something, dear," said Geraldine to Penelope, as she toyed with the meat on her plate. Lupin hoped that she did not appear unfeeling as she ate up her own meal with a good appetite.

"Isn't it awful having to eat?" said Elaine, looking at Lupin's fast-emptying plate.

"Oh, I don't know," replied Lupin. "I am rather hungry."

"Well, of course, it is different for you."

Lupin wondered how many times Elaine had seen her great-uncle. She could not imagine them ever being great friends, and she considered it rather affected of her to pretend that she did not want her nice saddle of mutton and Brussels sprouts. If Penelope liked to toy with hers, that was different. After all, it was her father who was dead, and she had the right to appear off her food if she wished, although Lupin had an uneasy feeling that if she had been alone she would have cleared up her plate and very likely taken some more. Alice had put down the glass of Guinness which she always took in the middle of the day. Penelope gave her a wan smile and said, "Thank you so much, Alice. It was kind of you to think of it."

Any of the other maids would have returned the ball, but Alice merely replied, "I thought you would have it the same as usual, miss," which wasn't exactly tactful.

Dick marshalled the party into the waiting cars. "You come with us, Auntie Boots," he said, as he held open the door of the front car for his wife and sister. Geraldine took half a step forward, her face furious, while the aunt muttered, "I should have thought, as the only sister of his dear wife—"

"Great friend, great friend," muttered the uncle. "Always thought they would make a match of it some day."

"Really, John!" said his wife indignantly. "I am sure he would never have put anyone in the place of my dear sister."

"As a blood relation—" said Geraldine emphatically, but was interrupted by Dick who ushered his uncle, aunt and cousins into the second car before taking his own place in the first. Andrew and Lupin slipped into their own car and started off while the procession was forming, as Andrew had to be at the church before it arrived.

"Well, I think it was a good idea taking Mrs. Dashwood with them," said Lupin, "because the aunt and cousin would each expect to be the one, and would be furious with the other."

"Now they are both furious with Mrs. Dashwood."

"I suppose so, and with poor Dick. I really feel sorry for that man. He was awfully fond of his father, and when you are in trouble it must be frightful to have masses of relations drooping all over you and thinking you are heartless if you are the least bit natural."

"I don't expect he minds what his relations think of him."

"No, but Penelope looked a little bit hurt, and he would mind what she thought. Do you really think she is so very sorry about her father?"

"I couldn't say."

"What I mean is, I don't think if you are really in trouble you seem quite so sad—not that I have ever been in trouble, so I can't really tell. But I have met a good many people who were, and Dick and Betty and that nice Mrs. Dashwood all seem much sorrier than Penelope and her relations."

"I think you are right. Penelope is very sorry that her father is dead but she isn't heartbroken. That is quite natural, but she feels she ought to be heartbroken and is trying to act accordingly without knowing how to do it."

"That is what I meant. You are a comfort, the way you always know just what I mean and put it into proper English. I wonder if Mr. Stevenson ever did think of marrying Mrs. Dashwood," and she repeated the uncle's words which she had overheard.

"Well, I don't expect we shall ever know. They may have just been great friends."

"It would have made all the difference to Penelope if he had married her, wouldn't it?"

"Yes, I suppose it would, and incidentally to Dick and Betty—but here we are at the church, dear."

They parted. Andrew went round to the vestry and Lupin tried to slip unostentatiously into a pew beside Mrs. Baker. The church was very full, for Mr. Stevenson had been immensely popular. Lupin saw the Deerings across the aisle. Sir Henry stared in front of him with a wooden expression. He was obviously regretting the passing of his old friend. Lady Deering, beside him, looked pleasantly sad, while Bob was genuinely wretched at the thought of Penelope bereft of a loving father's care and left all alone to fight for herself in a hostile world.

Behind the Deerings stood a good-looking gray-haired man whom Lupin had not seen before. As the procession came into the church, she saw him look at Penelope and she guessed who he was. She had had too many men in love with her in her life not to recognize the look when she saw it. His was not the gaze of tender admiration that illuminated Mr. Baker's rather prawn-like eyes, nor the look of humble reverence which transformed Bob's homely features, but just the normal look of a man in love with a woman.

Penelope and Dick were the only mourners to follow the coffin, and a very touching sight they were. Dick, young and strong, supporting his sister, as with her arm through his she faltered up the aisle, dry-eyed but pale, in a very becoming black hat and coat. Everyone's eyes were on her and there were very few in the church whose hearts were not wrung for her. Her whole life had been spent in the service of a beloved father, and now he had been taken from her.

They all went back to the Limes to tea. Penelope sat in a big armchair with all the female relations hovering around her, pressing her to eat. Mr. Baker stood near in an attitude of admiring sympathy, while Bob hurried backward and forward with plates of sandwiches and scones and the air of one who was facing lions for the sake of his beloved. Very likely he would have preferred lions to the aunt and cousins.

"Lupin, may I introduce Colonel Graeme? Lady Lupin Hastings," said Betty.

Lupin looked up eagerly at the gray-haired man. Yes, he was very nice indeed. He and Penelope would make a very good-looking couple. They must have been a charming pair when they walked beside the wild roses. They would be even more attractive now when they chatted beneath the hips and haws or whatever it was. (Bother, she had never got that hip stuff for Jill, after all. What a nuisance! However, the winter was more or less over now and the child was still alive.) She recalled herself from her poetic and motherly thoughts and shook hands. She noticed that Colonel Graeme had nice lines at the corners of his eyes, which showed that he could laugh when occasion offered, in spite of his whole life having been blighted by Penelope's unselfishness. "How do you do?" she said. She was just going to say, "I have heard a lot about you," when she realized that she did not even know for certain that it was the right man.

"Yes, I am the one," said Colonel Graeme.

"How did you know what I was thinking?" asked Lupin.

'You have a very transparent face."

"I suppose I have," she sighed. "It is a great drawback."

"I say," said Dick, "I wonder if all these ghouls are ever going? I don't mean you, Lupin, but all the female relatives. They will finish Pen off between them. She is being awfully sweet to them, but it must be a ghastly strain. Do you think you could get her to go out a little way with you, Charles? It would do her all the good in the world."

"I can but try," said Charles.

"Good luck," said Lupin.

He smiled, then strolled across the room to where Penelope sat among her female relations, while Mr. Baker and Bob stood by as if on guard. "I wondered if you would care for a breath of fresh air," he remarked, undeterred by hostile glances. "Dick thought it might do you good."

Penelope gave a wistful smile. "Not this evening, Charles," she said. "I feel a little tired."

"I've got my car here if you would care for a run."

"Oh no," she said.

Geraldine glared at him. "I should lie down, dear, if I were you. I am afraid Elaine and I will have to go very soon, if we are to reach home tonight, but I will see you tucked up with a hot-water bottle before we go."

"You needn't bother," said the aunt. "I will see that she is all right."

"Everyone is so kind," murmured Penelope.

"Well, I am afraid we shall have to be going," said Lupin. "Can we give anyone a lift as far as the station?"

The aunt and Geraldine stopped glaring at each other in order to glare at Lupin. "No, thank you," they both said firmly.

"Perhaps Mrs. Dashwood would like a lift," said Geraldine.

"She is staying the night," said Dick, who had joined the group.

"Oh, Dick," said Penelope reproachfully.

"I asked her to stay," said Dick. "I thought you would be glad to have her."

"Well, really," said the aunt, "considering she is no relation!"

"Goodbye," said Andrew, shaking Penelope's hand.

She looked up at him out of her large hazel eyes. "Goodbye, Andrew. You have been such a help."

"Goodbye," said Lupin. "If there is anything we can do any time, let us know."

"I wish you would go for a little stroll or a run in the car with Charles, Pen," said Dick. "It would do you such a lot of good."

"Penelope has just lost her father," said Geraldine.

"You don't say," retorted Dick, and he left the room with the Hastings.

Within a few minutes Andrew and Lupin were on their way home. "What a party!" sighed Lupin.

"Well, it was supposed to be a funeral," pointed out Andrew.

"I know, but all those women! I liked Mrs. Dashwood and I am glad she is staying the night. She will cheer Dick up. I don't think Penelope likes her much. I say, Andrew."

"Yes?"

"Do you think that Penelope really will marry Charles this time?"

"I can't think of any reason why she shouldn't."

"Nor can I. But I shouldn't put it beyond her to sacrifice herself once again."

CHAPTER 12

DICK sat in his father's library going through his papers, but his mind was not on his work. He was thinking of the future. He would sell the Limes and take a nice little house somewhere near, since there was not one available in the village. There might be one in one of the neighboring villages. He and Betty would start life all over again. He remembered the flat in London and what fun they had had both there and in those early days in the cottage. Naturally he could not expect Betty to be the same lighthearted companion as she had been in the early days before Christopher was on the way, but Christopher would soon be old enough to be left for a few days at a time. Gladys Browne was very reliable, although she was so young. He and Betty could go up to London and have some fun and recapture some of the old excitement.

Perhaps it was a queer thing to think of within a week of his father's death but he knew that his father would understand. He and Betty had had so many silly little squabbles lately. What they both wanted was a real change. Once Penelope was married they would have a fling. The last time they had gone up to London all together was some time before Christopher was born and it had not been a success. Penelope had been awfully sweet and had insisted on taking them to dinner at the Savoy, but when he and Betty had gone about alone they had always sat in the Upper Circle and had meals in little restaurants in Soho and that kind of thing. Somehow it had been much more fun, but of course one could not expect Penelope to sit anywhere except in the stalls, nor could she be expected to go on an omnibus or in the tube.

"Still working?" and Dick looked up to see his sister standing in the doorway.

"What are you doing prowling about the house at this time of night?" he asked. "It's time you were in bed and asleep."

"I know I shouldn't go to sleep. Oh, Dick! Doesn't the house feel empty and lonely without him?"

"Yes, frightfully," agreed Dick. "One does miss him most awfully. I shouldn't care to stay on here without him. I thought if it were all the same to you I'd put the house into the agent's hands tomorrow."

"Put the house into the agent's hands! What do you mean?"

"Well, I don't think we could afford to go on living here—at least, it would take all our income. My idea is to take a small house somewhere and to have plenty of money for holidays and all that sort of thing."

"What about me?"

"Well, my dear, I don't want to butt into your private concerns, but I expect you will be getting married before very long."

Penelope looked at him wistfully. "No, no, Dick, the time for that has gone by. I shall never marry now. All I want is to be of use to you and to your children. You don't think I'd let you leave your home, do you? The home that will one day be Christopher's? I thought we would all go on living here just as we did when Daddy was alive, but with the children growing up around us." She caught sight of Dick's dismayed expression, which he was unable completely to subdue, and added, "Unless you don't want me, of course."

She did not for a moment think that that was what was causing his dismay. She knew that he would always want her with him and that he would be unable to face life without her. He was probably worried about money, but if she lived with him and contributed to the expenses there would be nothing to worry about. What had she to do with her money except to help her brother and her nephew as well as any other nephews and nieces who might arrive to grace the old homestead? She smiled at Dick as she made her humorous remark about not wanting her.

But to Dick the remark was not humorous. He suddenly realized what he had tried to keep from himself before. He did not want his sister at all. In fact, he had never wanted her. His mind went back to his boyhood and he thought how happy he would have been if she had married Charles while he was a boy at school instead of staying and making a home for him. Recollections came to him of the last evening of the holidays with its long-drawn-out feeling of sadness, when in reality he was really looking forward to getting back to the other boys. He remembered the feeling of guilt he had always had if he made other arrangements in the holidays. The myth that had grown up and which he had come to believe himself was that he was never happy except when he was with his sister. He had often heard her say, "I do wish I could get Dick to go about with other boys and girls of his own age," and the queer intangible feeling he had always had that she would be hurt if he did.

He did not remember when he had first heard that she had made a very great sacrifice for him, the greatest a woman could make. But he knew it before he went to Rugby and all his time there was tinged with the feeling that he must make up to her for it. He refused invitations to stay with other boys in the holidays and spent them with her at the Limes or accompanied her to places abroad when she was able to leave their father, which seemed now, on looking back, to be whenever she wished.

He tried to pull himself together and to recapture the old feeling of uncritical gratitude and admiration but, once given rein, his thoughts were getting out of hand. Had Penelope ever given up anything for her father? He had been a useful excuse for getting out of anything she did not want to do: dull parties, parish work, war work, except for occasionally driving a car for the W.V.S. She had registered, of course, but had been granted exemption on the grounds of an invalid father. He thought of his own time in the army. He had enjoyed it, on the whole, but when he came on leave he would have liked to have 'beaten it up' with his companions, but he had always felt that he must hurry home to Penelope.

Still, it was through Penelope he had met Betty. He must be grateful to her for that. She had never encouraged him to meet girls. If he had ever seemed attracted by one she had been very sweet and understanding but had somehow always managed to destroy the attraction. But she had actually seemed to want him to marry Betty. Perhaps she had guessed that he might marry one day and felt that in Betty's simple heartfelt admiration she had found the ideal sister-in-law, one who would allow her still the first place in Dick's affections. It had not worked out quite like that. He had fallen wholeheartedly in love with Betty, she was the ideal companion. Yet all the time he felt he was being disloyal to Penelope. He had tried to be extra considerate to her to conceal the fact that she no longer came first. All these thoughts took but a few seconds to race through his mind. As he stooped to pick up a piece of coal that had fallen into the grate and straightened himself up again, she was still looking at him with a half humorous, half wistful expression. He mustn't start getting fanciful.

"Of course we always want you," he said.

Betty sat by her gas stove. The weather still remained cold and gray and the heat was very welcome. She was feeling happy, in spite of her father-in-law's death. She had been very fond of him and she would miss him, but he would have been the first to realize what it would mean to her to have her own home at last. He had left her a sum of money bringing in two hundred a year free of income tax. It had been very sweet of him to think of her in that way and to give her a little piece of independence. Dick had been very nice the last day or two. He had seemed to turn to her in his sorrow at his father's death and he had made plans with her as to what they would do when Penelope was married. Except for a few legacies, including the one to Betty and one to Mrs. Dashwood, everything had been left equally divided between Dick and Penelope.

"We will sell the house," Dick had said. "It is too big for us and Charles isn't likely to want to live in it. We will take a little house, something like the cottage, just within nice distance of my work and not too far from this neighborhood. After all, we have got quite a lot of friends round here and you really will be happy, darling, won't you?"

"Of course I will, darling," she had replied.

What a dear he was! She had been rather beastly to him lately, but living in Penelope's house had got on her nerves. Once they had their own home together she would never be beastly again, and, of course, they would have a spare room for Penelope and Charles and she would make them welcome whenever they liked to come. She and Penelope would have much more in common once Penelope was married. She was still fond of her, whatever Dick might think—she had never changed toward her. It was just that she wanted her own husband and her own baby to herself. She felt pleasantly sleepy and stretched herself lazily as she stood up. How late Dick was! She supposed that there was an awful lot of business to see to. Well, she would get to bed. Perhaps there would be something she could help him with tomorrow.

The door opened and Dick came into the room. "Hullo, darling, you are late," she began, but the words froze on her lips. How odd Dick looked! For a moment she thought he had been drinking, but his words, when they came, were quite clear. It was only the expression on his face that seemed different, and that wasn't like Dick at all.

"Well, I have got good news for you," he said, in a hard but perfectly clear voice. "Penelope isn't going to marry Charles after all."

"Not going to marry Charles! Do you mean that he hasn't asked her again?"

"I don't know if he has asked her again or not but he has been hanging about the place waiting to ask her, I imagine. No, she says she doesn't want to marry him. She wants to spend the rest of her life with you and me and Christopher."

"But she can't."

"So we shall all go on living at the Limes happily ever after," and he gave a short laugh.

Betty looked at him again. He seemed very unlike himself but she still did not think that he had been drinking. "I am not going to go on living at the Limes, Dick. You know quite well that it doesn't work, us all living together."

"You'll have to make it work. The Limes belongs to both Penelope and me. I can't sell it unless she agrees."

"Then give her your share. What does money matter? You get quite enough from the works for what we need and I've got my two hundred a year. We don't want a lot of money. We always used to enjoy ourselves most when we went about London doing things on the cheap."

"If we don't go on living here, Pen will think it is because we don't want to live with her."

"Well, we don't."

"She must never guess that."

"She will guess I don't want to, because I shan't do it. I am leaving this house, Dick. I have had quite enough of it and this is the end. I have three hundred a year of my own now, all together, and I could always do some part-time typing to help things out. I shall have enough for Christopher and me."

"You wouldn't leave me, Betty?"

"Yes, I would and I shall. I am serious this time."

"But don't you understand?"

"Yes, I understand all right. It is a case of choosing between your sister and your wife and you have chosen your sister."

"Oh, very well," said Dick. "Go away if you want to. I don't care."

"I know you don't," replied Betty, but the door had slammed behind him.

CHAPTER 13

LUPIN turned in at the vicarage gate. She had had rather a strenuous morning as she had awoken to the news that a pipe was leaking, and while she was trying to get hold of a plumber, the Sunday school superintendent, the organist and the piano tuner had all arrived, none of whom knew anything about leaking pipes, which was the only subject in which Lupin was interested at the moment. When at last she had managed to get out to do her shopping she had been stopped first by the doctor's wife who had lost her cook, secondly by the church cleaner who had lost her teeth, and thirdly by one of the Sunday school teachers who had lost her faith.

At last, rather tired but feeling pleasantly virtuous, she had arrived home, bearing triumphantly a parcel of vests for Jill, some fresh herrings, or so she hoped, and a bunch of tulips which had begun to wilt. "Hulloah, darling, has the plumber been? I've had such a morning. Everyone seems to have lost something but I have got some lovely vests for Jill and the man said these herrings all had soft roes. I got these tulips off a barrow, but they do seem to have got a bit tired *en route*—not that I blame them, because I have myself, and these vests smell a bit queer, or is it the herrings? It is funny about me and fish, isn't it? It always seems to go bad on me. Is anything the matter? Has anything happened to Peter or Jill?" And she hurried toward the staircase.

"No, darling, of course not, they are perfectly all right. Come into the study. There is bad news but nothing to do with the children or any of your family. Penelope Stevenson has been found shot."

"Shot? Why?"

"I don't know, dear. Mrs. Baker rang up. She thought it would be a comfort to Dick and Betty if we were to go to them. Do you feel up to it? I have been ringing up Dawson about the arrangements."

"Of course I feel up to it but I think I am going to be sick. For pity's sake get rid of those herrings. I'm not good with fish. We must go at once, Andrew. How too frightful! Will you get the car while I put a few things into a case?"

"We will have something to eat and drink before we start. No, not herrings. Cold beef if you like, it's simpler. We don't want to arrive there feeling sick. That won't help anyone."

Within an hour they were on their journey. It was a lovely May day. The sun shone from a clear blue sky on to fields of golden buttercups and all the trees and hedgerows were covered with fresh green leaves. It was very good to be alive on such a day, but Penelope wasn't alive, she was dead. It was extraordinary to think of Penelope dead. How had she died? Had she shot herself or had someone shot her? This last thought was so terrible that Lupin shied away from it. She must have shot herself, though it did not seem like the Penelope whom Lupin knew. Had something unforeseen occurred? Had Charles proved faithless after all? No, Charles loved Penelope, of that she was sure. Then why, oh why, after all these years, when at last her love story was going to have a happy ending, had she committed suicide? If it were suicide!

CHAPTER 14

ALICE opened the door to them, looking neither more nor less grim than usual. She ushered them into the drawing room where Mrs. Baker was sitting with Betty.

"I am so glad you have come, Lady Lupin," she said. "It has been very terrible for Betty. What a dreadful thing to have happened! And to Miss Stevenson, of all people! Everybody loved her, she had such charm, such tact. Lancelot will miss her terribly—in the parish, I mean."

Lupin had expected to find Betty in tears—naturally she would be distraught. To have such a tragedy enacted in one's family was enough to unbalance anyone, and Betty really was fond of Penelope underneath all her resentment, plus she would feel for Dick's sorrow. Lupin was prepared for a sobbing, frightened Betty. She was prepared to hug her and comfort her as she might hug and comfort Jill. Betty was such a simple, childlike person. It was easy to guess how she would react. But she was not reacting like that at all. She was dry-eyed and on the defensive. Lupin had expected her to be frightened—sudden death was frightening—but she had not expected to encounter that look of stark terror in Betty's honest brown eyes. Nor had she expected to be greeted with what almost amounted to coldness. Still, shock took people in different ways. It was no use being surprised at anything.

Mrs. Baker took her leave shortly after Lupin's arrival. As soon as Andrew had had a cup of tea he went out to look for Dick, leaving Lupin and Betty alone.

"I suppose you want to know all about it," said Betty, rather defiantly.

"Not unless you want to tell me," replied Lupin.

"I don't mind telling you, not that I really know much myself. They are having the inquest tomorrow."

"How beastly for you ! Did she...? I suppose she, or. . .I mean, she did it herself?"

"I don't know, it looked like it. The revolver was lying beside her. If there had been a murderer, he wouldn't have left it lying there, would he?"

"Unless he wanted to make it look like suicide. Of course, it might have been a thief. I suppose nothing was stolen? Her pearls or anything?"

"No, but it might have been a lunatic, or someone who had mistaken her for someone else, or, of course, they might have been aiming at a pheasant or something and hit her accidentally."

"Of course," replied Lupin soothingly. She did not feel that it was necessary to point out that people did not usually shoot pheasants on a May evening, nor did they usually shoot them with a revolver, nor would they have chosen this garden in which to do it, nor did Penelope look at all like a pheasant. Betty was talking nonsense but it was something that she was talking at all. She gradually became more like herself as she unfolded the story.

She herself had left the Limes within a week of her father-in-law's funeral, on being told by Dick that Penelope had decided not to marry Charles but to stay on with them at the Limes for the rest of her life. Naturally, she had lost her temper and had left the house the next day.

"I suppose I was a bit of a fool and ought to have been patient, but I felt I couldn't bear it any longer, so I took Christopher and went up to London to a friend and I got some typing to do. But I missed Dick all the time, and then I wanted some summer things so I came down for the week-end. I wanted to make it up, and I think he did, too, though he was a bit stiff at first. But by lunchtime on Sunday he was quite like himself and

Charles arrived and Penelope was cheerful, too, so I thought that perhaps everything would come all right after all. Oh, I forgot to tell you, I had an awful quarrel with Penelope the night before—at least it wasn't exactly a quarrel, since Penelope would never quarrel with anyone, but I told her I thought she was awfully mean to come between Dick and me instead of marrying her own man. When I saw her so nice with Charles at lunch I thought perhaps she had taken it to heart and decided to marry him after all, but instead she shot herself, and I feel it may have been my fault."

"You mustn't feel like that," said Lupin. "I don't expect it was anything to do with you. What could Charles have said or done?"

"I wonder," replied Betty. "We haven't seen him since. It is rather queer. Could he not have wanted to marry Penelope after all?"

"I am sure he was in love with her at the time of her father's funeral," said Lupin, "but something must have happened. Did they come in together?"

"I don't think so. I never heard Penelope come in. I had been resting, and I couldn't find anyone so Dorothy brought me some tea into the drawing room. Afterwards she said Penelope had come in a few minutes before and gone straight to her room, and she had taken a tray up there. She had seemed very tired and upset and told Dorothy not to say she was in. I suppose, poor thing, she was thinking about it then. We have not seen or heard anything of Charles since."

"It must have been something to do with him," said Lupin thoughtfully, "though I must say I am surprised." She could have banked on Charles' devotion, but the great thing was to prevent Betty from blaming herself. She obviously thought she was responsible for the tragedy, owing to having spoken so freely the night before. "It is queer his not having come forward," she said. "He must have seen about the tragedy in the papers."

"We haven't seen him since half past two on Sunday when he and Pen started out together. I was in the nursery putting Christopher to bed when I heard the shot. I ran out into the garden and there was poor Penelope shot through the head and a revolver lying on the ground. I felt so awful, and then I ran to the house for help and luckily Dick was just coming in and he rang up the police."

"You poor old thing. You must be feeling rotten. What about going up to see Christopher?"

"It is a queer business," said Andrew, as he came into Lupin's room before dinner. "Dick is in a terrible state about it. He seems to blame himself. He says that he had made it plain to her that he did not want her to go on living with them and that is why she killed herself—and then, of course, it was his revolver that she used.

He said he had left it lying on his writing table when he had cleared up some papers, so he feels it was his fault. She might not have thought of it unless she had seen it lying about. Of course it was careless but one would think that he had murdered his sister from the way he is going on."

"Betty is rather the same. She treated me as if I had come to arrest her when I arrived. She unbent a little toward the end but it was a pretty good strain."

Lupin had had some disagreeable meals in her life, but dinner that night was worse than anything she had ever known. Dick and Betty looked more like two criminals than anything one could imagine, with the possible exception of Alice the parlormaid, who handed each dish and filled each glass with the air of one who was in the pay of the Borgias. Looking at Alice, Lupin thought the odds were very good that at least one of the party, if not all, would wake up during the night in the most ghastly agony. In spite of this, Lupin and Andrew plowed conscientiously through each course, trying to make conversation, while Dick sat looking at his plate, making no attempt either to eat or speak, and Betty pushed her food about as if she knew it was poisoned, occasionally joining in the conversation in a queer, high-pitched voice.

At last the nightmare meal was over, and Lupin managed to persuade Betty to go up to bed almost at once, whereupon she broke down and cried and begged Lupin not to leave her. Eventually, as Lupin was resigning herself to an all-night session, Betty fell into an exhausted slumber and she tiptoed thankfully from the room.

Well, if either of them appears at the inquest, she told herself, they will be arrested for murder before anyone has time to do anything else! Could she with any decency go up to bed now herself? she wondered. No, she had promised to take Andrew for better or worse and sitting up with Dick in his present mood was certainly for worse. She reluctantly went down to the library where, to her great relief, she found Mrs. Dashwood sitting by the fire drinking tea and eating sandwiches and looking quite placid.

"Oh good!" Lupin cried. "I am glad you have come. It is all too frightful! Where are Andrew and Dick?"

"They have gone for a walk. Poor Dick! I have never seen him look like this. I am afraid he blames himself for Penelope's death. I am glad your husband is with him."

Lupin was not sure that she was so glad. If Dick really had turned into a homicidal maniac she would have preferred him to choose someone else's husband as his walking partner but she thought it might sound selfish to say so, so she sank down into a chair and lit a cigarette in silence.

"Have you any idea what has happened?" asked Mrs. Dashwood.

"Penelope seems to have committed suicide," replied Lupin, "and Dick and Betty both blame themselves for it. I suppose they let her see that she was in the way and that is why she did it. It doesn't seem a bit like Penelope, though, at least not like the Penelope I knew. I don't really think it was anything to do with Charles, though it is funny his having disappeared, but if only Dick and Betty would be a bit more come-at-able! Betty has unbent a bit but no one can say we were greeted with cordiality. Mrs. Baker asked us to come. She said we would be a comfort to them, but our entrance was rather like that of the first and second murderers. At least, I am not sure whether they thought that we had murdered Penelope or whether they thought that we thought they had."

"I saw about it in the evening paper so I came along at once, but I was not very welcome, either."

"No one is," said Lupin gloomily. "And their trouble doesn't seem to have drawn them together, either. And this used to be such a happy house! Now Mr. Stevenson is dead and Penelope's committed suicide and Betty and Dick will probably do the same thing before the night is out. I only hope he won't kill Andrew first. Anyway, I'm glad you are here,"

"You don't think that I am likely to commit suicide?"

"No, but then I shouldn't have thought Penelope was likely to, so you can never tell."

"You are sure it was suicide?"

Lupin stared at her. "I don't see what else it can have been. I mean, why should anyone murder her?"

Mrs. Dashwood looked at Lupin out of her bright blue eyes. "I could think of a lot of reasons," she said, "but one does not often murder people in real life."

"They do if I am anywhere about," replied Lupin. "I don't know why it is, exactly, but there must be something queer about me, like those people in Greek tragedies, you know. The minute I appear upon the scene everyone cries, 'Let's have a murder!' First there was the curate at Glanville. It wasn't anything to do with me, but I feel it wouldn't have happened if I hadn't been there—I mean, no curates had been killed until I married Andrew. Then I went to stay with a friend for a rest cure and a nut was loosened in her car and she was very nearly killed—as a matter of fact, it turned out to be an accident but the principle is the same—and now Penelope has gone and shot herself or else someone else has shot her."

"Well, I don't want to seem callous," said Mrs. Dashwood, "but it is Dick that I am worried about. It is no use pretending that I liked Penelope, but I am very fond of Dick, and I don't like the way he is taking this."

"One would feel rather awful if one's sister had committed suicide."

"If she did!"

"But who would murder her? I know they are both going about looking as if they had done it but I am sure they didn't. If they had really murdered her surely they wouldn't give themselves away so obviously. Did you say you say you didn't like Penelope? I thought everyone did except me and Mrs. Baker—and I didn't murder her because I wasn't here."

"I suppose I had as much reason as anyone," remarked Mrs. Dashwood briskly, "and at seventy-five, being hung wouldn't matter so much."

"They might not hang you though," pointed out Lupin. "They might imprison you for life like Petain and you might go on living for ages. It would be rather awful."

"Yes, that wouldn't be so good," agreed Mrs. Dashwood, "and of course it would be a pity to blot one's copy-book so near the end. All the same I suppose I am the most obvious person—and I haven't got an alibi."

"Why should you want to murder her?"

"She did me out of twenty years of happiness," explained Mrs. Dashwood. "Her father and I were very fond of each other. As soon as Penelope got engaged to Charles Graeme he asked me to marry him, and we should have had a very happy life together."

"Did Penelope know?"

"Know! Of course she knew! She had a fit of hysterics at once and locked herself in her room. Then she broke off her own engagement."

"But if you had married her father, she could have married Charles and gone to India with him quite comfortably."

"She broke off the engagement before there was any talk of going to India. She had an idea of marrying Charles and still spending most of her time here. She would not care for the life of a soldier's wife, moving from place to place. She probably hoped to persuade Charles to retire from the army and settle down here with her. After she broke off the engagement he managed to get himself sent out to India. He was heartbroken, poor man!"

"But wasn't she in love with him?" asked Lupin, bewildered.

"Penelope never loved anyone but herself. If she had been fond of her father I could have gone off with a good grace, but she never cared for him except as a sort of adjunct to herself. She always went away whenever she felt like it. There was a great deal of talk about her unselfishness and of what a wonderful daughter she was, but it never seemed to interfere with her pleasure."

"What happened?"

"What could happen? Penelope always got her own way. She implored her father not to marry and in the same breath said that she would go away and live by herself in a boardinghouse. I could see that he was worried to death, so I took myself off. I think I was a fool, but there it is."

"Didn't Dick know about it?"

"I am not sure how much he knew or guessed. He was only a little boy at the time, but he has always been a perfect dear to me. I think he may have had some kind of a notion."

"What did she say to Charles when she broke it off?"

"That I don't know, either, but I think she held me up as the villain of the piece, as a wicked stepmother who would ill-treat Dick! Anyhow, they had a frightful quarrel and he went off to India where he got married. They met again when he came back to England and she got hold of him once more."

"If she were murdered it might be by some relative or old flame of his first wife."

"It might have been. I hadn't thought of that. All the same, murder does seem such an *outré* sort of thing."

"I know. I think she committed suicide, though I should have expected her to have left a letter saying why she had done it and forgiving everyone and that sort of thing. I mean, she would never just go quietly."

"Unless she hoped that someone else would be blamed for it!"

"Would she be so awful as that?"

"No. I ought not to have said that. It is dreadful to be so vindictive at my age, but I was really very fond of her father and she was not at all nice to him. If he had been happy, honestly I don't believe I should bear her any grudge."

"Dick and Betty really were very fond of him, weren't they?"

"Yes. I was hoping that Penelope would marry Charles when his wife died and leave her father to those two. He would have been very happy with them, but of course that would not have suited her at all. She had to be mistress of this house and she would have hated to think of anyone being happy without her."

"If only Dick and Betty would stop looking like criminals for a few minutes," sighed Lupin, "things would not be so bad. Naturally they feel rather awful, but I don't see that they have really anything to blame themselves about. One would expect them to look sad, but they needn't look so furtive. Then there is the parlormaid, Alice. She has a guilty look."

"Oh yes, Alice! She did not like Penelope."

"No, she didn't, did she? The others were devoted to her, but I always noticed that Alice wasn't."

"She saw through her—she was devoted to Richard."

"Who? Oh, Mr. Stevenson, you mean? Yes, she was. And I'll never forget what a brick she was that day—or rather night—when Christopher was born. I wonder if she did it. I don't blame her at all if she did—at least, of course it would be very wrong, but if it were all out of loyalty to Mr. Stevenson one can quite understand it. I wonder if we could get her away to America."

"What would your husband say?"

"Oh, I see what you mean. Naturally he would think murder very wrong. So do I, as far as that goes, but there is a difference in murdering someone as a punishment and in murdering them for gain. Though, of course, it isn't our place to take the law into our own hands. Still, one could excuse her a bit. She might even have thought Penelope was responsible for Mr. Stevenson's death or something. Oh, I don't know, of course. If she did, it was very wrong. . .but I don't want her to be hung. Christopher would not be alive now if it hadn't been for her. I should have done everything wrong, though I have had two children and Alice has never had any so far as we know, but of course when you are having them yourself you don't notice much. In any case, why should she shoot Penelope? Surely she could easily have slipped something into her Guinness at lunch! Do you remember the day of the funeral?"

"It was funny, wasn't it?" agreed Mrs. Dashwood.

"Those frightful cousins! I wonder if they shot Penelope?"

"I don't quite see why they should have done."

"Nor do I, but they were so awful I wouldn't put anything beyond them."

Andrew and Dick came into the room. Andrew looked tired out and Dick still looked as if he were planning crimes and stratagems. Lupin looked back to her first visit a year ago when Dick had been a young man bubbling over with youth and good spirits. Now he looked an old man burdened with many crimes. How awful it all was! And only this morning she had been pursuing her lighthearted way among lost teeth, and faiths and cooks. Had Dick murdered his sister? Everything pointed to it. His guilty manner, Betty's terror, motive, opportunity, everything. On the other hand if she had committed suicide because she had discovered that Dick did not want her any more, he might well feel himself guilty of her death and behave like a murderer. Lupin did not want to think hard thoughts of the dead but she did feel it was a little unkind of Penelope not to be content with ruining Dick and Betty's lives while she was alive but still to go on doing it after she was dead. Feeling there was nothing more she could do to help she said good night to Mrs. Dashwood and went upstairs to bed.

Andrew joined her after what seemed a very long time. "I do hate forcing myself where I am not wanted," he remarked. "Dick was wishing me to the devil this evening. He wanted to go for a walk by himself. I insisted on going too and in dogging his footsteps until I nearly collapsed. My extra fifteen years told on me and I felt myself wheezing, as we went up the hills. Dick was relying on shaking me off but I hung on like the British bulldog. It was an unpleasant feeling. I don't mean the wheezing, I didn't mind that so much but the being where one wasn't wanted."

" 'O'er moor and fen, o'er crag and torrent till,' " said Lupin. "Sorry, I didn't mean to be irreverent."

"I know you didn't, bless you, and it was rather like that."

"You poor old thing. It must have been frightful. I do hope you haven't strained yourself or mixed your kidneys up with your liver or anything. But if you hadn't been there he would have tried to commit suicide, though I don't see what is to stop him doing it now—or are you going to sleep in his room? You needn't, need you? I don't think I could bear a night alone. Besides, if Dick really did murder Penelope, surely it would be kinder to let him commit suicide than to have him hung."

"Darling, I am sure there is no question of Dick having murdered Penelope, but I won't sleep with him—Betty might not like it."

"I don't think they are together. I am afraid they have had a quarrel."

"Oh!"

"Yes, I know. If Penelope really had come between them, one of them might have killed her. I should, if someone came between you and me—though I don't see how they could. I saw it coming on some time ago. I don't mean killing her but hating her. It was when Betty was expecting Christopher and Dick was always wondering whether Penelope were tired! Then there was that awful time Betty came to us and he came after her and we hoped they had made it up, but I don't think they really did. I mean they had a lot more squabbles. Then after Mr. Stevenson's death they thought Penelope would marry Charles and they would all live happily ever after, but she decided to devote her life to Dick and Betty. Of course, Charles hadn't asked her again then, but Betty went off the deep end about it and flung out of the house and took in typing."

"I didn't know about that," said Andrew. "But all the same, darling, you are imagining things because you are tired. Perhaps Dick and Betty let Penelope see their feelings and that is why they blame themselves, but anything else is absurd, as you would be the first to agree if you were feeling yourself. I don't think there is any doubt that Penelope took her own life. It is very, very sad and naturally Dick and Betty are terribly distressed."

"Absolutely," agreed Lupin. "But it is all pretty grim, and I do wish they wouldn't behave like something out of Edgar Allan Poe. Then of course there is Alice. I wouldn't put it beyond her to have murdered Penelope and she certainly looks as if she had done it. But why should she shoot her in that noisy way when she could so easily have poisoned her without anyone knowing? And I don't think it was Mrs. Dashwood, either."

"Why on earth should it be Mrs. Dashwood?" asked poor Andrew, wondering if his wife had taken leave of her senses on top of everything else.

Lupin told him Mrs. Dashwood's story. "Well, really," said Andrew, "talk of melodrama! We have mixed ourselves up in it this time."

"Not for the first time, either! But everyone here seems to have a love story. I expect Alice is in love with Mr. Baker and Mrs. Baker with Sir Henry Deering, if only we knew all. Oh dear, it has been a long, long day and tomorrow will be longer still. Isn't there something about the longest river reaching the sea? I suppose we will, too, if no one murders us first, and then there will be the Sunday school treat!"

"Put the idea of murder out of your head, dear. I should take a couple of aspirins, if I were you."

"Andrew," she suddenly exclaimed half an hour later.

"Yes, dear," he replied in a resigned voice. "What is it now?"

"I can't remember what I did with those herrings which I bought this morning."

CHAPTER 15

LUPIN and Andrew accompanied their friends to the inquest the next day. Dick formally identified the body as that of his sister, Penelope Stevenson. He stated that he had been out to tea and that as he returned to his own house he heard a shot and hurrying into the garden found his sister lying dead, shot through the temple, his own revolver lying beside her. As he approached the body his wife arrived, also summoned by the sound of the shot. She came from the house as he came from the side gate. They reached the body almost simultaneously but he was a few seconds in advance.

Mrs. Stevenson stated that she had heard the shot while in the nursery with her son. She had run straight down and out through the back door and had found her sister-in-law sitting slumped in a deck chair. Her husband arrived almost at once but she felt convinced that she was the first on the spot.

"I do wish they had decided on the same tale," thought Lupin. "They must really know who arrived there first."

Dorothy, the housemaid, stated that Miss Stevenson had come in round about four-thirty. She had said she was tired and wished to lie down as she had been for a long walk. Dorothy took up some tea to her room and that was the last she had seen of her. Just before six o'clock she had heard a shot ring out from the garden. She was on the landing when the nursery door opened and Mrs. Stevenson came out. She asked Dorothy whether she had heard a shot and told her to stay with the baby while she went to see what it was. As they were speaking the church clock struck six.

On being recalled Mr. Stevenson said the last time he saw his sister alive was as she was starting out for a walk with her friend Colonel Graeme at about half past two. On being shown the revolver he identified it as his own. He said he had been tidying his desk that afternoon and had left the revolver on the top when he went out for tea. It was not loaded.

The coroner asked whether Colonel Graeme was in court. The answer was in the negative.

Sergeant Wells said that he had been rung up at 6:12 P.M. and had proceeded straight to the Limes, leaving orders that the police doctor should be notified and asked to join him at once. The dead lady was sitting in a garden chair with a bullet wound in her right temple. The revolver lay on the ground beside her. One bullet had been fired from it. The doctor had arrived within a quarter of an hour.

Dr. Headlam had been playing golf at the time of the telephone call, but his wife had rung up the club at once and the steward had come out himself to find him. He had arrived at the Limes just as the church clock was striking the half-hour. He had examined Miss Stevenson and found that she was dead. He did not think she could have been dead much more than half an hour. Later he and Miss Stevenson's own doctor, Dr. Maud, had performed a postmortem and were confirmed in the knowledge that Miss Stevenson had died as the result of a bullet passing through the brain. Death was instantaneous. They had extracted the bullet, which they had returned to the police.

Sergeant Wells stated that it had obviously been fired from the revolver found at her side.

Then Dr. Maud gave his evidence.

He said that he agreed with his colleague in all his findings. He also stated that Miss Penelope Stevenson was a healthy woman of thirty-nine. On being questioned he said that he would be surprised at Miss Stevenson committing suicide, he would not have expected it. She was a woman of splendid constitution and he would have said a well-balanced mind. But he agreed with Dr. Headlam that the wound was perfectly consistent with suicide.

Then Sergeant Wells threw his bombshell. The revolver had been taken to the police station and examined for fingerprints, but there were no fingerprints at all

A stunned silence fell on the court as the meaning of this sank in. The coroner looked uncomfortable and Lupin felt as if someone had suddenly and unexpectedly struck her across the face. She glanced at Andrew. He looked very sad. Dick and Betty alone showed not the slightest surprise.

The inquest was adjourned until further evidence should be obtained. The coroner said that it was essential that Colonel Graeme should be present, as he was a very important witness. Telegrams were sent to his home address and to his club in London. There were notices in all the newspapers and messages from all wireless transmitting stations.

"How nice to see the sun," said Lupin. "Oh, is it raining? What a pity. I thought I saw the sun a few minutes ago. But I expect the farmers will be glad of the rain."

"Yes, won't they," said Mrs. Dashwood eagerly. "They always want rain for the crops, don't they? Or else fine weather. You must find it difficult to know which to pray for, Mr. Hastings."

"Very difficult. What do you think of the government's new bill for national insurance, Dick?"

"What bill?" asked Dick.

"There are such a lot of bills, aren't there ? I can never keep up with them all," agreed Lupin. "Education, too—such a good thing!"

"Yes, isn't it?" said Mrs. Dashwood.

"I suppose," said Lupin, "it means they are going to educate people.

What a pity they didn't have it in my day."

"Oh, do be quiet, Lupin," snapped Betty. "What is the good of making conversation?"

"Well, it is so awkward to sit in silence. One is sure to make a noise eating or drinking or something," protested Lupin.

"I know what you are thinking about, what everybody is thinking about. Why pretend you are not? I hate tact!"

"There are some things one can't talk about and if one could, it wouldn't make it any better. By the way, I suppose she couldn't have been wearing gloves?"

"That is a good idea," said Mrs. Dashwood.

"She might have been," said Betty, almost animatedly. "She did sometimes."

"She wasn't," said Dick shortly.

" 'Oh why do you walk through the fields in gloves, Missing so much and so much, Oh fat white woman whom nobody loves,' " murmured Lupin. She pulled herself up short at the third line and blushed. How awful of her! Not that Penelope had been fat and Charles had loved her even if no one else had, so the poem didn't really apply. But where was Charles? Had he shot her? And if so, why?

The rest of the meal was eaten almost in silence. Mrs. Dashwood and Andrew made a few disjointed remarks to each other but Lupin felt herself in disgrace. Neither Betty nor Dick made the least effort to make a difficult meal easier.

After luncheon Lupin thankfully retired to her own room and tried to lose herself in a novel but she could not escape from her present environment. She pictured Penelope lying dead in her deck chair, having been shot through the head with Dick's revolver lying beside her. Who could have shot her?

She can't have shot herself and then wiped off the fingerprints, she told herself. Charles was the obvious person. He was so maddened by her refusal to marry him after all these years of devotion that he had whipped out a revolver and shot her. Yes, but why Dick's revolver? And why did he come back to do it in the garden? They had left the house at half past two and she had come home alone, according to Dorothy, at half past four. Had he followed her and waited for her in the garden? What had they done during those two hours? Had it taken him two hours to propose and had she then said she must have a little time to think it over but would tell him at six? She could hardly have said, "Oh, Charles, this is so sudden!" after twenty years! Surely she knew her own mind before they started out.

Perhaps she had refused Charles during the walk and he had come back to try once again and had hidden in the garden till she came out, having in the meanwhile walked into the library and picked up Dick's revolver, which had been lying on the table. He had waited until Penelope was sitting in the chair and had then approached her and said, "Will you marry me?" She had said, "No," and he had said, "Very well, take that," and had shot her through the head.

Yes, that must be it, though she would have thought it a silly story if she had read it in a book. He might have been enraged with Penelope when they were out, if she had refused him again when there was no earthly reason to prevent her accepting him. He might even have shot her or strangled her then and there in an excess of passion but all that following her home and pinching Dick's revolver seemed farfetched. But what was the alternative? Lupin shuddered. If only Dick and Betty would behave like reasonable beings and talk things over, how much easier it would all be.

Was there anything she could do? Could there be some clue which everyone else had missed? Could there be anything among her papers that might give some help? Had anyone been through them? Of course it wasn't Lupin's business to do that, but if she went into the sitting room she might get some sort of an idea. She did get ideas sometimes, although they were mostly silly ones, such as Penelope wearing gloves in which to shoot herself. Lupin got up from the armchair and walked across the landing.

CHAPTER 16

IT WAS very unpleasant staying in a house which was overrun with police. As Lupin said, she never felt really safe from inspection even when in her bath but this afternoon everything seemed very quiet and peaceful. She could see the constable on duty outside the house. There was probably another one somewhere about but there was no sign of him. She slipped across the landing and tried the door of Penelope's sitting room. Rather to her surprise it was not locked. She opened it and walked in. The room was in semidarkness but she could make out a figure standing by the writing desk, hurriedly taking out drawer after drawer and searching feverishly through the papers. She supposed at first it was one of the police or a detective but surely they would be doing the work in a more methodical manner! The ways of the police were not unknown to her. But this visitor seemed in a terrible hurry. He turned as she shut the door behind her and she saw in the dim light the greenish face and distorted features of Mr. Baker.

"Are you looking for something?" asked Lupin, inanely.

"No—I mean yes. I thought I might light on a clue, you know, and help the police. It is the duty of every citizen to help the police and in such a case, such a woman . . . leave no stone unturned. . . just an idea . . . I might have found something." He dropped a handful of papers on the floor and stooped to pick then up.

"What are you looking for?" asked Lupin.

"Nothing, nothing at all. I mean, I thought there might be an incriminating piece of evidence—incriminating to the criminal, I mean, something among her papers."

"Did you suggest to the police that you should come and look for it?"

"No, no. I thought I would just try what I could do on my own. Amateur detective, you know, Sherlock Holmes, Hercules Poirot and so on." He gave what was meant for a laugh, though it came out rather like the croak of a raven.

Did Mr. Baker murder Penelope? wondered Lupin. He looked simply terrified of being found out. Why should he murder her? He thought her too marvelous for words. If it were Mrs. Baker who had killed her, it would be more understandable. Was it Mrs. Baker and did her husband know? But why ransack Penelope's desk? Perhaps he had written her a compromising letter. Yes, that was it, and Mrs. Baker had found it and killed her. No, she couldn't have found it, because if she had it he wouldn't be looking for it here. She may not even have known about the letter but just that her husband was in love with Penelope. The letter, however, would be evidence of his guilty love and would prove a motive against her and he, still fond of her in spite of all, wanted to destroy this.

On the other hand he might have killed Penelope for fear she would betray him. Blackmail? Lupin had come up against that before. But no, one could not associate Penelope with blackmail, nor even with such a mean act as showing a letter that had been written to her. But Mr. Baker might not have realized that, he wasn't a good judge of character. He might have written her a silly letter, then 'got the wind up' and murdered her for fear of the letter being made public.

"I should leave the police to do their own work," she said. "They won't thank you for trying to help them. After all, you wouldn't want them to come preaching sermons for you and if they find you in here it won't look too good."

"You are in here too, if it comes to that," pointed out Mr. Baker.

"So I am," agreed Lupin. "Let's go somewhere else," and she led the way out of the room. Mr. Baker hesitated and then followed her. "Did you unlock the door? Because, if so, you had better lock it again," she suggested.

"How could I have unlocked the door? How could I have got hold of the key?"

"I expect all the doors on this landing have the same locks."

"Oh well," he said, as he produced a key.

"That's right," said Lupin. "Where did you get it from? Oh, my bedroom, how funny! I never noticed it was on the outside, but then I never lock my door. Thanks," and she took it.

"We are both in the same boat, Lady Lupin. You can't say you saw me in that room without incriminating yourself, you know."

"How awkward! Are you staying for tea? Oh well, goodbye for the present." She went to her own room and sat down in the easy chair and lit a cigarette while she tried to think things out. She wished that she were not always getting mixed up in criminal affairs. She always felt so sorry for everyone concerned and she hated the idea of giving anyone away. Still, one could not afford these feelings in the case of murder. One had to find out who really was the criminal, otherwise suspicion hung about innocent people. Betty and Dick were both frightened, she could see that, though surely no one could seriously suspect them of having murdered Penelope. Yet things did look bad for them.

Dick would come in for quite a lot of money at Penelope's death and that was the sort of thing people always thought about. And then Betty—

well, of course, there was the money motive there, too. As if either of them would commit a murder for money! But there was no getting away from the fact that Penelope had been badly on Betty's nerves for a long time, and she had never really regained her strength since Christopher's birth. Penelope had seemed determined to ruin her life. Why? Why couldn't she have married Charles and made a happy life for herself? If she hadn't had the chance of a husband, it would have been different. A thwarted woman might try to wreck the happiness of others. But had she had the chance of marrying Charles?

That brought in another line of thought. She had declared to Dick that she wasn't going to marry Charles and that she was going to give up her life for him and Betty. Had she said that to save her face, knowing that Charles was tired of her, knowing that he did not want to marry her after all? But did she know? Perhaps she wasn't sure and said that in case, then she would look all right if Charles did not come up to scratch. But she was not sure until Charles came to see her that afternoon, then he had said he was tired of her and didn't want to marry her, so she had committed suicide. That would be quite understandable. After loving one man all her life, to be turned down at the end—especially to a conceited woman like Penelope—would be a bitter blow, enough to drive her to suicide.

But she hadn't committed suicide. She could not have shot herself, got up and wiped off her fingerprints, resumed her seat and died. Besides, if Charles wanted to get out of it he would not have come down specially to tell her so, he would have just stayed away or slipped off somewhere without saying anything. He could have been called away and then his letters would have become few and far between till they ceased altogether. And what was more, Lupin was sure that as recently as Mr. Stevenson's funeral he really was in love with Penelope and wanted to marry her.

Where *was* Charles? That was the question.

CHAPTER 17

"GOOD God!" exclaimed Dick.

"What has happened now?" asked Lupin. "Look!"

A car had been driven up to the door and in the act of alighting from it were Geraldine and Elaine.

"I suppose they have come to the funeral," said Lupin. "Where the carcase is there shall the vultures be gathered together, as they say." She then realized that this had not been a very tactful reference and lapsed into silence, while Dick burst out laughing, rather to her surprise, and Betty collapsed into an attack of hysterical giggling. At this inopportune moment Geraldine and Elaine pushed past Alice into the room.

"My poor, poor Dick," said Geraldine.

"Ha, ha, ha!" shouted Dick. "Hullo, Geraldine. Ha, ha, ha!"

"Umph, umph, umph!" giggled Betty.

"This is all too, too terrible," said Geraldine. "Who would have guessed at dear Uncle's funeral that anything like this was going to happen?"

"We had no idea, had we?" agreed Lupin, feeling it was beholden on her to keep the conversation going.

"Dear, dear Penelope! Although we were only cousins, I always felt as if she were my own sister. I think two sisters were seldom as devoted as we were. Such a daughter, such a sister! But tell me, Dick, it isn't true, is it? I mean, I can't put it into words but it must all be the most hideous mistake."

"It can't be true," agreed Elaine, "not in Uncle's house!"

"It was in the garden, actually," said Lupin.

Dick lurched toward the door. "Ha, ha," he said. "So sorry, got to see someone."

"The whole affair has been too much for him," said Geraldine kindly. "He seems quite unhinged—temporarily, of course."

"Of course—temporarily, I mean," agreed Lupin. "But it has all been such a shock."

"Naturally! I should not think there have ever been a brother and sister so devoted. They were the whole world to each other. Many a time when we were girls and I wanted Penelope to come to some little gaiety with me, she would say, 'No, Geraldine, dear, I am sorry but I never go out in the evening, Dick would miss the reading aloud.' He was always her first thought. Why, she might even have been a wife and mother herself if it hadn't been for Dick."

This was really too much! On the other hand, quarreling with Geraldine would not make things any better. Lupin looked nervously at Betty, who had got over her giggles and was gazing out of the window with a glassy stare. "Poor Dick and Betty have had a dreadful time," she said. "They are both feeling pretty awful. Shock is a queer thing, isn't it? I remember once when I was in a raid. I felt quite all right and scrambled out of the place—it was in the grocer's and I had been under a counter with one of the assistants, a very nice man—and I was only worried because I had ruined my suit and I had no more coupons. I had finished my shopping so I went home and ate a huge lunch, but in the evening the curate came in and started telling funny stories and I began to cry and couldn't stop. I must say the curate was frightfully decent. He stopped being funny at once and went out and borrowed some whisky from a parishioner—not to say borrowed, exactly—so everything ended up well. It was really a case of good coming out of evil, I suppose. But it just shows what a queer thing shock is."

"Were you here when the tragedy took place?" asked Geraldine, fixing Lupin with a cold and suspicious eye.

"No, it was at Glanville where I live—we had a lot of those tip-and-run raids. On the other hand, I think on the whole we got more to eat than the people in safe places. I remember a friend of mine, who came to stay, saying she would give anything to live in a danger area. They couldn't get a thing where she was and the laundry only called once in three weeks. I should have rather liked that personally," she went on. She had not the vaguest notion of what she was talking, but felt that she must keep the ball rolling at all costs. "The laundry always scorns to be coming at home and I never have the money to pay for it—it is such an awkward sum as a rule, fourteen and sevenpence halfpenny and so on. Then it is so tiresome when something is missing and one writes to complain and it turns out you never sent it."

"I meant were you here when my dear cousin, my dear cousin—" Geraldine's voice broke.

"Oh, I see what you mean. No, I wasn't. It was a frightful shock to us when we heard about it, so what it must have been to Dick and Betty . . .! Yes, I should if I were you," as Betty muttered something unintelligible and left the room. "Poor Betty, it is too awful for her!"

"I should not think that she is a young woman with very strong feelings," said Geraldine.

"I didn't think she seemed very sad at dear Uncle's funeral," put in Elaine.

If only one of them had done it, how gladly I should see them hanged, Lupin thought to herself. But I don't see how they could have done or why. They were nowhere near here that evening—or were they? No one knows where they were. They might have been lurking about somewhere and popped in and done it. I don't know why, I am sure, but it is a wonder no one has ever murdered them!

"Tell me," said Geraldine, obviously trying to subdue her distrust of Lupin in her eagerness to learn something from her, "what has Dick said to you about this tragedy? Has he confided in you at all? I know that you are a great friend of the family."

"He hasn't confided that he murdered his sister, if that is what you mean," replied Lupin bluntly.

"Murdered his sister!" shrieked Geraldine.

"Murdered his sister!" squeaked Elaine.

"How could you say such a thing? Do you realize that you are talking about my cousins?"

"Sorry, but I thought that was what you meant when you asked if he had confided in me. I don't see what he could confide. He doesn't know any more than the rest of us."

"He may know something, he may suspect something or someone."

"In that case he would tell the police. Why should he make a secret of it? Naturally, he is as anxious to know who murdered his sister as the rest of us—in fact, a good deal more so."

"There may be wheels within wheels," said Geraldine.

"What sort of wheels?" asked Lupin. "I never understand what that means, but then I never was much good at machinery."

Mr. and Mrs. Roberts, the uncle and aunt, were now announced, and Lupin felt that it was like one of those recurring nightmares. She knew what Mrs. Roberts was going to say before she said it.

"This is all very, very dreadful. My poor sister's child. I can't believe it!"

"My only comfort," replied Geraldine, "is that dear, dear Uncle was spared it. It would have broken his heart."

"So it would have done my dear sister's. I can't believe it even now. Who could have murdered my sister's child?"

"A burglar," suggested her husband. "Mark my words, I said at the time, 'It is a burglar.' "

"But he didn't take anything," objected Elaine.

"Are you sure?" asked Lupin. "Anyway, he may have been hovering round, waiting to take something when he encountered Penelope, so he shot her to prevent her giving him away."

"But why should he burgle in broad daylight?" asked Elaine, to whom this seemed a very tame ending to a thrilling experience.

"One often hears of burglaries being carried out in broad daylight," protested Mr. Roberts. "They have got very daring since the war and Penelope probably caught him in the act."

"I don't see how she could have done so in the orchard," argued Elaine, who was an uncomfortable sort of girl. "If it had been in the house it would have been a different thing but he could not have been trying to burgle in the orchard."

"Perhaps he was burying his booty," remarked Lupin, rather inanely. She liked the idea of the burglar. Surely, however improbable, that was more likely than that a friend or relation should have shot Penelope through the head.

Elaine looked at Lupin with the contempt that her remark had deserved. "If he buried the booty, why haven't the police found it?"

"Perhaps they haven't looked," ventured Lupin.

"Or, of course, it might have been a homicidal maniac," went on Mr. Roberts hopefully.

"So it might," agreed Lupin eagerly, "it is just the sort of thing a homicidal maniac would do."

"There was a homicidal lunatic who escaped near my brother's place in Kent. He killed three women before they caught him."

"I wonder how many people this one will kill?" asked Lupin.

"To think of my sister's child appearing at an inquest," broke in Mrs. Roberts.

"She did not appear, as matter of fact," said Lupin in an effort to console the aunt.

Mrs. Dashwood came in and Mrs. Roberts hissed, "That woman! What is she doing always hanging about the place?"

"Luncheon is served," said Alice gloomily.

Mrs. Roberts and Geraldine arose as one woman, "Will you come in to luncheon, Lady Lupin?" invited Mrs. Roberts.

"Will you come in to luncheon, Mrs. Dashwood?" asked Geraldine.

Betty and Dick joined them in the dining room. Dick had pulled himself together. He looked white and ill, but he talked politely to his aunt or at least listened to her and made fairly suitable rejoinders.

Betty toyed with her food and hardly seemed to notice what was going on around her. Luckily she was sitting between Andrew, who gave his entire attention to Geraldine, and Mr. Roberts, who was kept well in hand by Lupin. He told her about all the new laws concerning lunacy, which she felt most appropriate, as there seemed little chance that they would not all end up in a lunatic asylum. It was cheering to hear that the inmates were so well-treated and even encouraged to do handicrafts. She had never been very good herself with her hands but perhaps if there were nothing else to do she would become quite interested in making raffia bags and woolen mats.

"And leatherwork, too, I suppose," she suggested.

"They tried that," said Mr. Roberts, in a low voice, "but they let one man have a knife to cut the leather and he gouged out the warder's eyes."

"How unpleasant! So I suppose they gave it up—leatherwork, I mean."

The funeral seemed to be a repetition of Mr. Stevenson's. It was in the same church with the same mourners and the service was taken again by Andrew and Mr. Baker. But there is something different, thought Lupin. What is it? Something is missing. Then she remembered there was no graceful, tragic figure in the front pew. That was what made everything so strange and, as it were, disjointed. Wherever Penelope had been she had been the central figure, a focus for all eyes. Nothing seemed real without her, there was no center any longer. How powerful was the impression she had made on all who came near her. Whether you liked her or not you could not help noticing her. That pale sad face, those lovely deep-shadowed eyes, and that low, moving voice. The doctor had stated at the inquest that she had been a strong healthy woman but appearances had been very misleading. Lupin supposed that it was just the way her eyes happened to be set that gave her that look of delicacy. Penelope saw herself as fragile and everyone else had seen her so, too. She had also seen herself as unselfish. Did she realize now that she never had been? Lupin remembered that Andrew had once said that he was sorry for her because she was deluded about her own personality. He thought that one day she might have a terrible awakening. Well, she had been spared that. Or had she? Did the murderer say anything to her to break down that carefully constructed fabric before he fired the shot? Had she known that the end had come and with that knowledge had knowledge of herself come, too, in one blinding flash before she went? Lupin felt a pang of sympathy for her, although she had never liked Penelope. She had sometimes longed to tell her what she thought of her, but now that she was dead she realized that there had been something pitiful about her. She had been fooled by everyone into thinking that she was a wonderful character, just as Christopher Sly had been fooled into thinking that he was a lord.

Lupin looked round the church. Betty and Dick sat in the front pew. They were not sitting very near together, and they both sat rather stiffly, gazing straight before them. Surely it would have been natural in these circumstances for them to have drawn together, even to have sat hand in hand, as they had walked so gaily across the fields. Was that only a year ago? She remembered that time, and how she had thought of the well-known lines from "Pippa Passes," and had in her muddled way mixed it up with "Penelope Passes."

She had not realized then that as Pippa made everyone happy as she passed on her way, poor Penelope had left a trail of trouble behind her.

Lupin sighed. Oh dear, she thought, it is all like a Russian play or a Greek tragedy or something. Ever since I saw Dick and Betty so happy together last June I had a feeling that something would happen to them—a sort of foreboding, I suppose.

Mr. Baker was standing up and saying a few words. Lupin expected him to spread himself a good deal. He had been fulsome enough when Penelope was alive. What would he be now that she was dead? But, no, he spoke, but his heart did not seem to be in his words. He said that they were all mourning the passing of a good woman. She would be much missed in the parish but her memory would remain green. He said a little more, touching on the sorrow of her bereaved relatives but they were all set phrases and might have applied to any woman who was not actually a notorious sinner. He did not allude to her wonderful sympathy, her unselfishness, her personality, nor to any of the qualities that he had admired so much in the old days. He spoke mechanically and as if it were something of an effort. He seemed relieved when he had finished and the organ broke into the opening bars of "For all the saints who from their labors rest."

Lupin could not ever remember having seen Penelope labor. The picture stamped on her memory was of Penelope leaning back in a chair, looking tired, while all her friends and relations gathered round her begging her to rest. She did occasionally play a round of golf or even two rounds, and when at the seaside would enjoy a swim, but one could hardly call those labors. Lupin checked herself sternly and went back to her previous thoughts of pity. Betty was crying. Lupin thought perhaps it was as well, tears often did one good. Wouldn't Dick reach out a hand now? No, he stood staring at his book and taking no notice of anyone. Behind him stood Geraldine and Elaine singing shrilly. Lupin remembered how she had told Betty that next time they met they would be singing "Oh, Perfect Love," and instead they were singing "The golden evening brightens in the west." She remembered walking home from the evening service with Penelope and talking of the wild roses and the hips and haws (she must remember that hip juice for Jill next winter).

Mrs. Roberts made a valiant effort to sing as loudly as Geraldine and Elaine, who after all were no relation to Penelope's mother, and it was the mother who counted most, but her voice cracked badly. Mr. Roberts boomed away cheerfully in a somewhat tuneless bass.

Lupin glanced across at the Deerings. There they stood, the four of them, as they had stood at Mr. Stevenson's funeral. Yet there was something different about them . What it was she could not say. At Mr. Stevenson's funeral they had looked sad, but now they did not look anything at all. Their four faces were entirely expressionless, as if the blinds had been, pulled down. Lupin had expected Bob to look heartbroken. She remembered the last time that she had seen him standing there, with his eyes fixed on Penelope with a look of worship. Now his face registered nothing, but he seemed to have turned from a boy into a man.

Mrs. Baker's eyes were fixed on her husband. She looked almost scared, as if she were frightened of something. Suddenly she realized that Lupin was looking at her and, dropping her eyes to her book, she sang out in a shrill scream, " And hearts are brave again and arms are strong," just as the rest of the congregation were singing "Sweet is the calm of Paradise the Blest." Did Mrs. Baker know of her husband's search through Penelope's papers? wondered Lupin. She either knew or suspected something. Surely they could not have murdered Penelope between them! Mr. Baker, though he was so hearty, and though he was rather silly about Penelope, was really a religious man. He wouldn't deliberately commit a murder.

But poor Mrs. Baker, poor silly, adoring, little Mrs. Baker, could she be guilty? Her husband was the mainstay of her life and more to her than her religion, Lupin guessed. If she really had believed that Penelope was stealing him from her she might have murdered her. She certainly had a furtive look, glancing up every now and then from her book and throwing a sidelong look at Lupin to see if she were watching her. Poor Mrs. Baker! That is the worst of it, thought Lupin, whoever it is I am so dreadfully sorry for them. How can one know what one would do oneself if one were tempted! I do hope that it was a homicidal lunatic, as Mr. Roberts suggested.

"Will you come to tea with us, Lady Lupin? Or must you go back to the Limes?" asked Mrs. Baker, as they were moving away from the graveside.

"I should love to come to tea with you," replied Lupin. She was surprised, for in church Mrs. Baker had seemed to avoid her eye and now she was asking her to tea. What about Mr. Baker? Did he know that she was being asked? He could not want to meet her again after their encounter yesterday afternoon. But she could not resist the chance of having a little conversation with them. She might find out something—not that she wanted to find out that they were the murderers but it would be better to know definitely one way or the other. Betty and Dick would never make a fresh start until the matter was settled. Also she was very glad to escape from the Limes for a little while. She was sure that both Cousin Geraldine and her daughter Elaine considered her the murderer-in-chief.

"Then, will you come on with me? Lancelot will bring your husband."

CHAPTER 18

LUPIN and Mrs. Baker slipped out of the churchyard through a side gate and made their way down the little path to the vicarage. Mrs. Baker was unusually silent as she took Lupin into her rather fussy drawing room and left her while she went to get the tea. "Mrs. Payne, my daily woman, went to the funeral and she won't be back yet—they love funerals, don't they? Personally I think they are very sad, though Lancelot says we oughtn't to be sad if we believe in an afterlife. All the same, I think there is something very distressing about them."

Lupin looked out of the window, then she strolled round the room. There were a great many photographs about. There was one of Mrs. Baker as a bride. She had been quite pretty. Lupin looked at the girl's face and tried to reconcile it with that of the Mrs. Baker of today. The features were the same but the happy expression had been replaced by a harassed one. The pretty hair that showed beneath the white veil had long since gone a mousy nondescript color and was no longer waved nor set but hung in untidy wisps beneath the drab mushroom hats that she always affected.

Why had she let herself go? She needn't look as she did. Of course, she was probably pretty poor but mushroom hats were no cheaper than any others. Adoring her husband as she did, surely she might have made more of an effort. Lupin turned to another photograph of Mrs. Baker, still young, with a child on her knee. She did not know she had any children, as she had never mentioned them. Funny, because she was always talking about Lancelot. If she had a child she would talk about it, too. Had she lost it?

Poor, poor little thing! If anything happened to Peter or Jill, Lupin was sure she would never take any interest in anything again, she would let her hair hang in wisps and wear mushroom hats, too. There was a large photograph of Mr. Baker sitting at a table with a book before him and a rather fatuous expression on his face. He was quite good-looking, but his chin was weak. What was he doing in Penelope's sitting room yesterday?

Mrs. Baker came in with the tea. She was more herself now and began to talk, though Lupin sensed that she was nervous, or was that her imagination?

"We'll start tea. I expect Lancelot and your husband will be some time, speaking to the relatives and so on. It is a terrible business. Penelope Stevenson, of all people! She will be very much missed. Lancelot always said she was his right hand in the parish."

"What did she do?"

"Do? Oh, I don't know, she was always very helpful."

"Whom did she help?"

"She brought some beautiful flowers for the Easter decorations—lilies. She looked very beautiful carrying them. And she came to the Mothers' Union once."

"She wasn't a mother?"

"No, she wasn't. Lancelot always said it was a tragedy she wasn't a mother, she seemed cut out for one. I believe she gave up marriage for the sake of her father, though I don't expect he wished it. After all, marriage is natural. There may be a lot of troubles in married life but I always say it is better than remaining single."

"I agree with you. Did you like Penelope, Mrs. Baker?"

Mrs. Baker's mouth fell open and her eyes nearly popped out of her head. "What do you mean, Lady Lupin?"

"Oh, I know she's dead, and it's not done to say anything about the dead. *'Nil bonum desperandum,'* or do I mean something else? But all the same it is no good pretending that I liked Penelope Stevenson and I believe there are several other people in the same boat."

"Anyone could be lovely if they had masses of money and nothing to do. She never cooked a meal, nor lit a fire nor washed her husband's shirts, nor bore a child, and. . ." Mrs. Baker's voice broke.

Lupin caught her hand. "My dear," she said, and vowed that if Mrs. Baker were the murderer she would help her to escape from justice, even if it meant being an accessory after the fact.

"It's hard when you have drudged all your life, when you never have a minute to call your own, when you are so tired you wish you were dead, and then you have someone held up as an example of goodness when you know they have never done a hand's turn in their life, never even mended their own stockings. And to hear of her having had so much sorrow, what can anyone know of sorrow when they haven't lost a—"

Lupin was crying by this time. She hugged Mrs. Baker. "Men are such awful fools, aren't they?" she sobbed, "though of course frightfully clever in most ways. But I suppose it's that they take their wives for granted. But suppose your husband cut his finger, or lost his money, or. . .er. . .got into trouble with the bishop, whom would he go to then? After all, that is what really counts."

Mrs. Baker drew herself upright. A look of pride came over her harassed face. For a moment fear was banished. "It is me he comes to in trouble," she said.

"That's everything," said Lupin.

"Lady Lupin, I know that you found him yesterday looking for something in Penelope's room. That's really why I asked you to come to tea today. I wanted to tell you about it."

"If you feel like telling me, I shall be very glad. In a case like this it is best to have everything straight and aboveboard. It saves trouble in the long run. I mean, all sorts of little things become important—if one has a bath in the evening instead of the morning, the police think that you are washing off the guilty signs. If Mr. Baker's fingerprints are found among Penelope's papers it will look sort of queer."

"Did you suspect him of having had any part in the murder?" demanded Mrs. Baker.

"Well, I thought that you might have murdered her and that he might be trying to protect you in some way, as a matter of fact."

Mrs. Baker laughed. "I suppose I might have murdered her," she said, "but, no, I wouldn't really have done." She glanced at her baby's photograph and Lupin knew what she meant.

"I don't have to tell you," went on Mrs. Baker, "that Lancelot was besotted with Penelope. Of course, there was nothing wrong. I don't think he looked on her as an ordinary woman, and anyhow he has very high ideals, he would never . . . I mean, it wasn't anything like that."

To Lupin's disgust a line from the *Idylls of the King*, read long ago, flashed into her mind at this juncture. "For when was Lancelot wanderingly lewd?" Why was it that when she was feeling particularly serious such frivolous thoughts assailed her? It wasn't as if she were particularly poetical, either.

"It was the Saturday before Easter," said Mrs. Baker, "that Penelope came into the church carrying some lilies, as I told you just now. She simply walked in with them, laid them down and walked out again. It didn't occur to her to offer to help us with the decorating, though some of us had been there all the morning and had got our dinners to cook. But Lancelot was so struck with her goodness in bringing the lilies, and with the picture she made carrying them—as a matter of fact he said she looked like the Madonna—that he wrote a poem to her that night when I thought he was writing his sermon. And he sent it to her. I don't know what was in it but after he sent it he was ashamed of himself. He said it was very silly and the least bit blasphemous too, he was afraid. It was only last night that he told me about it, after you had found him searching in her desk. But he said after writing and sending the poem his admiration for Penelope got fainter—he had worked it off, I suppose—and he rather tried to avoid her. But of course when she was killed he was terrified of it being found and perhaps read in court or printed in the newspapers. He has been in a terrible state. I didn't know what had happened till last night."

"I am glad you know about it now. Anything is better than not knowing, isn't it? Besides, you can share it with him."

"Thanks very much, you are an understanding sort of person. I thought you were worldly when we first met."

"Did you really?" asked Lupin, surprised. "I am glad we have got to know each other. Here are the men coming. I do hope Mr. Baker will tell Andrew about it all, he will advise him what to do."

Mr. Baker shook hands diffidently with Lupin. "How do you do, Lady Lupin, I am glad to see you," he said, not very convincingly.

Mrs. Baker poured out the tea and they all sat down and made polite conversation.

Suddenly Mr. Baker broke into Lupin's halfhearted account of a Mothers' Outing. "Lady Lupin," he said, "I have told your husband what I was doing in Miss Stevenson's room yesterday afternoon."

"Oh, good!" said Lupin. "Now we all know about it we can discuss what we had better do next. It is so difficult to think of one thing when one is thinking of something else, if you know what I mean. And now I come to think of it, it wasn't the Mothers' Outing that went to Canterbury, it was the Church Cleaners' Guild, not that it matters. But about that paper. I wonder if there is any way of getting hold of it?"

"I am so ashamed of myself."

"I don't see why. After all, everyone did admire Penelope, and why shouldn't one write a poem? I expect it was awfully clever but I know how you feel about it being seen. The whole thing is, where is it now?"

"I should think very likely Penelope burned it," said Andrew. "She would have guessed that it might be embarrassing for you, if it were found."

"And after all," said Lupin, "whether one liked her or not, one must admit she would always do the right thing. She might have learned the poem by heart before committing it to the flames with a sad, wistful smile."

"Darling!"

"Oh, of course, I keep forgetting she is dead. One can't think of her as dead, somehow."

"There is the possibility that it is somewhere among her papers. I have advised Mr. Baker to mention the matter to the police, so that if it is found they will have their explanation and, all being well, it will go no further."

'That is a good idea," said Mrs. Baker.

"I will go round to the police station this evening," said Mr. Baker. "You are very good, Hastings, and you, Lady Lupin. I do not deserve that you both should be so kind."

"Oh rot!" said Lupin. "How dull life would be if we were all perfectly sensible all the time!"

"And as for my wife . .. " said Mr. Baker, giving her a look of devotion.

"Absolutely," agreed Lupin. "You are jolly lucky, if you don't mind my saying so. You and I are alike in that, each being married to someone so—"

"Much better than ourselves," finished Mr. Baker.

"I didn't really mean to say that," apologized Lupin.

"Well, it is true as regards me, but I hope I shall grow more worthy of her."

"Ditto," said Lupin. "As regards me and Andrew, I mean. Oh, and by the way, it was Chichester, not Canterbury, we went to!"

CHAPTER 19

DICK did not appear at breakfast the next morning, and as Lupin had managed to persuade Betty to stay in bed, she and Andrew and Mrs. Dashwood were able to have a fairly peaceful meal. None of them had slept much and they were all feeling very tired and jumpy, but at least they did not have to try to make conversation or be tactful with each other. They did not speak much, and just as Lupin was lighting a cigarette

Alice came in to tell them that there was a police-inspector in the study.

"Oh dear," sighed Lupin. "I seem to spend my life among police inspectors. They are very nice, of course, but I get so nervous of contradicting myself and getting had up for perjury."

Andrew went into the study, "Good morning, Inspector," he said. "I am Andrew Hastings, a friend of Mr. Richard Stevenson."

"He has just given himself up for the murder of his sister," said the inspector.

"Has he?" replied Andrew. He looked out of the window where the sun shone on an apple tree. He remembered, as Lupin had done, the first time that he had met Dick and Betty. What a happy carefree couple they had been then. How full of gaiety and insouciance. He was silent for a few minutes, then he said, "May I come round and see him?"

"Please do. He won't say anything to us except that he murdered his sister. He said he didn't want a solicitor."

"I will ask my wife to break it to Mrs. Stevenson," said Andrew, going to the door and calling to Lupin. As she and Mrs. Dashwood approached the study, Betty ran down the stairs in her dressing gown. She brushed past them and, reaching the door, said, "Are you a police inspector? Because I want to tell you that I shot my sister-in-law."

"I don't see how you can have done," protested Lupin. "You said you were in the nursery when you heard the shot. If you had shot her yourself you would have been in the garden, not in the nursery."

"I was in the garden. I invented that about the nursery to put you off the scent."

"I will ask you to come along to the station, madam, to make a statement."

"Why the station?" asked Lupin with interest. "Oh, the police station, of course. How silly I am! Well, darling, you go along and tell them what you remember but I am sure you are wrong about being in the garden at the time of the shot. I daresay it will all come back to you by the time you reach the station."

She saw Betty off and walked back into the dining room, where she drank a cup of black coffee in silence. "What about Mr. Borden, Andrew?" she asked.

"That is an idea," he agreed. He turned to Mrs. Dashwood. "A private detective and a friend of ours. He might get people to tell things to him that they would not tell to the police."

"Get hold of him, do," begged Mrs. Dashwood. "Anybody, anything. This is just like a nightmare."

"I'll ring him up," agreed Andrew. "I am afraid I shall have to go home tomorrow, at any rate for a day or two, but if you are staying here perhaps Lupin might stay on with you, in case there is anything she can do for Dick and Betty."

"I shall stay here till Dick and Betty are safely back," replied the old lady, "and I shall be very grateful for Lupin's company. She can help Betty, if anyone can."

"Right you are," said Lupin sadly. She thought of home and of her children longingly. She hated being parted from Andrew even for a day or two but when one's friend was in prison for murder one must rally round.

Andrew got in touch with Borden, who promised to come down. He also asked Dick's solicitor to come for a conference.

Although May, it was a chilly evening, and they were all glad of a fire in the library as they sat together after dinner discussing the awkward business. Dick and Betty had both been detained, although Betty had been lodged in the prison hospital.

"I don't really see what line we are to take," said Mr. Douglas the solicitor, "as neither of them will say anything, except that they killed Miss Stevenson."

"They neither of them did," said Mrs. Dashwood.

"I suppose they each think the other did," hazarded Lupin.

"But why should they?" objected Andrew.

"Don't ask me," said Lupin. "They have been reading too many detective stories, I suppose. We will each be saying it was us in a minute, I expect, for fear the other one gets accused—still, we must do something."

"Dick's story," said Mr. Douglas, "is that his sister had come between him and his wife and that on Sunday evening he could bear it no longer, so he took out his revolver from its drawer and shot his sister as she sat in the garden. He left the revolver lying beside her to make the murder look like suicide."

"Then why did he wipe off the fingerprints? He ought to have pressed her fingers on to it, that is what they do in books."

"He says that he had the presence of mind to wipe off his own fingerprints, but did not think about hers."

"What a silly story!"

"Betty says that her sister-in-law had come between her and her husband and, feeling that she could not bear it any longer, she left her baby in the nursery, went down to the library, took her husband's revolver, went out to where her sister-in-law was sitting in the garden and shot her through the head."

"Rot! She did not leave her baby alone in the nursery! I know she would never do that, however many people she might murder. And Dorothy, the housemaid, is ready to swear that she came out on to the landing just after the shot and said, 'Did you hear a shot?' and then asked Dorothy to stay with Christopher while she went to investigate."

"And she couldn't very well have gone into the library to get the revolver while Dick was sitting there," objected Andrew.

"I think the police are satisfied that Betty did not commit the murder," said Mr. Douglas, "but she might be an accessory after the fact—that is why they are detaining her. It points to Dick, I fear, but personally I do not think that he did it. However, it is very difficult to know what defense to put up when he insists that he did."

"A friend of ours is coming tomorrow," said Lupin, "a Mr. Borden. He is a private detective and I am hoping that he may be able to find out something. Of course, no one will know he is a detective, but I thought I ought to tell you."

"Yes, of course Mr. Douglas must know everything," agreed Andrew. "I expect you will like to see him. I have to go back to Glanville tomorrow, unfortunately, but my wife will explain things to him and bring him round to see you, if that suits you."

"Thanks very much. A good idea. Some people will not talk freely to the police. He may manage to learn something of which they do not know. It is very good of your wife to stay here."

Mrs. Dashwood and Lupin went up to bed, leaving the two men to have a little more conversation. On her way to her room, Lupin caught sight of Alice. On a sudden impulse she called to her, "I say, Alice, could you spare me a minute?"

"Very good, miss—I mean, my lady," replied Alice, rather grudgingly.

"Come in here," said Lupin, leading the way to her bedroom. "Now look here, Alice, do sit down a minute. I do so want to know what you think."

"What about, my lady?"

"About who killed Miss Penelope, of course."

"Do you think I did, my lady?"

"No, I don't think so. Did you?"

"I did not."

"I didn't think you had because, after all, why should you shoot her? It would be as easy as pie for you to slip something into her glass at dinner and then wash it up yourself."

"Why should I want to murder Miss Penelope, my lady?"

"You hated her pretty badly, didn't you?"

Alice stared at her for a moment, then her face broke into a grim and unwilling smile. "That's true," she said. "I hated her all right. She was a bad woman."

"You mean that she wasn't good to Mr. Stevenson?"

"That's what I mean. She treated him shamefully—never thought of anything but herself and yet pretended to be so good. Poor old Mr. Stevenson wanted to marry Mrs. Dashwood, but Miss Penelope would not hear of it, though she was engaged herself at that time. She wanted her father to sit at home alone waiting for her to deign to come and stay with him, so she broke off her own engagement and made the poor old gentleman break off his, too. But she didn't try to make up for it to him. She just went away whenever it suited her and he must always be sitting waiting for her. It was the same with Mr. Dick, too—she must come first with him. Poor Mrs. Dick—I have often felt sorry for her."

"Alice, do you think either Mr. or Mrs. Dick did it?"

"No, I am sure they didn't. Not that I'd have blamed them if they had, she was always trying to make mischief between them. Still, neither of them could have hurt a fly. They were devoted to the old gentleman and very good to him. But they had to be careful in front of Miss Penelope, she was as jealous as the devil and had to come first with everyone."

"Well, it's like this, Alice. I am a great friend of Mrs. Dick and I do want to help them both if I possibly can. I know you do to, so if you can think of anything that can help, you will let me know, won't you? We might talk things over together each evening." Alice looked at Lupin suspiciously but ever since that night of Christopher's birth she had admired her. She had rather despised her to start with for being good-looking and an earl's daughter but she had been wonderfully handy that night. She hadn't minded what she did and kept her head, what was more. Alice trusted her.

"Very good, my lady," she said.

CHAPTER 20

MR. BORDEN arrived the next day and visited the local police station. He always got on well with the police, and the inspector and his sergeant welcomed his cooperation. "It's a very rummy case," concluded the inspector. "Two people going and giving themselves up for murder—and what's more, I don't believe either of them did it. The young woman didn't, I'm pretty certain of that. The maid swears that she came out of the nursery just as the shot was fired, and I don't think she is lying. Besides, the shot was fired at very close range. Surely there would have been a struggle?"

"I suppose that applies to whoever did it?"

"If it had been a man she might have known struggling was no use, she might have hoped to get round him. Or, of course, the most likely explanation is that she was taken by surprise. But Mrs. Stevenson doesn't seem the sort of young lady who would be able to keep up an amicable conversation and then suddenly whip out a revolver and shoot her unawares. She would have bungled it somehow."

"I suppose Miss Stevenson might have been asleep and one or other of them might have slipped up and shot her without waking her?"

"I suppose so," agreed the inspector grudgingly, "though you'd hardly expect a sportsman like Mr. Stevenson to do that. Then if they wanted it to look like suicide why did they wipe the gun? They should have pressed her fingers on to it."

"Whoever did it seems to have been an inexperienced criminal."

"Well, these two are inexperienced all right, I should think. They can't have conspired together to tell the tale. He says that he was sitting in his library brooding over things and that he went into the garden to have things out with his sister and that she told him that she intended to live with him and his wife for the rest of her life. He knew his wife would not agree to it, so he whipped out his revolver, which happened to be in his pocket, and shot her, after which he wiped off the fingerprints and rang up the police. He met his wife on the way back to the house. She had been in the nursery with her baby.

"She says that she had had a quarrel with her sister-in-law the night before because she thought she was trying to come between her and her husband, so she went downstairs, leaving her baby with the house-maid, Dorothy, went into the library, which she swears was empty, took her husband's revolver out of the drawer, loaded it and went into the garden, shot her sister-in- law, wiped the revolver, and returned to the house. On the way back she met her husband, who had been out to tea and had only just returned. She told him that his sister was dead and left him to ring up the police."

"Weak!"

"Very. And, as I say, the maid heard the shot and went to the nursery just as Mrs. Stevenson came out. As for Mr. Stevenson, his story is just as silly. After all, if he did not want his sister to live with him, surely he could tell her so, instead of shooting her!"

"Money?"

"Yes. There is that snag, I am afraid. He comes in for a good bit at his sister's death, but . . . well, you will see the chap for yourself. I shall be interested to know what you think."

"Any other starters?"

"Yes, there is a Colonel Graeme. He seems to have been the last person to have seen her alive, except for Dorothy the maid. They went for a walk together at about half past two. She came back, according to the maid, at about half past four, and he has disappeared entirely."

"That looks rather fishy, doesn't it?"

"It does indeed. He seems to have been an old suitor, from what I have gathered. You may be able to glean more in the course of ordinary conversation. Whether she refused him and he shot her out of pique, or whether she tried to hold him to some promise and he shot her to get out of it, I don't know. But he seems the most likely solution."

"What about the revolver?"

"That is Mr. Stevenson's, all right."

"How did the Colonel chap get hold of it?"

"Yes, that is the weak part, but still, he has disappeared. If he is innocent, why has he done that? We've advertised in all the papers, broadcast an S.O.S and are in touch with all the police stations in this country and at the channel ports on the other side."

"You are bound to get him in the end. In the meanwhile I'll go round to the Limes, or whatever the scene of the crime is called, and try to get some of the inside dope."

"They may let on a bit to you where they wouldn't tell the police. Oh, there is a parson chap there, quite decent on the face of it but he's got a flighty sort of wife, Lady Lobelia or something. Seems a bit phony to me."

"She is all right. I've met her before. She is not as flighty as you would think. She has quite a shrewd head if you can get at it—and a heart of gold, as a matter of fact."

"Well, you should know. Come round this evening and tell us how you have got on."

Mr. Borden rang the front doorbell. He looked at Alice as she appeared to answer it. "Old retainer," he thought. "No good saying I am a friend of the family or anything of that sort."

"I believe Lady Lupin Hastings is staying here," he said. "Her husband asked me to look her up as he says she has had some trouble and I happen to be staying in these parts for a few days."

"I will ask Lady Lupin if she will see you," replied Alice, ushering him in.

"I do hope I'm not butting in. I saw something of your trouble in the paper and I wouldn't have come, but Mr. Hastings said he had to get back to his parish and his wife would be glad to see a friend. But of course I'll quite understand if it is not convenient."

"Thank goodness, you've come," said Lupin a few minutes later, coming into the drawing room where Mr. Borden had been waiting. "We are in the most ghastly mess. Two of our best friends have been arrested for murder. At least they have given themselves up, which is the same thing, though rather worse, because there is nothing you can do to help them when they will keep on saying they did it, so the only thing is for you to find out who really did it as soon as possible."

"Sounds easy! Have you suspicions of anyone else?"

"Yes, masses. There are heaps of people who might have done it, frightfully nice people, too, but that can't be helped—we simply must clear Betty and Dick. Oh, who did you say you were, by the way?"

"A friend of your husband's. I hesitated over whether to say I was a brother or an uncle of yours but remembered in time I should have to be a lord or something and I should have got terribly tied up."

"You might have been a nephew of Mrs. Dashwood's if we had thought of it sooner but it doesn't matter much. I expect Alice guessed everything from the word go."

"She is rather grim-looking."

"Yes, but she is a perfect dear. I do hope it wasn't her. But whoever it is I feel terribly sorry for them. I really don't think it was Betty or Dick and I'm not just saying that because they are friends of mine. It's not a bit like them, somehow."

"You seem to feel more sympathy with the murderer than with the victim."

"Well, I think I should rather be murdered than murder someone else, wouldn't you? I should simply hate to be hung. Besides, one would feel so awful if one had actually committed a murder, even if one weren't found out."

"Would you mind telling me something about all the people involved?"

"Absolutely. Well, of course, first of all there is Charles Graeme. He has been in love with Penelope for practically the whole of his life and she has kept on putting him off. First she said she couldn't leave her father and brother so he went off to India in a rage and married someone else—you know the way men do. I don't think women do so much, on the whole. They droop about looking wistful and pressing violets in their prayer-books instead.

"Then he came back to England and they met and he fell in love all over again. At least I suppose he had never fallen out. Anyhow, she must have rather encouraged him because they kept on meeting and he asked her to run away with him and one can't blame her for not doing that because of course it wouldn't have been right. All the same she might have avoided him altogether, instead of working him up again. Still, she is dead now, so one mustn't blame her. And talking about being dead, his wife died a little while ago and it seemed as if they—Penelope and Charles—were going to live happily ever after. Dick and Betty were so delighted. For Penelope I mean, of course. They were sorry about his wife but it did seem as if everything were going to come all right at last and that Penelope was going to be rewarded for her years of self-denial.

"Dick and Betty knew she would still hesitate about leaving her father so they left their own cottage and came to live here, for Mr. Stevenson was devoted to Betty and would have been as happy as anything and everything would have been all right. But it was N.B.G. by Penelope. She couldn't bear to think of anyone being happy without her, so her conscience forbade her to marry Charles—her father must come first or she would never forgive herself. It was all the most awful rot but I suppose she had got so used to sacrificing herself that she could not bear the thought of stopping.

"Well, it was frightfully tiresome, especially for Betty, because she had given up her own home and here she was parked as Penelope's guest for the rest of her life, as far as she could see. She just felt she couldn't stand it, and she came to us for a bit, which was very nice, of course, only Dick came too and they quarreled a good deal—and then Mr. Stevenson died, so we all thought everything would come right at last, though of course we were frightfully sorry about Mr. Stevenson, because he was an absolute darling. I hadn't really heard anything from them since his funeral and then suddenly I heard that Penelope was dead, and when we got here Dick and Betty were going on in the strangest way. I expected them to be arrested at any moment and wasn't really very much surprised when they both gave themselves up."

"You think that one of them, or both of them, murdered Miss Stevenson?" asked Borden.

"Good heavens, no! I am absolutely certain they didn't. Dick was simply devoted to his sister. He could not bring himself to tell her he didn't want her living with them, so he certainly wouldn't be able to bring himself to shoot her. As for Betty, I am sure she wouldn't have done it. For one thing she has an awfully nice nature and for another the maid, Dorothy, swears that she did not leave the nursery until after the shot. Besides, if she had gone out into the garden to shoot Penelope, Christopher would have been alone in the nursery, and she would never have done that. She was a perfect fool as a mother, just like me, so I know how she felt."

"About this man Charles, as you called him—what was there to stop them getting married once Mr. Stevenson was dead?"

"Nothing on earth, but Betty told me that she told Dick—Penelope, I mean, not Betty—that she wasn't going to marry Charles, but was going to devote her whole life to Dick and Christopher. Pretty sickening for Betty, you must admit."

"Most trying."

"Well, anyway, Charles came over and they went out together, and then she was found dead in the garden and he has never been heard of since. It does look pretty fishy. My idea is that he was so furious at being put off again that he whipped out his revolver and shot her. On the other hand he was obviously expecting her to accept him or he wouldn't have been so furious, so why was he carrying a revolver? And whatever they do in books, I do think a revolver would make rather a big bulge in one's pocket. Besides, it was Dick's revolver."

Mr. Borden waited a moment, as those talking to Lupin often found necessary, and then replied, "There is that, of course."

"All the same," went on Lupin, "where is he now, and why?"

Borden hesitated again, said "Quite," then went on, "As regards your friend Mr. Stevenson, what were his feelings when his sister told him that she intended to devote the rest of her life to him and his family?"

"Mr. Stevenson? Oh, you mean Dick. He never said a word about it to me—in fact he never said a word to me about anything, so far as I can remember. He was furious with us for coming. Most uncomfortable! But I think he would have been thankful if Penelope had married and lived happily ever after and had some children of her own. In fact, I am sure the situation was beginning to get beyond him even before his father died, because he really is fond of his wife, though he was so maddening about his sister, always asking her if she were tired, even when she was expecting a baby. His wife, I mean, not his sister. I could have gladly murdered him myself but you see his whole trouble was that he was afraid of hurting his sister, so he would hardly be shooting her, would he? I mean, if he were the insensitive sort of person who went about murdering people, he wouldn't have minded telling her that he didn't want her."

"The trouble is that one can't write anyone off as the sort of person who would commit murder or not," said Mr. Borden. "It is just possible that someone might commit an act foreign to their real nature under great stress or nervous strain."

"I know what you mean," Lupin agreed. "I adore my children, but when I had been up all night with Jill and had at last got her off to sleep, and then Peter woke up and started to sing, I could have murdered him quite easily. But I didn't. And I am sure Dick didn't, or Betty. Besides, I don't really see how she could have done. I mean, suppose she had gone downstairs leaving Christopher alone in the nursery, gone into the library, loaded the revolver, which I don't expect she could have done for a moment, and then walked into the garden and shot Penelope, would Penelope have sat there quietly waiting to be shot?"

"I suppose that applies to whoever did it."

"Well, a man might have shot from a distance but Betty couldn't hit a haystack unless she were touching it with one hand. She was perfectly rotten at darts."

"Might Miss Stevenson have been asleep?"

"Oh no! I am sure Betty would not shoot someone while they were asleep. It would be a horrid thing to do, wouldn't it?"

"Who else was staying in the house at the time?"

"No one. Mrs. Dashwood came over when she read about it in the evening paper, but she is over seventy and as she says herself, she wouldn't go blotting her copy-book so near the end. Besides, if she had done it she would have said so. She is so fond of Dick she would never sit still and watch him being hung."

"I don't see how she could do that, in any case," remarked Mr. Borden thoughtfully, "but had she any motive for shooting Miss Stevenson?"

"Yes, rather! She and Mr. Stevenson wanted to get married and Penelope got round him to prevent it but then, if she had been going to murder her, why not do it while Mr. Stevenson was alive and she could still marry him? I mean she can't now, however many times she murders Penelope."

"No, it doesn't seem a very good motive. Revenge, of course but I don't think a woman of seventy would murder someone for revenge. Any other candidates?"

"Well, I am telling you everything, so it is no use pretending that Alice—the parlormaid, you know—didn't absolutely hate the sight of Penelope. But hate isn't a motive, is it? I mean, one can't like everyone but it would be awkward if one went about murdering everyone one didn't fancy, wouldn't it?"

"Very awkward. Was this maid the one who saw Mrs. Stevenson

coming out of the nursery just after the shot?"

"I see what you mean. How clever you are! That would fit in very well. I am sure she would tell any amount of lies for Betty. She was devoted to her—she helped her have Christopher, you know. Hating Penelope as she did, she naturally wouldn't mind but it was Dorothy, the housemaid, who adored Penelope, and thought she was too wonderful for words. She would never help anyone to murder her, but she absolutely sticks to her statement about Betty being in the nursery, and I am sure she is speaking the truth."

"I see. But about Alice—did she really hate Penelope? And why? You used the word hate, which is pretty strong."

"Well, it was a pretty strong form of dislike. You see, she was devoted to Mr. Stevenson and she didn't think Penelope was a good daughter."

"Was she?"

"If the woman weren't dead, I'd say she was about as bad a one as ever stepped. She always gave the impression that he led her an awful life and that he was exacting and selfish. Really he was a perfect darling and frightfully unselfish. Of course he spoiled Penelope, she had her own way over everything and he even gave up marrying Mrs. Dashwood for her sake. In return she lived here doing exactly what she liked, going away when she liked, chivvying him about, talking to him as if he were a child and never considering him at all. I am sure my father would have chucked something at me ages ago if I had talked to him as she did to hers. But Alice was the only one of the maids who saw through her, because of course she always put in a lot of 'Daddy dears,' and all that rot, and they thought she was ever so sweet. But Alice didn't and I am sure she must have been tempted time and time again to pour some hot soup down her neck at dinner, but so far as I know she never did. If she had wanted to murder her it would have been as easy as winking to have poisoned her. She wouldn't have needed to shoot her."

Mr. Borden looked at his notes. "Charles Graeme seems the most likely candidate," he said. "It is difficult to see his motive but his disappearing in this way seems highly suggestive."

"Yes, doesn't it? I am sorry for him in a way because he looked rather nice and I am sure he was very much in love with Penelope. At least he was at her father's funeral, though he seems to have changed his mind since, because otherwise why should he shoot her? But the great thing is to clear Betty and Dick. I daresay Charles may get off with a *crime passionnel,* if you know what I mean. His love must have suddenly turned to hate. Oh, that reminds me. If you are going through Penelope's papers and you find an awkward piece of poetry likening Penelope to the Madonna, you might let me have it back quietly because I am sure the person who wrote it didn't do it and it would be awkward for him if it appeared in the newspaper."

"Do you mind being more explicit? I thought it was agreed that you should tell me everything."

"He was of course. I had really forgotten about the Bakers, and in any case I don't see how they could have done it, because they would have been in at evening service. But here goes." And she plunged into the Bakers' story. "I think that's all," she concluded. "He was an awful ass, but it wouldn't have helped him to murder her. He'd be less likely to get back his poetry. And she didn't do it, either. She admitted that she had sometimes felt like it but she is awfully nice really. And she lost her baby, poor darling, so I am sure she didn't. It's hard to explain and I am afraid I don't express myself frightfully well."

"Thank you very much indeed," said Borden. "I will go somewhere quiet and read through my notes, if I may."

"Make yourself at home in the library," begged Lupin. "There may be some police about, but I don't expect they will disturb you."

"Lady Lupin is not a clear thinker," Borden remarked to the superintendent that evening, "but there is not much that escapes her."

CHAPTER 21

LUPIN was pushing Christopher along the village street. It was a pretty kettle of fish, whichever way you looked at it. Someone must have murdered Penelope, there was no doubt about that. Dick and Betty had every reason to have done it but she was sure they hadn't. She did hope Mr. Borden would find out something, as she couldn't stay here forever. Andrew had gone back to Glanville and she was longing to go back, too. There was not much point in hanging about any longer, so she would go tomorrow and take Christopher with her. She supposed Christopher would live with them always now. Well, she wouldn't mind that, if it weren't for such a sad reason . She would quite enjoy another baby in the house. But how could Betty bear to leave Christopher?

"Hullo!" Agnes Deering was walking along with young Harry and a couple of dogs. Lupin liked Harry. He was about the same age as Peter and very friendly.

"Good morning," he said politely, "may I push the pram?"

That was like Peter, too, he had loved pushing the pram.

"Yes, but be very careful, won't you? Christopher is so young."

"He is young, isn't he?" agreed Harry pityingly. "Do you think he'll get older soon?"

"Just going for a walk?" asked Agnes.

"Yes," said Lupin. "I was sort of trying to think, you know, but I'm not very clever and the more I think the less seems to happen."

"It doesn't seem much good anyone thinking," said Agnes. "It is a beastly muddle."

"Isn't it? I mean, why kill her?"

"I can think of a good many people who would have liked to but one doesn't as a rule, in a civilized country."

"Did you ever want to kill her?"

"Oh yes! She was engaged to my husband once."

Lupin started. "Was she really?"

Agnes looked at Harry. He was walking ahead of them along a lane. He was walking very carefully on the left-hand side and talking to Christopher, who chuckled up at him in a sociable manner, even if he didn't give audible answers.

"I'd always liked Henry. I'd known him all my life. We didn't know the Stevensons very well then. I lived ten miles away at Little Fenmore, but my mother was a friend of Lady Deering's and my father of Sir Henry's, and we all saw a lot of each other. Henry and I were both awfully keen on hunting and most out-of-door things. We would tramp for miles, sometimes. I—well, I thought an awful lot of him and I was proud when he said I could do things as well as a man," and she gave a bitter little laugh.

"I used to see Penelope occasionally, of course. Bob and Dick became very friendly but I never noticed her much. Then the Deerings gave a dance for Henry's coming of age and she was there with Charles Graeme. I remember thinking what a good-looking couple they were. I never noticed looks much but Penelope was perfectly lovely—she was wearing a dress of very pale green and she quite took one's breath away. Henry was struck 'all of a heap.' He kept saying, 'Isn't she lovely?' I thought he was being rather tiresome. We usually talked about horses and dogs but he seemed to be able to talk about nothing else but Penelope that night. I got rather fed up.

"Then we heard that she had broken off her engagement to Charles. Everyone was talking about it. She couldn't leave her father and Dick. She had promised her mother to look after them and with Charles in the army there was no knowing where he might be sent, so she wouldn't be able to do her duty to him as well as to her father and brother. Well, you know what it is like in the country. Some people said how selfish it was of Mr. Stevenson while some suggested that Charles should give up the army and live at the Limes with Penelope and her father."

"Like Mr. Knightly!" exclaimed Lupin.

"What?"

"Oh nothing, do go on."

"Well, everyone agreed how wonderful Penelope was—although I didn't. I thought she was a fool. If she loved the man she ought to have married him. I expect her father and brother would have got on all right without her. But of course I was prejudiced because it was just about then that I realized I was in love with Henry. We still went about together but he was always going on about how wonderful Penelope was and how he hadn't realized that there were women like that and I found it wasn't much satisfaction, after all, to be looked on as another man.

"Lady Deering was all over her. She thought her such a sweet girl, so pretty and such a good daughter. And of course it would have been a great pity if she had gone to a foreign station and lost her complexion. I don't think Sir Henry was so keen. He was very nice to her but not blindly adoring like everyone else. Well, anyhow, we all went to the Hunt Ball. Penelope didn't want to go, or so she said, but Lady Deering begged her to and she said something about not wanting to spoil the pleasures of others. Of course she looked too lovely in a sort of gray affair. I am not much good at describing clothes, but Henry proposed to her and she accepted, and Lady Deering was delighted. Sir Henry said Henry was much too young to settle down and so he was—he was only twenty-one. Well, anyway, Penelope said she didn't want to have it known, so only the Deerings and her father knew of it—and me, of course. Henry told me I was his best man-friend!

"I went out to India. I was thoroughly miserable and a school friend who had married a man in the Indian army asked me to stay and I was thankful to go. I only heard about what happened next some time later from Henry. It seems that Penelope had never ridden. She had always been so busy with her father and Dick that she had never had time to learn or some rot. Well, naturally Henry was not happy until she had learned—he was more at home on horseback than on his feet and naturally he wanted his wife to ride with him. I suppose it is very seldom that anyone learns to ride really well if they wait until they are grown up and I gather Penelope was not much good. Henry used to tease her a bit and she was not used to being teased. One day, he said, 'It is funny that someone who looks like a goddess on the ground should look like a sack of potatoes on a horse.' "

"She didn't like that," hazarded Lupin.

"No, she didn't, but I can't think why. Henry often used to chaff me—ragging each other is part of the fun when you are fond of someone."

"I know," agreed Lupin, "but I don't think Penelope thought so. I don't think she'd like being ragged." She thought for a moment or two. "Dick never ragged her. He ragged Betty but he and Penelope weren't a bit like a brother and sister. Her father-in-law teased Betty and he teased me but he didn't tease Penelope. She lived a dull sort of life in a way."

"I don't know about that. She had plenty of admiration, which was what she liked, but she was a dull woman."

"She could be quite amusing," said Lupin, impartially. "In fact I have heard her being very funny, but one was so anxious to laugh in the right place that one sometimes missed the joke, if you know what I mean. One felt 'Penelope is being funny, how amusing she is!' and one felt how awful it would be if one missed the point."

"Um, I never bothered much myself. We never liked each other, though I don't know why I should bear her any grudge. Henry and I were very happy together."

"Was it long after? I mean, did you get engaged soon after he and Penelope had the quarrel?"

"Five years. He was frightfully upset and his father sent him out to

New Zealand to study their farming methods. He had a cousin out there and I was in India for two years. I met Charles and his wife."

"What was she like?"

"Quite a nice little thing. She and Charles seemed happy enough. He asked me about Penelope. He had heard that she was engaged to Henry. I don't know how those things get about. I never told anyone. I didn't like talking about it. But Charles liked talking to me. I don't know whether he guessed we were in the same boat, but anyway I heard that the engagement was broken off. I didn't tell him. I thought it might unsettle him but he heard from someone and, poor fellow, he seemed quite demented. He came to see me one evening and said, 'Is it true, is it true?' And I said, 'Is what true?' And he said, 'About Penelope and Henry—have they broken it off?' So I said, 'Yes,' and he said, 'What a fool I've been, what a fool!' I suppose he meant he wouldn't have married Ruth if it hadn't been for thinking Penelope was going to marry Henry. Anyway, I felt sorry for Ruth, but I only saw them once or twice again, and never Charles alone. Well, I came home and Henry came home and we started meeting again and in the end we got married—then the war came along and he was killed, so that's that."

Lupin said nothing. There was nothing to say. They walked for some way in silence, then Agnes said, "I don't know why I've been talking so much, but I was trying to explain why I didn't like Penelope. I suppose one is always jealous of the woman one's husband falls in love with first. I think he always admired her but she was very aloof with him. Of course, we had to meet her pretty often. And then young Bob got quite besotted about her. It was really too much."

Had it been too much? Had Agnes just felt she couldn't bear it and popped along and murdered her? No, one would hardly murder someone for the sake of a brother-in-law. It wasn't even as if Penelope were in any danger of marrying him. She would never have done that. There is always something that calls for slight amusement when a woman marries a man a great deal her junior and Penelope did not like to cause amusement. No, Lupin could not see any reason why Agnes should have killed Penelope. As a matter of fact, as she said, she had good reason to be grateful to her, better perhaps than she realized, for if Henry had not been first in love with Penelope he might never have learned to love Agnes.

She must have appealed to him by her very difference. Having once been misled by a lovely face he chose a plain face the second time; having once been misled by lofty sentiments he chose someone matter of fact. No, Agnes could have no real grudge against Penelope.

"Come in and have a glass of sherry," invited Agnes. "Christopher can sleep in his pram as well in our garden as in the Limes."

"Better, I should think," agreed Lupin, "with the police all over the place, not to mention the most ghastly relations you can possibly imagine liable to pop in at any moment and talk about dear, dear Penelope, dearest Uncle and my sister's child."

Lady Deering was pleased to see Lupin. "How nice of you to look in, dear, and you've brought little Christopher. Isn't he a lovely child? How sad to think that both his parents are in prison! And poor Penelope, too —to think of her being dead. Such a nice woman! She was engaged to my son for a time," she added, as Agnes went in search of sherry. "His father thought him too young and I daresay he was, but she was such a pretty girl. However, I daresay it was as well as it was, for he learned quite a lot about farming in New Zealand and brought back such interesting photographs of his cousin's family, six children—such a big family for nowadays!—and some wool. I had it made up into a jersey suit."

"What color was it?" asked Lupin.

"Green, bluish-green. *Eau-de-Nil,* we used to call it. I was very pretty but I could not get a hat to go with it. I got one but it faded almost at once, went quite a different color—much more blue, you know."

"I should think *eau-de-Nil* would suit you awfully well," said Lupin.

"Would you, dear? Yes, I think it did. You always dress so charmingly yourself. Agnes isn't very interested in clothes. She is a very dear girl. I was glad when she married Henry. I had known her mother for years and of course I did not know Penelope's mother. Still, they were both very nice girls. I hope Bob will choose as well when it comes to his turn. Not that there is any hurry. He is very happy as he is, helping his father-in-law."

Lupin wondered if anyone could be such an idiot as Lady Deering. Well, she knew one. Herself. Was she quite as idiotic? She wasn't sure. Suppose Lady Deering put it all on? Suppose she had never forgiven Penelope for throwing over her son? Suppose she thought that she had got Bob into her clutches?

It was an idea. She looked at the pretty, placid, pink-and-white cheeks and wondered.

CHAPTER 22

LUPIN walked in through the side gate of the Limes, past the house and into the garden. The flowers seemed to mock her. Everything was at its very best. As usual she was haunted by lines of poetry that she could not remember properly. She supposed it was because she had no brains and could not assimilate things, that disjointed bits and pieces were always haunting her, like food one could not digest, as she told herself inelegantly.

> And May with her world in flower,
> Seemed still to murmur and smile.

What on earth was she to do? What she wanted to do and what common sense told her to do was to go home tomorrow. She would take Christopher with her and there would be Andrew and Peter and Jill! It wasn't as if she could do any good here. Or could she? Was there anything left for her to do? Surely Mr. Borden would be able to clear up everything. She probably made things much worse with her cockeyed notions. Lady Deering, for instance! One could hardly imagine Lady Deering strolling into the garden on a Sunday evening, shooting Penelope and returning to the hall to sit at the head of the dinner table, looking charming in gray chiffon.

"Who is my beautiful?" said a voice, and Lupin looked up to see Gladys Browne approaching.

"I'm sorry we are late, Gladys, but he has been asleep for the last hour. I went in to see Lady Deering and he slept all the time, so rude! I remember Mr. Hastings doing it once, when we went to dinner at the archdeacon's. He had been fire-watching the night before and the archdeacon's wife would tell us her experiences in Czechoslovakia, or it may have been Yugoslavia, before the war."

"Lor, mum—I mean, my lady—shall I take baby in?"

"Please do, Gladys," and Lupin walked rather wearily into the house.

She looked at the library door. What a relief it would be if Mr. Stevenson were to come through it now. She felt that he would know just what to do. Moved by an impulse, she walked into the room, as if by merely looking at his furniture she might gain something of an inspiration.

Leaning back in the big armchair lay Charles Graeme. "Thank God," said Lupin. "We have been waiting for you."

"So I gathered. I picked up a continental *Daily Mail* yesterday morning and found that the police were looking for me, so I hired a car to the nearest aerodrome and flew back to be met on arrival by the police. After several hours of cross-questioning they let me loose, but I understand they are keeping an eye on me and that I may be arrested at any moment."

"Did you shoot Penelope?"

"No."

"Then who did?"

"I don't know. I hear that both Betty and Dick say they did."

"But they didn't."

"No, I don't expect they did."

"Then who did?" she repeated.

"You are hoping that I did it, aren't you? So that Betty and Dick will be cleared. Even if I didn't do it, I expect you think I might have the decency to say I did and to give myself up. But is that really going to help us very much, all of us saying that we have done it? They will have to prove it, you know. If it were just a case of being hung, I don't think I should mind particularly, but it is not so simple as that."

"I say," said Lupin, "I am most frightfully sorry that I am being so unsympathetic. I have been thinking so much about Dick and Betty and Christopher, especially Christopher, that I forgot all about you, except as a means of clearing things up. But of course, now I come to think about it, it is much worse for you than it is for anyone else."

"Thanks very much. You see, I loved Penelope."

"I know you did," replied Lupin.

"When I say I loved her, I mean that I loved her for twenty years and I think I was the only person who did love her, as she was. I was under no delusions about her, I never thought that she was unselfish or a wonderful character or anything like that. I loved her just as she was. I didn't want to see her different, except I wanted her to be my wife. I always thought she would be that one day and now she never will be."

"That is what I thought the first time I saw you—that you loved her, I mean."

"Well, I fell in love with her and we got engaged and we were as happy as it is possible for two people to be—at least, I was. Then Mr. Stevenson and Mrs. Dashwood decided to get married. Before they made the engagement public or anything, they told Penelope and me. Naturally they thought she would be pleased."

"But she wasn't?"

"She went off the deep end, said it was sacrilege to put someone in her mother's place, that Dick's life would be ruined by having a stepmother and all the rest of it. It was a ghastly time and I made things worse by losing my temper and telling her what I thought of her and—well, we parted. I managed to transfer and got sent to India. Why Mr. Stevenson gave in I can't think."

"Nor can I, he always seemed so sane."

"Of course, Penelope always gave the impression of being frightfully delicate and the old doctor they had then encouraged her. And by that time Mrs. Dashwood was pretty fed up, I should think—I don't know and we never shall know now. Anyway, we all acted like a lot of fools. If Mr. Stevenson had insisted on marrying Mrs. Dashwood and I had been a bit patient, everything might have turned out all right. Penelope was young and she might have been able to adapt herself. But there it is, there was a regular flareup and I went off to India. Soon after I got there I heard that Penelope was engaged to Henry Deering, and I nearly went off my head. Ruth, my wife, was very decent to me at that time. I mean she never said anything but she was always ready to do things with me when I wanted someone and—oh, I don't know. I felt she liked me and that is something when you are feeling raw all over from being turned down by someone you care for. I thought we could make a life together. She liked children, and—well, I was pretty wretched."

"I understand."

"Everything went all right to start with. We fitted in well together. It wasn't romance but it was a happy companionable sort of business. After all, as I told myself, Ruth had the nicer nature of the two. But sometimes when the moon shone over the mountains or I heard some music or smelled some flower—you know what I mean—I realized that

I didn't give a damn for a nice nature. I wanted Penelope. However, as I say, I was getting more sensible and I hoped soon to forget. Then I needs must run into Agnes Martin."

"Mrs. Deering?"

"Yes. Well, the last time I'd seen her was at a dance when Penelope and I were engaged. I danced with her, Agnes, once, and I was treading on air. And here I was dancing with her again. I kept remembering that night: the garden in the moonlight, the night-scented stocks and the tobacco plant and Penelope. Penelope! Sorry, you must think me driveling at my age, but there are some things one never forgets.

"I tried to avoid Agnes and yet she drew me like a magnet—a link with the past, you know—and then I guessed that she was miserable, too. She cared for Henry. I don't know how I guessed but somehow I did, though we never talked much. In fact, I did not see her very many times but I think we had a sort of fellow feeling.

"Then I heard that Penelope's engagement was broken off. Agnes did not tell me. I heard it through another man, I forget who. But I asked Agnes point blank and she had to tell me. I guessed it, really, as soon as I saw her. She looked different, cheerful, almost good-looking. But she was sorry for me. I knew then what I had thought before—she cared for Henry. Now she could hope that one day he would care for her. But I had dug my own grave! If only I had waited, if only I had been patient!

"I tried not to let Ruth know what I was feeling but I daresay she did. She was very good to me. Poor Ruth. I wish I had been a better husband to her. I had been settling down before I heard this news, but now I felt all churned up again. I tried to keep Penelope out of my thoughts and when we came home on leave I made up my mind to keep right away from anywhere where I might run into her or even hear about her. But one day I met her at a friend's house in London.

"She was lovelier than ever. Everything else faded out of my mind. Ruth, my career, all my other interests. She was looking sad and I wondered if she had suffered. She came out to dinner with me and she told me that she had. She had become engaged to Henry out of pity, because he had seemed to need her so. But it was no good. She realized that she did not love him and that it would be a mockery for her to marry him. She loved me and she would never love anyone else. I did not really believe it all but what did that matter? Here she was, close to me, being kind to me.

"She was up in London most of that winter and we met constantly. Then in February, on St. Valentine's Day, I told her that I couldn't go on. She must come away with me or we must break it all off. It was a wonderful winter's day, just touched by early spring. We went to Hampton Court and the crocuses were showing. She had on a gray fur coat and a little gray velvet cap. I gave her a bunch of early violets and she pinned them on her coat. I carried that picture in my heart for years.

"I got the war office to send me abroad again. Ruth and I agreed to live our own lives. If we had had children it would have all been different, but we hadn't, and it was no good going on. There was no question of divorce. She did not want it and it wouldn't have helped me. We saw each other from time to time and were on quite good terms. She spent most of her time with a sister. And—oh, well, so life went by.

"Then Ruth died—poor Ruth. I should never have married her. I waited until the year was up, then a week or two longer to bring it to St. Valentine's Day. I thought Penelope would like that. I hadn't seen her for fifteen years. My last recollection was at Hampton Court in a gray fur coat and cap and a bunch of violets. She was in gray again."

She would be, thought Lupin.

"Tweedy things! She was older, but lovelier—far lovelier than ever. I brought her some violets, and I said, 'Is it too late, Penelope?' And—oh, well, we had it all over again. Her father was very old. He would die if she left him.

"I pointed out that I had retired from the army and we could live quite near. Dick was grown up now. Surely he and his wife could help look after him. I tried everything but it was all no good. She was very, very sweet, she would never love anyone else, but duty came first. Again I did not really swallow a word of it but it made no difference—nothing she did could ever make a difference—and I resigned myself to waiting for her father's death. It was an unpleasant situation because I liked him and I hated having to look forward to it but there it was. As a matter of fact he died quite soon and I felt that perhaps after all Penelope had been justified in waiting. Now she could feel that she had sacrificed herself up to the hilt and she could marry me at last without any regrets.

"That's what I felt, everything seemed rounded off so tidily for her. I looked at her in church on the day of the funeral and I felt that we had come to the end of a long journey, and that now . . ." He stopped and Lupin looked out of the window.

"Naturally," he went on after a short pause, "I waited for a month before I said anything. I don't know whether she thought I ought to have waited longer, she might have thought it more artistic. But I had waited a pretty long time already."

"I suppose she might," replied Lupin thoughtfully. "She saw things as sort of pictures, tableaux, and she liked everyone to play their part properly. All the same, you had absolutely out-Jacobed Jacob. She couldn't really expect you to wait any longer."

"Out-Jacobed Jacob?"

"Perhaps you call him Yarcup," suggested Lupin, helpfully. "I know some people do, but I always think it sounds like a hiccup."

"Oh, Jacob, I know who you mean. I didn't know anyone called him Yarcup. He was the chap that served seven years for Rachel, wasn't he?"

"And then got put off with her sister with bad eyes. Still, even then he only did fourteen years and you'd done twenty."

"Yes, twenty years—and then she said it was too late, that she had made her life and that she was too old to change."

"I think in a way she was right. I don't mean that she was too old but she had made her life. I can't describe what I mean but she had somehow made herself into a sort of person, someone who had had great sorrow and whose only pleasure was in sacrificing herself for others. And she could not see herself as starting out as a new person without any sorrow and no sacrifice being called for and no one being sorry for her any longer."

"I know what you mean. She always saw herself, could never forget herself. I suppose she never really loved me. I was just one of the players, the faithful lover. Well, I've always known that inside me but, like a fool, I went on hoping that one day she would love me."

"In her own way I think she did," said Lupin.

"In her own way, yes. If only she had married me I would have been content with very little, for I knew she wasn't capable of much. But I had always hoped that one day she would be ready to play the part of the perfect wife instead of the perfect daughter."

"And would that have contented you?"

"I think so."

Lupin looked at him and thought what a fool Penelope had been. Here was a man, and a very nice man at that, who had loved her for twenty years, who knew her and understood her and who would never be put off however she behaved, with whom she would never have to put on an act. And yet she let him go, so that she could keep up her stunt of sorrow and renunciation. What did she think would happen to her as she grew older? Did she think that Dick would go on worshipping her blindly? Lupin had seen signs in Dick even before his father's death that he was beginning to wonder a little. In fact, she suspected that ever since Christopher's birth he had been getting restive, realizing how much he loved his wife and how difficult it was to be happy with her without hurting Penelope.

Why would she not marry Charles? Lupin frowned, hardly listening to what he was saying. She remembered that Penelope had broken off her engagement with Henry Deering because he said she looked like a sack of potatoes on a horse. Charles would never say anything like that. She would always look lovely to him but he did not think her a wonderful character. Perhaps Penelope realized that her husband would have to think she was perfect in every way. It wasn't love she wanted, it was admiration.

"We walked through the wood and she turned me down. I said, 'Do you really mean it, Penelope?' and she said, 'Yes.' I said, 'This is the last time that I shall ask you.' Then she started about friendship and that I should always be a very dear friend and I said, 'Friend be damned, Penelope! I am not going to hang round like a tame dog any longer. If you won't marry me, you won't, and there is an end of it. I have wasted twenty years of my life being in love with you.' I don't quite know what I said, but I told her that I was the only person who had ever really been in love with her. Other people were in love with the pretty picture of herself that she showed them but I loved her in spite of herself. I had never thought she was a wonderful character. In fact I had always known she was horribly selfish but yet I loved her, fool that I was!

"I told her that even after the time that she behaved like a fiend to her father and to Mrs. Dashwood and to me I went on loving her, angry though I was. I knew that she could not bear the idea of anyone else coming first with her father, even though she was going to get married herself. I tried to stop loving her. I went away and married someone else, and though I never forgot her, I was fairly content with my wife until I met her again. I reminded her of how she soon worked me up again and made me madder than ever. She encouraged me up to the last minute and then her virtue, or rather her sense of self-preservation, came to her aid, and there was a lot of talk about my dear wife and her dear father but it was her own dear self she was thinking of, I told her. No breath of scandal must touch her. She was a good woman, a noble woman who had known much sorrow and whose happiness came from helping others! I gibed at her, I jeered at her, and now I shall never see her again." His voice broke.

Lupin was crying, too, but she managed to turn away her head so that he should not see. Then she tried to stifle a sob. It turned into an undignified snort but he did not notice.

Charles went on huskily, "I said everything, everything I had been thinking for years. It was a relief in a way to get it off my chest but how was I to know, how could I guess. . . I pointed out that she was trying to wreck Dick's marriage because she realized that he cared for Betty more than he did for her. She had to be the center of everyone's devotion and admiration. She liked have me as the pining lover but as a husband I should be dull. Besides, she would never forgive me for seeing her as she was. And yet, fool that she was, she would be safe with me as she could never be with anyone else, for there would never be any danger of me finding out about her and being disillusioned. I suppose," he said abruptly, "that you won't believe that I loved her. No one would believe it, if they had heard me talk that afternoon."

"I believe it," said Lupin. "I know that you loved her. I knew it the first time that I saw you. I can't describe it. I've seen other men looking at her with admiration, as you say, obviously thinking her too wonderful for words, but you were different. I knew at once that you loved her in spite of herself, not because of herself, if you know what I mean."

Charles nodded. "If only I hadn't been so beastly to her that last time! I'll never forget it, but I was feeling like a madman. I told her she had had a long run for her money but that it wouldn't last forever and that one day she would be left alone, that her friends would drop from her one by one as they began to see through her, but that with me she need have no fear of that, for though I had always seen through her, I loved her just the same."

"I don't think she saw through herself," said Lupin.

"No, I suppose not. I hadn't thought of that and I was the one to tear down the picture and hurt her. I who loved her. She"—he shuddered—"she—well, she asked me to leave her and I just went breaking through the undergrowth, not knowing what I was doing. I got up to London somehow, and I caught a plane to Croydon. When I landed in France I went straight to a place in Brittany that I knew about, miles away from everywhere. That's why I never heard the news till yesterday. I came as soon as I could, not that there was anything I could do. I will never see Penelope again."

CHAPTER 23

"WELL, I am afraid I am not much forwarder," said Mr. Borden, as he sat down in the chair indicated by Mrs. Dashwood and accepted a whisky and soda.

It was evening. Charles had refused Lupin and Mrs. Dashwood's invitation to luncheon. He had met the latter as he was about to take his leave and the meeting had moved them both. If it hadn't been for Mrs. Dashwood, he thought, he might have been married to Penelope. It had been her engagement to Mr. Stevenson that had caused the break between them. If only Charles had been patient, thought Mrs. Dashwood, Penelope might have changed her mind and I might have been married to Richard. Yet she had felt sorry for Charles. He had loved Penelope faithfully for many years and now he had lost her for good. She had asked him to stay to luncheon and had been seconded by Lupin but he had made a hurried excuse and had left them and they had not seen him since.

It had been an endless day. They had talked and Lupin had told Mrs. Dashwood all that she had learned and all that she had surmised. They had both tried to rest in the afternoon, but Lupin had soon given up the struggle and gone for a walk in the woods. Never had she felt so depressed, never had she longed so for home. If only she could have been safe in the vicarage garden she would not have minded how many parish workers had disturbed her; she would have welcomed all the little problems of everyday life. How easy of solution would have been the quarrels between the Sunday school teachers, the servant shortage, the food question and the pension papers.

She returned to tea and she and Mrs. Dashwood once more discussed the question of Penelope's death until it was time to play with Christopher and watch him in his bath. At dinner they had been too tired to talk much. As they were finishing their coffee Mr. Borden had been announced.

"I have seen Colonel Graeme," he told them. "He says he went for a walk with Miss Stevenson and left her at about four o'clock."

"Then what was she doing till six?" asked Lupin. "She can't have been shot before six. Or do you think that Colonel Graeme shot her in the wood at four, then dragged her body into the garden and sat it in the deck chair?"

"The doctor seems certain that she could not have been dead for more than half an hour when he saw her."

"He might have been mistaken. They are sometimes, though I don't see why he should have used Dick's revolver."

"He might have shot her with his own, then got hold of Dick's, shot into the air to account for the used cartridge, and laid it beside her to make it look like suicide."

"Then why did he wipe off the fingerprints?" demanded Lupin.

"Murderers do sometimes make very childish mistakes."

"Then you think it was Charles?"

"No, I don't really. I don't think the doctor could have been so far out in his calculations. Besides, there is Dorothy's evidence. The police have checked up on Graeme's statement and it seems pretty certain that he caught the four-forty-five up to London. I am sorry, but I am afraid at present Dick Stevenson seems the most likely person. He had the only really clear motive apart from Mrs. Stevenson and I think we can wipe her out. Here is a list I made out: Dick Stevenson. Motive—his sister was making trouble between him and his wife and he stood to inherit a considerable sum of money at her death."

"I am sure that would not influence him at all," put in Lupin.

"Opportunity—he was in the garden when the shot was fired. He had a gun and it is practically certain that that gun was used. He could have got very close to his sister without her suspecting anything wrong. He might even have put an arm round her or something of that sort."

"What a horrid idea!"

"No one seems to have seen him since he left the Deerings' house at five-thirty, until his wife saw him just after the shot was fired. Why did she say that she had committed the murder? Because she saw him shoot his sister."

"Oh no," said Mrs. Dashwood. "I'll never believe it."

"Next we have Mrs. Stevenson. Her motive was the same as her husband's, but her opportunity was not so good. She was in the nursery with her baby. If she had left him it was more than likely that someone would have heard her. The child himself would very likely have cried out. She may have known how to load and fire a gun but was probably not very proficient at it. She wouldn't have had a pocket into which to hide it as she approached her sister-in-law. In any case we have the maid Dorothy Piper's statement on oath that she was in the nursery when the shot was fired.

"Charles Graeme. Motive—thwarted passion. Opportunity—he was alone with her for an hour and a half but would he have a weapon on him? We know that he left the neighborhood by 4:45 and the ticket inspector at Paddington recognized his photograph as one who had passed the barrier at 5:50. So he could not have killed Miss Stevenson at six o'clock, and if he had done it at four he would not have had time to drag her to the garden, put her in the deck chair, get out her brother's revolver, arrange it by her side, and get to Morely by 4:15. In any case if Dorothy is speaking the truth she saw her and spoke to her at about 4:30, at which time we can be pretty sure Graeme was in the train."

"Go on."

"Mr. Baker. Motive—fear. He had written a very foolish poem and was afraid that Miss Stevenson might show it to someone. She might even have blackmailed him, but it seems very unlikely as she was a wealthy woman or at any rate very comfortably off and he was a poor parson. She may have had some sort of hold over him of which we do not know. Opportunity—he may have known where Stevenson kept his revolver and he could have approached Miss Stevenson without being suspected. He might have gone on his knees to her or something of that sort, then whipped the revolver out of his pocket and shot her. Against that, he had to wipe the revolver, lay it beside her and get back to church and into his surplice by six o'clock. The verger says that he was in the vestry by five minutes to. And everyone seems agreed that the shot wasn't fired until just before six, whatever that may mean. The verger does admit that the vicar did not seem quite himself and he might have been running.

"Mrs. Baker. Motive—jealousy. She thought her husband was in love with Miss Stevenson. Opportunity—she might or might not have known where Mr. Stevenson kept his revolver, she might have slipped into the house and taken it, or she might have taken it a day or two before. On the other hand, Mr. Stevenson said it was on his table on Sunday afternoon and he has no reason that I can see for lying about it, unless of course he thought his wife had it.

"That is an idea! Let us say that Mrs. Baker came in one morning and was shown into the library. She extracted the revolver from the drawer, took it home, then on Sunday evening, watching from the vicarage, saw Miss Stevenson enter the garden. She followed her and shot her, put the revolver beside her and hurried across the road to the church and slipped into her pew just as her husband and the choir came in. Though the evidence is that she was in her place in plenty of time and that she spoke to the organist about a chant before the service."

"And she wouldn't have been shown into the library," objected Lupin. "People who came to see Penelope or Betty were shown into the drawing room."

Mr. Borden looked at his list and hesitated. "Go on," said Mrs. Dashwood.

"Well," he said apologetically, "I am afraid you are next."

"I supposed I would be appearing soon."

"Motive—revenge. Is that right?"

"Quite."

"Opportunity—you were staying with friends at Little Frampton, seven miles away. They went to tea with some other friends and you pleaded a headache and stayed at home. They left their house at 3.30 approximately and returned just before seven. The maid took you some tea at 4:30 but no one saw you between then and seven o'clock. You would have had plenty of time to drive over if you had previously hired a car or you could have caught the 5:10 bus arriving at 5:50, come into this room you know so well, taken Dick's revolver, shot Miss Stevenson, wiped the revolver, caught the 6:10 bus back, arriving at 6:50, and retired to your room. If you were seen in the road you could have said you had taken a little walk, thinking the air would be good for your head."

"How clever you are!"

"Unfortunately, neither of the conductors recognizes you from your photograph and both deny having had an elderly lady as a passenger either way. The hired car is the only possible alternative and we are circulating all the garages."

"Thanks."

"Alice Martin, parlormaid. Motive—revenge. Fancies that Miss Stevenson behaved badly to her master. Opportunity—she would know where Mr. Stevenson kept his revolver. She would know who was in and who was out and the movements of everyone in the house. She was out herself on Sunday evening but there was nothing to prevent her returning. Mrs. Clarke in the village says she had tea with her but is very vague as to when she came and when she left. Mrs. Pedly, also of the village, says Alice came in to see her some time in the evening and that they had some supper together but she is also vague about the time. It seems that it would have been easy enough for Alice to have slipped home and shot her mistress between her two parties. But revenge is a pretty poor motive, and if she did shoot her as a punishment for her treatment to her father, surely she would have told her what she thought of her and why she was doing it, in which case there would have been a struggle. Miss Stevenson would hardly have sat quietly in her chair waiting to be shot and I can't believe Alice could have resisted telling her what she thought of her. There is not much satisfaction in shooting someone quietly without them knowing you are doing it, so to speak."

"No, there isn't, is there?' agreed Lupin. "And Penelope would have had to be asleep for Alice to get near enough without her noticing it and, as you say, there wouldn't be much revenge in shooting someone while they were asleep. All the same she does seem the most likely. Poor Alice! But there it is—wherever we go we come up against someone and feel sorry for them but, after all, if they really murdered her they must be dreadfully wicked, and I suppose one shouldn't feel sorry for them. Just think what one would have to go through before one got to murdering someone! And, by the way, what about the Deerings? Have you considered them at all?"

"The Deerings? Do you mean Sir Henry Deering? I have heard of him—he is a magistrate, isn't he?"

"I believe so, but they all have a sort of motive—nothing much, but

I suppose we might include them in our list. I mean, Penelope was engaged to Agnes's husband—Henry Deering, you know—but she jilted him so that Agnes was able to marry him herself, so I don't quite see why she should have a grudge against her but of course his father and mother might have had. I mean, I am sure I should murder anyone who jilted Peter. But why should they wait till now to do it? I mean, he was very happy with Agnes—at least, I don't know whether he was or not but I have no reason for thinking he wasn't and the Deerings would really prefer her as a daughter-in-law. Her mother was at school with Lady Deering and all that sort of thing. But then there is Bob, he worshipped Penelope. They might have been afraid of his marrying her, though I don't know why they should mind, or of course they may have thought she was playing with him, or he may have murdered her himself because she wouldn't marry him—like Charles, you know."

Mr. Borden looked at her, frowning slightly, and jotted down some notes.

"I don't know if that is quite clear," apologized Lupin.

"Very lucid!" commented Mrs. Dashwood. "It is lucky Mr. Borden is a detective, otherwise he might have difficulty in following your train of thought."

"I dreamed I was in a train last night," said Lupin. "I had to change at Reading and every time we passed Reading the train dashed through and I couldn't get out and I could hear Betty crying for Christopher but he was in my handbag. Oh, what were we talking about?"

"Sir Henry Deering," said Mr. Borden. "Motive: one, revenge; two, fear—fear for the happiness of his son Bob."

"But when one comes to think of it," said Lupin, "even if he were afraid of Penelope turning down Bob, it wouldn't make it any better for him to murder her. I mean, as long as she were alive there would always be a chance, whereas if she were dead there would never be a chance and the same applies to Charles."

"Would Sir Henry Deering have liked his younger son to have married Miss Stevenson? If she jilted his other son he wouldn't have a very high opinion of her."

"No, I don't believe he did like her very much, though I've only just thought of it. But I can't remember his ever having made a fuss of her or gazing at her in admiration as most people did. Lady Deering was always very sweet to her but she always is to everyone, so that doesn't mean she liked her. I wonder if she has hated her all the time for first jilting her elder son and then making a fool of the younger, because she did make a fool of Bob—it is no use saying she didn't just because she is dead. And I must say Lady Deering did seem sort of abstracted this morning, as if she had something on her mind. But it may have been indigestion, or the cook giving notice, or lack of fats, not murder at all."

"Motive? Perhaps if they thought she was going to ruin their son's life! But I don't quite see the opportunity. Stevenson had tea with them. I suppose if they were in it together one could have kept him in talk while the other hurried back to the Limes, took his revolver out of the library, and went in search of Penelope—after all, though, they weren't to know they would find her sitting in the orchard. If they wanted to kill her they would have had better opportunities than that but I agree they want watching."

"I do hate suggesting people, it is all so beastly," said Lupin. "But I want to get Betty and Dick home again, and I don't know how else to do it than by finding someone else."

"I'll do my best, Lady Lupin, but I am afraid things do look pretty bad for young Stevenson." He said good night and after going over everything for the thousandth time and agreeing that neither Dick nor Betty could possibly have murdered Penelope and that it must have been someone else, with the usual difficulty of deciding who that someone else could be, Lupin and Mrs. Dashwood parted for the night.

Lupin had just turned out her light and was wondering if Andrew were in bed and whether her children were asleep and whether she would ever see any of them again, when a sudden frightful thought passed through her mind. Slipping on a dressing gown, she hurried across to Mrs. Dashwood's room and knocked on the door.

She found the old lady sitting up in bed, clad in a pretty blue dressing jacket and reading a novel. "Hullo, my dear," she said. "Has anything happened?"

"It suddenly dawned on me," explained Lupin, "just as I was settling down, that you would probably commit suicide during the night and leave a note saying that you had murdered Penelope." She looked anxiously at the bedside table. There was no note, but the aspirin bottle was suspiciously empty.

"No, I haven't taken an overdose of aspirin, if that is what you are thinking," said Mrs. Dashwood. "That is an old bottle. I suppose that is what I should have done if I had been a really noble character but I am ashamed to say that such a thought never entered my head."

"I am glad," said Lupin, "because it wouldn't really have helped. I mean, if everyone says they have done it no one will be any forwarder. Well, I suppose we had better try to catch up with our beauty sleep. Good night."

"Good night," replied Mrs. Dashwood, and she went on with her novel.

CHAPTER 24

ON LEAVING the Limes, Borden walked to the inspector's house at the other end of the village. He was welcomed cordially and he related the pieces of information he had picked up.

"Colonel Graeme seems all right," commented the inspector. "As I told you, we checked his story and there is no doubt that he left Morely at 4:45 and arrived at Victoria at 6:50. That lets him out all right."

"I suppose Miss Stevenson could not have been shot earlier," hazarded Borden. "Suppose Colonel Graeme had returned with her to the Limes, shot her and put the gun beside her, then fixed up some sort of time bomb to explode at six o'clock, left her and caught his train to London?"

"Rot, my dear fellow!" returned the other good-humoredly. "My chaps had a good look all over the garden. They would have found a time-bomb if there had been one. Besides, why should the fellow go to all that trouble, carrying time bombs about with him? If he had murdered the woman it would have been in anger at being refused after all those years. It could hardly be a calculated crime."

"You are quite right. It was an idiotic suggestion but, as I told you, I have been called in by the Hastings to try to clear poor Dick Stevenson, so I have to think of every possible and impossible contingency."

"I am afraid you are going to be unlucky. I am sorry, he always seemed a nice young chap."

"What about the Deerings?"

"The Deerings? Are you suspecting them, now?"

"Not seriously, but had you ever heard of young Deering being keen on Miss Stevenson?"

"Now you come to mention it, I think I have heard something of the sort, but she was very much admired by everyone. I admired her myself, if it comes to that. Now I suppose you will be suspecting *me* of the crime," the inspector said.

"I am ready to suspect anyone. It is curious that practically everyone in this place seems to have had some reason for wishing the poor lady dead."

"It has been an eye-opener to me. A very charming lady I always thought her, very easy on the eyes and with a pleasant word for everyone."

"Well, thanks very much. It seems a pretty hopeless business from my point of view. I'd better go and try to get a night's sleep and leave you to do the same."

In the lounge of the hotel, Borden found Charles Graeme sitting with a whisky beside him and a book on his knee, gazing before him with a look of blank despair on his face. He greeted him and Charles seemed glad to see him. He invited him to have a drink and they talked for some time of India and the war and the government policy, ignoring by tacit consent the subject of the murder. At last they parted, and Borden, who had accustomed himself to switching off his mind from his problems, fell fairly soon into a refreshing sleep while Charles went upstairs to get through the night hours as best he could. But even when he fell into a troubled sleep toward dawn it was to dream of Penelope and to wake thinking he heard her voice calling to him out of a deep despair.

The next morning Borden paid a call on Sir Henry Deering. He received him courteously enough but his manner was reserved, not to say wary. Borden laid his cards on the table. "You will forgive me calling on you like this, I hope, sir, but the fact is I am a friend of Mr. Hastings and his wife, and they asked me to come down and see if I could do anything to help their friend Mr. Stevenson."

"Are you a detective?"

"Yes. I don't want it known in the village—people would not talk so freely if they knew my profession—but I thought it better to tell you the truth."

Sir Henry looked at him keenly for a moment, then looked away. "It is a bad business," he said. "Poor Dick! We should all be glad to see him cleared, but what can one do? He confesses to the murder himself."

"So does his wife, and it is pretty certain that she is innocent."

"I suppose she knew it was her husband and gave herself up in a hysterical fit of devotion."

"Was she a neurotic sort of woman?"

"No, not normally, but she had been very nervy since the birth of her child. It altered her strangely. She was such a jolly little thing when she first came here but she had been different lately—had actually left her husband, I believe. I was surprised when I saw her on Sunday. I hoped that they had made it up."

"What sort of a woman was Miss Stevenson?"

"Very charming."

Was it Borden's imagination or was the old man's voice slightly satirical?

"She was engaged to your son, I understand."

Sir Henry started. "Who told you that?"

"Lady Lupin Hastings. She heard it from your daughter-in-law."

"Yes, it's quite true. The boy was dotty about her, but it was broken off. I can't say I'm sorry. There was something about her I never cared for. Her father was a great friend of mine. I miss him and I am sorry for Dick. They both spoiled Penelope, made her think there was no one like her. Well, she's gone now, poor woman," he sighed.

"Dick came to tea with you on Sunday?"

"Yes, he dropped in to see us. We were always very fond of him, and he seemed more cheerful than he had been for a long time. I hoped things were going all right for him and that he had made it up with his wife. His sister was out with that fellow Graeme. He had been keen on her for a very long time. She was engaged to him before she was engaged to my poor son. I never knew the rights and wrongs of that. It was given out that she couldn't leave her father, but my old friend wouldn't have wanted such a sacrifice. Besides, I always had my suspicions that he would have married again himself if Penelope were settled. However, it is all a long time ago. Anyhow, the chap had turned up again and we all took it for granted that she would marry him—at least, there was nothing to stop her. The next thing we knew was that she was dead and that he had disappeared. It looked as if he had done it but he doesn't seem to have been arrested yet, though I gather he has returned."

"It has been proved that he can't have been in the garden of the Limes between 5:30 and 6:10, during which time the shot was fired."

"Dick didn't leave here till 5:30—it may have been later. It would have been a bit of a rush for him to have got back, loaded his revolver and gone into the garden."

"You don't know the exact time that Dick left this house?"

Sir Henry hesitated. "Not the exact time, no, but it was after 5:30."

"Well, thank you very much, Sir Henry, you have been very kind to me. I do hope you didn't think my questions impertinent, but I have to find out everything, relevant and irrelevant."

"I understand that, and I hope you will get the boy off. I don't believe he did it." He glanced away again.

The old man has got something on his mind, thought Borden. He is the type who would naturally look you straight in the eyes. He paced out into the drive and walked slowly along, deep in thought. As he reached the gate a young man passed him with a dog, a tall young man with broad shoulders and close-cropped fair hair. "Mr. Deering?" questioned Borden.

The young man turned. He was very sunburned but was disfigured by an unhealthy pallor, and he had a mouth which seemed by nature intended for laughter but which was now fixed and grim. The bright blue eyes were sunken and he had the same wary look as his father. "Yes," he said, "I am Bob Deering. Did you wish to see me?"

"I have just been to see your father," replied Borden. "I told him that I was a private detective called in by Mr. Hastings to try to find out who killed Penelope Stevenson. They are sure that it was not her brother."

"No, of course it wasn't, he adored her."

"Then who was it?"

"That is what we should all like to know."

"What about his wife?"

"I don't think so."

"Colonel Graeme?"

"I don't think so."

"Well, if you do think of anything you might call and let me know. I am staying at the Golden Crown." He watched Bob striding off down the road. He knows something, he thought. So does his father.

He turned in at the Limes, where luckily he met Lupin starting out for a walk. "Is there any way I could speak to Dorothy without causing suspicion?" he asked.

"No one can speak to anybody these days without causing suspicion," she replied. "When I went into the post office to buy some stamps I felt that they all guessed my guilty secret, and the organist was coming out of the church. . .and—oh, of course! I know, the piano tuner."

"What about the piano tuner?"

"You, of course. Oh, bother! I suppose Alice would naturally let you in but I'll tell her to pretend she's dressing or something and send Dorothy."

"Do you mean that I have got to pretend to be the piano tuner?"

"That's the idea."

"But I can't play 'God Save the King!' "

"Why do you want to?"

"I mean I shan't sound like a piano tuner."

"Oh yes, you will, if you just play a few odd notes—can't you do a scale or anything? I don't expect Dorothy will notice, anyway, and if Alice does it won't matter, as we have no secrets from each other."

"Is that wise?"

"I think so. I look on her as one of ourselves, the same as Mrs. Dashwood. They both had the same motive and you admit yourself it isn't a good one. All right, Christopher, just amuse him for a moment," and she disappeared.

When she came back Borden and Christopher were having a lovely game and Christopher was chuckling with delight. "I expect he will be sick," she remarked ungratefully. "Just ring the bell and ask if you may tune the piano. I told Alice to say that we were expecting the tuner today. Good hunting!"

Mr. Borden rang the bell. He wished he had a professional card. He must have some printed as a piano tuner, also as a seller of vacuum cleaners and as a wireless expert—one never knew when one would want such things.

"Good morning," he said. "I have come to tune the piano."

"Oh," said Dorothy, "I had better ask. Will you come in?" She left him in the hall while she called up to Alice, "It's the piano tuner. Is it all right?"

"There now," said Alice, "of course he was to have called today. I clean forgot. Take him into the drawing room, Dorothy, and you might take him in a cup of tea when you have your elevenses. I am busy with Mr. Dick's clothes. He will want them when he comes home."

"Oh, I do hope he will come home," said Dorothy. "I am sure he never went murdering Miss Penelope. I only wish they'd find the real murderer—the horrible thing, I'd hang him."

She took Mr. Borden into the drawing room, and he tried to remember the scales he had learned as a boy. Shortly after, she returned with a cup of tea and a biscuit.

"Well, you have had some exciting doings in these parts," he remarked, as he took the tray from her hand.

"Oh, it has been awful," replied Dorothy. "I never thought to stay in a house where there had been a murder. My mother wanted me to leave at once but I thought it would be Miss Penelope's wish that I should stay on here and I would have done anything for her. And I like to feel I am keeping the house as she liked it and that if Mr. and Mrs. Stevenson get back they'll find everything the same as usual. And poor little Master Christopher, too—his auntie fair doted on him."

"Do you think Mr. and Mrs. Stevenson will come back?" enquired Borden idly, as he took a bite of biscuit.

"Oh, I do hope so," said Dorothy. "I am sure they never killed Miss Penelope. I told the policeman who came—two policemen, one of them was ever so nice. I said, 'Well, whoever it was it couldn't have been Mrs. Dick, because she was in the nursery with Master Christopher. She wouldn't have left him without telling me to listen for him. Besides, I heard the shot and I wondered what it could be and I went up the stairs and Mrs. Dick she came out of the nursery and she said, 'Did you hear a shot, Dorothy?' and I said, 'Yes, ma'am,' and she said, 'Whatever could it have been? It sounded as if it were in the garden,' and I said, 'Yes, it did, ma'am.' White as a sheet she was, and she said, 'You stay with Christopher and I'll go down to see,' and I said, 'Do be careful, ma'am, it may be an escaped convict,' and that's what I think it was. Mr. Dick, he'd never have shot his sister—why, I never saw a brother so devoted, it was lovely to see them together. So down she went and Christopher started to cry and I played with him and then Mrs. Stevenson came in, looking fit to drop, and she said, 'It's Miss Penelope, Dorothy, she's dead. Mr. Dick is ringing up the police.' "

"That doesn't look as if she could have murdered her sister-in-law. Did they get on together?"

"I couldn't say as to that, I'm sure," said Dorothy. "They always seemed very devoted but Mrs. Dick had been away for a bit—I never rightly understood about it. She was a very pleasant-spoken young lady, though of course she wasn't a patch on Miss Penelope. But she couldn't have murdered her, that I'll stick to whatever anyone says. I saw her come out of the nursery with my own eyes, just as I'd heard the shot."

"When did you last see Miss Stevenson alive?" asked Mr. Borden, after striking a tentative chord on the piano.

"At about 4:30. She came in just as I was making tea. She looked very bad, I thought, but she was ever so delicate. She said she was going to lie down and she didn't want me to tell anyone as she was going to have a nice sleep. I got her to let me take her up some tea and she lay on her bed. When I came down, I saw Mrs. Dick and I gave her some tea and then she went up to the nursery and I cleared away and went back to the servants' hall, as I'd got my auntie to tea."

"And you never saw her again?"

Dorothy looked at Mr. Borden. He had a very sympathetic expression and she gave way to a longing to unburden herself and blurted out, "Well, I did and I didn't."

"How do you mean?" inquired Borden, taking his hands off the keys and looking at her with kindly interest.

"I was taking the tea things out of the drawing room and the library door was open. I thought I heard someone moving and I looked in, in case it was Mr. Dick and he might want some tea, and there she was standing by the writing table, and yet I don't rightly know if it was her."

"Miss Penelope, do you mean?"

"Her or her ghost. She took something off the table and then she turned round. She must have seen me and yet she looked right through me, her as always had a smile and a kind word for everyone. Ugh, it wasn't like her face at all . . .it. . .was almost as if she were dead already. The next thing I heard was the shot and I thought it must have been her ghost I saw and I've never mentioned it to anyone."

"Was she wearing Miss Penelope's clothes?"

"Yes, a gray frock it was with little black spots, ever so pretty. She always wore such sweet things but I was dreadfully scared. And when the police asked me when I last saw her I didn't like to tell them, because if it weren't her it would look as if I were batty or something, seeing things!"

"I quite understand. It must have given you a terrible shock."

"Oh, it did. Even now I come all over queer when I think of it. I woke up last night and thought I saw her."

"I don't expect you remember what time it was. You were too upset to notice."

"I didn't notice rightly, I was too shaky, but I know I had just seen Auntie off. She was going to church and it was then I saw Mr. Deering."

Mr. Borden kept quite still. "Just before six, I suppose?" he said casually. "The service here is at six, isn't it?"

"Yes, but Auntie likes to get there in plenty of time and she walks very slow—she is stout, you know. She always likes to be in church about ten minutes before the service begins. She says she can't attend unless she has a bit of breathing space."

"Then she probably left here by twenty to six."

"Oh yes, I'm sure she would have done. I said to her, 'Auntie,' I said, 'you've plenty of time,' but she would go, and after she'd gone I went to get Mrs. Dick's tea things and saw Miss Penelope's ghost and was that upset I had to sit down when I got outside, my knees felt so queer. There was still a little tea left in the pot and I poured myself out a cup, I don't know how long I was, and then I heard a shot and I thought, 'Oh, dear, that's what it all meant' and I ran up to Mrs. Dick and she was just coming out of the nursery as I said,. She went out and the next I heard was that Miss Penelope had been shot. Her ghost must have come to warn me. If only I'd told someone at once perhaps they could have stopped it."

Borden patted her hand. "Now don't feel like that, my dear," he said. "I don't think you could have done anything, no one would have believed you if you had said it was a ghost. And I expect it was really Miss Stevenson you saw, only perhaps the light cast a shadow on her face and she looked different. Anyhow, I am glad you have told me about it, as it must be a relief to get it off your mind. Thank you very much for this tea, I must get on with the piano." Just as Dorothy reached the door, he said, "Oh, by the way, what was that you said about Mr. Deering?"

"Mr. Deering?"

"You said you saw him when you were seeing your aunt out of the door."

"Oh yes, he came strolling in at the side gate. Of course he was a great friend of the family and didn't bother to ring the bell. He passed quite close to Auntie and me. He said, 'Good evening,' but he didn't seem like himself either—sort of absentminded, if you know what I mean."

"You were seeing your aunt out of the back door, I suppose, and that opens on to the garden path?"

"That's right, he went on into the garden. I thought perhaps he was hoping to see Miss Penelope, he was ever so sweet on her, and I wondered if I should tell him that she was lying down but I didn't like to say anything. Auntie would have thought it forward, she is ever so particular, and he may have come to see Mr. Dick, so I went back into the house and I saw Auntie had left her umbrella. I wondered if I had better go after her with it and then I thought I oughtn't to leave the house as the others were out. And I wondered if I should go and ask Mrs. Dick if I might. Then I thought well it's not likely to rain and I can run round after supper, perhaps. Gladys Browne would be back by then and Alice very like and it's nice out in the evening."

"It is at this time of year and I shouldn't be very surprised if you had a friend who liked to see you in the evening."

Dorothy blushed. "Well, I have been walking out some time with a very nice boy. That is why I didn't want it to come out about me seeing a ghost. He wouldn't want to be mixed up with anything like that—he's in the post office, you see. He had to go and see his mother that day but hoped to be back in the evening and if he came we could have walked round together to Auntie's. But when the time came I didn't feel like it. The last few days I haven't wanted to see him. I felt as if I were deceiving him and yet I couldn't tell him and I have been very unhappy." Her round eyes filled with tears.

"You poor little girl!" said Borden. "It has been a very terrible time for you but I expect it will all be cleared up soon. Oh, was it after you thought you saw Miss Stevenson, or before, that you saw Mr. Deering?"

"I saw Mr. Deering when I saw Auntie out, then I went back and I thought about Auntie's umbrella and what I'd do about it. I couldn't quite make up my mind then, so I went to the drawing room to get the tea things, and then—"

"That's all right, my dear, don't you bother about it any more. Think about your young man—after all, you would have been leaving here soon anyway, wouldn't you?"

"Oh, I don't know, I don't believe I could ever have brought myself to leave as long as Miss Penelope was alive. But everything is different now."

CHAPTER 25

THE INSPECTOR was sitting in his office when the constable announced that the Reverend Mr. Baker would like to see him. "Show him in," said the inspector, and the vicar came into the office.

"Sit down, Mr. Baker," said the inspector. "What can we do for you?"

Mr. Baker ran his hand through his sparse hair. "It suddenly came to me this morning," he said. "I was a fool not to see it before, but Miss Stevenson's death came as a great shock to us all and I didn't marshal my thoughts clearly. Mr. and Mrs. Dick giving themselves up like that was an additional blow, for they were very great friends of ours, and of course I knew they couldn't have done it. I pinned my suspicion on Colonel Graeme, as his having disappeared like that was very suspicious, but I hear he is actually here in the village and is not under arrest. So I gather my young friends are still in custody."

"Yes, I am afraid so."

"And then I remembered what I should have mentioned sooner, fool that I am. The sergeant questioned me about Sunday evening, asked me if I had heard a shot and so on. He never asked me anything about Dick Stevenson and I never thought of him. He had not given himself up at the time. But this morning it all came back to me. I was rather late in starting for evensong that evening. I was sitting at my desk thinking about things when suddenly I realized it was five minutes to six and I ran across the churchyard. As I reached the main gate, Dick Stevenson passed by up the street on his way to the Limes. He waved his hand quite cheerily and called out, 'Sorry, Baker, I'm afraid I'm not sitting under you tonight.' I got into the vestry just in time to throw on my surplice and walk into church as the clock struck. It was a close shave. When I started to think about it, I guessed from the questions and so on that the shot was fired at about six o'clock, so Dick could hardly have had time to shoot his sister."

"Thank you, Mr. Baker. I will get you to repeat your story in front of my constable and to sign it. It may constitute valuable evidence. It is a pity you did not think of it before."

"I know. I am terribly sorry about it. But the events of the last few days have been so bewildering that I honestly forgot all about that encounter."

The vicar seemed perfectly sincere and the inspector rang for his subordinate. After Mr. Baker had gone he sat for a time in thought, wondering how this evidence affected the case. If Dick had had the revolver on him, he could just have reached the Limes in time to shoot his sister by six, but he would not have had time to go into the library to get it and load it.

As he was thinking over the fors and againsts, Borden was ushered in and he told the inspector Dorothy's tale.

"Um, I know the chap the girl is walking out with. He is a postman, decent enough but not much imagination. I don't expect he would care for his future wife to believe in ghosts. I wonder if it were really Miss Stevenson whom the girl saw."

"You don't think it was a ghost, do you?"

"No, but she might have imagined something or she may have made up the whole story to arouse your interest."

"Why should she, when she's got a perfectly good young man of her own?"

"My dear fellow, women always like to arouse men's interest, however many they have got. Besides, as I say, Horace West isn't much of a subject to waste that sort of thing on. I expect you put on a good bedside manner?"

"Not at all. I was the piano tuner. I didn't go anywhere near a bed—strictly piano side. But look here, about this Horace what's his name—I suppose you mean the postman. You'd better look into the way he spent his Sunday. He says he went to see his mother but as I was leaving, Dorothy confided to me that she didn't think she would have ever been able to leave Miss Penelope if she had lived—suggestive, rather!"

"Oh lord, what a case! It appeared clear enough at first, but everyone in the village seems to have had a motive, and the padre has just been in and told me that he saw Dick Stevenson at the gate of the churchyard within a minute or two of six o'clock."

Borden whistled. "That's a good bit of news."

"For you," grumbled the inspector. "But someone must have done it. By the way, the resumed inquest is on Friday. It was only held up for Colonel Graeme, but I managed to wangle a couple of days to give you a chance."

"You are a good fellow. I believe you would like to get young Stevenson off."

"A policeman can't afford to have likes and dislikes. My business is to discover the criminal."

"Well, I am inclined to suspect Bob Deering," Borden said, and he told the rest of Dorothy's story. "He was in the garden waiting for her, that seems fairly obvious. Miss Stevenson was in the library at about a quarter to six. She took something off the library table and went into the garden where Bob Deering was awaiting her and he shot her at six."

"How had he got hold of Dick's revolver?"

"I suppose he could have slipped through the library window and out again."

"What had Miss Stevenson taken off the library table?"

"Perhaps it was some letter he had written and she was going to blackmail him for it."

"Baker is supposed to have written some compromising letter or poem, though we only know it unofficially. I suppose you know all about that."

"Yes, and Lady Lupin Hastings is certain Miss Stevenson would never blackmail anyone."

"I can't imagine her doing so, I admit, but one can never be sure of anything. I am not a pretty young woman."

"Aren't you? Well, Lady Lupin has more sense than you give her credit for," Borden said.

"That is as it may be. We must certainly take Bob Deering into consideration."

"Funny Baker should have only just remembered about seeing Dick!"

"That's what I thought, but I thought he was speaking the truth, though I defy anyone to be certain," Borden said. "However, this is what we have at present:

"4:30. Miss Stevenson returns to house.

"5:45 or thereabouts. Deering is seen in the garden.

"5:50 or thereabouts. Miss Stevenson is seen in the library.

"5:55. Dick is seen near the church by the vicar.

"Six or just before. The shot is fired."

"I'll interview Deering, and I'll put a man on to see what Horace West was doing that afternoon," the inspector said.

"Thanks very much. At last there seems to be a ray of light for my nominee." And Borden went back to his hotel, while the inspector finished his routine work and gave some orders. Then he walked up to the hall.

He purposely arrived at lunchtime so as to catch Deering, and he was not kept waiting long. Bob came to him in the study, and the inspector noticed the difference in him at once. He had known him since he was a boy and had, in common with the rest of the village, liked his honest, homely face and candid manner. There was nothing candid in his manner now. His face was as if a shutter had been drawn down over it.

"Good afternoon, Inspector," he said. "Do sit down."

"Mr. Deering," said the inspector, as he took a seat, "I have been told that you were seen in the garden of the Limes between five and six on the evening of Miss Stevenson's death."

"Yes," replied Bob, "I was there in the garden of the Limes, talking to Miss Stevenson."

"At what time?"

"I don't know exactly, but it was after five. I should say it was about half past or a little later."

"And when did you leave?"

"I wasn't there more than ten minutes, if as much. I should think at a rough guess that I left at about a quarter to six."

"You were in all probability the last person to see Miss Stevenson alive?"

"I suppose so, at least, yes, I don't know."

"With the exception of the murderer, of course."

Bob clenched his fists and sat quite still. "Yes, I expect so," he said.

"You did not see the murderer?"

"No."

"You didn't see anyone after you left the garden?"

"No, at least I may have done. I don't remember seeing anyone."

"Try and think, Mr. Deering."

"No, I didn't see anyone. I wasn't noticing. I went out of the side gate into the village and then turned up the lane and went across the fields. There may have been some people in the street, I don't know."

"You were preoccupied?"

"Yes."

"Isn't it rather strange, Mr. Deering, that you never came forward to give evidence that you had seen Miss Stevenson such a short time before her death?"

"I didn't see that it would help," he muttered.

"That was for us to decide. You are the son of a magistrate, you must have known it was your duty."

Bob looked up. "Yes, I knew it was my duty but I didn't want to do it. I would have done it if it would have helped Dick but I didn't see how it would, and . . . and I didn't want to have to talk about it, to give evidence in court. I know I have behaved badly."

"Had you any special reason for going to see Miss Stevenson that evening?"

"She rang me up."

"At what time did she ring you up?"

"Soon after five, I should think. I went straight round and saw her in the garden."

"Had she anything special to say to you?"

Bob went scarlet, and his eyes turned away from the inspector's.

"No," he muttered, "nothing special."

"It was rather funny her ringing you up and then having nothing to say."

"Well, she hadn't anything to say," he repeated. "She just wanted a chat, she was feeling a bit depressed."

"Why?"

"She had just parted from Colonel Graeme, and though she . . . though she . . ." Bob groped for words. "Well, they were very old friends," he said lamely, "so I suppose she was sorry to say goodbye to him."

"And she wanted you to cheer her up?"

"Yes."

"But you didn't stay long trying to cheer her up."

"No, I had to go. My mother would have been wondering where I was. I had been out all the afternoon and when I got in Miss Stevenson rang up, and so I hadn't seen my mother and she had been expecting me in to tea."

"But when you left the Limes you went up the lane and across the fields, not straight home."

"No, I meant to go home and then I felt I wanted more exercise, so I went across the fields for half an hour."

"Although you knew your mother was expecting you and you had left Miss Stevenson to go straight home?"

"I know it sounds a bit queer."

"It does sound very queer, Mr. Deering. You had been out walking all the afternoon for between two and three hours, I should imagine, then you arrive home and get a telephone message from Miss Stevenson. You don't say anything to your people, though surely it would have been natural to have told your mother where you were going. Then you hurry along to Miss Stevenson and after a quarter of an hour you leave her, saying you must get back to your mother, then you decide you have not had enough exercise, in spite of having been walking all the afternoon, so you take a walk across the fields. Then when you hear that Miss Stevenson, one of your greatest friends, has been murdered, it doesn't occur to you to mention the fact that you were with her within a quarter of an hour of her death."

Bob clenched and unclenched his hands. He stared out of the window, and then he stood up. "Well, the fact of the matter is," he said, "that I asked Miss Stevenson to marry me and she refused. I didn't want to have to talk about it."

CHAPTER 26

BORDEN had managed to get permission to see Dick Stevenson. He was led down the corridor and ushered into the cell reserved for prisoners awaiting trial. Dick was sitting at the table with his back toward the door, and Borden had a shock. Surely that was Bob Deering sitting there, the set of the shoulders and the short fair hair? Then Dick turned, and the likeness faded. Their faces were quite different.

Dick was better-looking than Bob, but he was ill and drawn. The exercise was not enough for him, sitting still was very alien to his habits, and constant anxiety had brought him low. He smiled, however, and put down his crossword puzzle as Borden entered with the warder.

"How do you do?" said Borden, and then as the warder withdrew, went on, "I am a friend of Mr. Hastings and Lady Lupin. I am also a private detective. I helped Lady Lupin once before and she asked me to come and help her again." The smile faded from Dick's lips, and a hostile expression came over his face.

"What do you hope to find out?" asked Dick.

"Who killed Miss Stevenson."

"Well, I can save you that trouble. I did."

"But your wife says she did."

"I can assure you she is mistaken."

"I know that."

Dick looked up quickly. "I am glad you have that much sense," he replied.

"It seems quite certain that your wife did not murder her sister-in-law, so perhaps you have been mistaken too."

"No, I am not mistaken."

"Do you mind telling me the story in your own words? I am sorry to be so tiresome. You must be tired of it but I have promised Lady Lupin and Mrs. Dashwood to do all I can. There is no one listening to us, so you can talk quite freely."

Dick sighed. "I am sick of the whole thing," he said, "but I suppose Lupin means well, and she is a good sort. Here goes. I had been out for a walk, worrying about things. My wife and I had had a quarrel. She did not want to live with my sister and I didn't see what was to be done about it. You see, my sister was devoted to this house and she could not have afforded to go on living here on her money alone. She wanted us all to live together and my wife wanted to have a home of her own. It was very difficult to know what to do. I hated the idea of turning my sister out of her home where she had lived for so many years."

So you turned her out of life altogether, thought Borden, but he said nothing.

"I have always hated rows and hurting people's feelings and all that sort of thing and of course the money question was rather urgent. I mean, we had plenty of money together but not so much apart. I had been hoping that she would marry Colonel Graeme but she said she didn't want to, yet I still hoped. He came down that Sunday and they went for a walk. I trusted that he would persuade her and then we could all be happy. So I went for a walk on my own, then I went to tea with the Deerings—they are always very good to me. I stayed chatting for some time, then I started home. I still hoped that perhaps things would be all right. I walked into the garden, where my sister was sitting. I said to her, 'Well?' and she said, 'I have sent Charles away,' or words to that effect, and I saw red and shot her through the head."

What a silly story, thought Borden. Then another thought took form in his brain. The two young men were very much alike from the back. Suppose Betty had seen Bob shoot her sister-in-law and thought it was Dick? From the nursery it was quite probable. He must try an experiment there when he got back. She hurried down and in a panic wiped the fingerprints off the revolver thinking they would be her husband's. Yes, it all fitted in. "Had you your revolver on you then?" he asked aloud.

Dick hesitated. "No, I—er—had been cleaning it. It was on my table. I darted in and fetched it out, and—er—shot her."

Borden regarded him sadly. "I can't see it," he said. "If you had had the gun in your pocket, you might have nipped it out and shot her in a rage, but I can't see you saying, 'Half a mo',' and going back into the house to fetch it. Besides, what would she be doing during that time? Sitting quietly waiting to be shot? And in any case the vicar swears he saw you at five minutes to six, probably later. I think you had better come clean, don't you?"

"I don't know what you mean," said Dick stiffly. Like most good-tempered people he could be very stubborn.

"Well, shall I tell you what I think happened?" said Borden.

"If you like."

"Your wife was upstairs with her child. She looked out of the window and saw a man, resembling you from the back, shooting Miss Stevenson. She only had a very imperfect view but she was probably feeling wrought up. I gather there had been a good many quarrels and so on lately. She thought it was you, so she rushed down. The man had disappeared but in a fit of panic she picked up the revolver and wiped off the marks. You came, on hearing the shot, saw her wiping the revolver and took for granted that she had murdered your sister. You were both in a nervy state or you could not have imagined such things about each other. Don't you think that is somewhere near the true story?"

Dick lit another cigarette and pondered for a moment. "Why did Betty say she had done it?"

"For the same reason that you did. As Lady Lupin puts it, you are probably both suffering from lack of fats."

Dick laughed. "That girl is an ass."

"Yes, but a very shrewd ass."

"A jolly decent one."

"Well, what about trying to get at the truth? I give you my word that your wife could not have done it. She is being detained till after the inquest but the police are satisfied about her innocence."

"I don't know," said Dick, pacing up and down the small room, "but if you are a friend of Lupin's . . ."

"Oh, I forgot," said Borden, and he handed him a note.

Dear Dick,

Mr. Borden is a friend of mine, so do tell him everything. He is awfully clever and will find out what really happened if only you will help. No one thinks Betty could have done it, you can't really. Can you imagine her leaving Christopher alone in the nursery while she went down looking for revolvers and shooting people? Besides, can you imagine her loading a revolver and shooting anyone? She would miss them! I suppose she thought you did it but I am sure you didn't and you might think of poor Christopher. It won't be very nice for him if you are hung. Masses of love from Auntie Boots and me.

Lupin

Dick threw himself down on his chair, stabbed out his half-smoked cigarette and lit another one.

"It is difficult to know where to begin. I suppose, in common with everyone else in England, you know all about my private affairs by this time. It is hard to explain to anyone, but my sister had always been the most dominant personality in my life. I don't remember my mother and Penelope did everything for me. I was devoted to my father, but it was Penelope who arranged everything. I was always told how lucky I was to have her and how she was a mother to me and I always took it for granted. Children don't question things much—at least, I didn't. I was never given much to introspection or anything of that sort. I always took for granted I was lucky to have such a sister and I knew in a vague sort of way that she had given up a lot for me.

"Betty was her friend to start with, and I was so happy to think that I had fallen in love with someone who appreciated Penelope. We lived for some time in London, then Penelope wrote and said that the Limes Cottage had become vacant and she and Father thought it would be lovely to have us so close. It wasn't much further from my work, as it was on the Morely-London road, and she and Betty would be able to be together when I was working. It seemed ideal, because of course I am away most of the day and I thought it would be lovely for Betty to have Penelope. Then it would be nice for Penelope to have us near to help her with the old man." He hesitated. "I don't know how it was but I got the idea that Penelope had a thin time with him.

"As a matter of fact he was a brick and he was very, very good to her. Anyhow, it is no use going into all that now. Then the man to whom Penelope used to be engaged—well, I expect you know all about that by now—she gave him up because of Daddy and me, or so I had always gathered, now his wife died, and Betty and I thought he would come and ask Pen again and they would live happily ever after. I said, 'What about Dad?' and Betty said, 'Couldn't we live with him?'

"So we hatched a scheme. We would suggest coming to live at the Limes altogether, say that Betty found running our little place rather difficult now she had a baby or something, and then it would be quite easy for Pen to get married, knowing Dad would be all right with us, as he was always very fond of Betty. Naturally we did not like to say anything about Charles to her. Well, he came, proposed, was refused and went away.

"Then my troubles began. Even then, though I was very sorry for Pen's sake because I thought she would be happier married and I knew, or thought I knew, she cared for the chap, I thought everything would be all right. After all, it was more comfortable for Betty at the Limes, with maids and everything and no housekeeping. But it seemed she wanted her own home and didn't want to live with Penelope.

"She rushed off to Glanville to the Hastings. I was pretty fed up. I thought they were acing her on and I thought she was flattered by Lupin making a friend of her and that she had got tired of Pen and all that sort of thing. I was an awful fool, really, though I did see a bit when Lupin and Andrew both explained it to me. I suppose it was natural for a woman to want her own home but I got Betty to come back and we went on fairly well for a few weeks. But things weren't the same as they used to be. Betty and I were always quarreling, and I used to have a feeling sometimes that Pen was feeling hurt if Betts and I ever did anything on our own.

"Well, then my father died. It was an awful shock to us all. I missed him, miss him terribly still, though I am thankful he has been spared all this. There was a lot of business to see to, everything was left equally between Pen and me, with Pen's share to go to our children if she didn't have any of her own. Quite straightforward! Well, I hoped she would have some. She wasn't forty, and there was nothing to prevent her marrying Charles now if he still wanted to and I had a feeling he did still want to. I thought we had better sell the Limes and Betty and I would try for some smaller house in the neighborhood.

"Penelope came in when I was working one evening and I told her what I intended doing and she went off the deep end at my idea of selling the Limes. She said she would never marry, that she was going to devote herself to me and to my children for the rest of her life. It was an awful blow and I realized for the first time that I didn't want her devoting herself to me. I mean I was awfully fond of her and I know it sounds ungrateful but she really was too devoted. I was always afraid of hurting her. I went up and told Betty what she had said. I really wanted to talk things over but I expect I put it badly, I was a bit unstrung. She flew into a temper and I thought her unsympathetic. And I always knew—at least, I had lately—that she did not admire Penelope as much as I thought she ought, so we had another quarrel and she went off to London the next day, taking Christopher with her.

"I don't know how I got through the next month. Penelope was very sweet and said dear little Betty would soon be back and we must make allowances and we should soon all be happy together once more. Then she threw out hints that she was missing her nephew and that I ought to insist on having him home, even if Betty wanted to stay away longer. I wasn't going to do that. I thought it was unkind of Betty going off when I wanted her, but nothing would have induced me to use Christopher as a means of getting her back.

"Then suddenly I got a card saying she was coming down for the weekend. She wanted some summer things, but I felt she really wanted to see me. And yet when she arrived I couldn't say anything. I don't know if it were pride or resentment or just embarrassment, but we met as strangers or casual acquaintances. I had a sleepless night. I wanted to go to her and I kept hoping against hope she would come to me.

"The next morning I felt at the end of my tether. I went for a long walk. I just walked and walked, not noticing which way I was going, and at last, when I was beginning to feel a bit tired and all of a 'muck o' sweat,' I realized what I had got to do. I had been pulled this way and that, old associations and all that sort of thing, but now, when my body was so tired, my brain seemed to wake up, and I saw that everything was quite simple. It sounds as if I were a weak fool not to have realized it before, but early habits are hard to break and not to hurt Penelope had always been the first rule of life at the Limes. Now I realized that I had a wife and that I had a child and that my first duty was to them. It was a great relief. Naturally I had always wanted to put my wife first. I am—er—fond of my wife."

"Quite," replied Mr. Borden gravely.

"So now I came home feeling quite cheerful, although I could hardly drag one foot after another. My duty and inclination were the same thing. Betty and Christopher and I would have a home of our own, and Penelope must make her own arrangements. Of course she would always be welcome to come and stay with us, and I wondered if it would be possible to make her an allowance so that she could stay on at the Limes. But Betty and I could talk all that over. All that mattered was that I could go to her and tell her that I—that no one else mattered, that we would have our own home just as she wanted.

"And then who should be at lunch but Charles Graeme. Of course, naturally he would let a few weeks elapse after Father's death before asking Penelope again. Anything else would have offended her terribly, but I had rather wondered when he was going to turn up. Perhaps I thought he would be able to persuade her to marry him after all. Perhaps the reason she had told me she wasn't going to get married was because she wasn't sure he would ask her again and she wanted save her face. Well, I didn't know and I didn't care. I drank quantities of beer and felt very cheerful. Everything would turn out all right after all and I shouldn't have to break it to Penelope that I didn't want her, because she would be getting married herself and wouldn't want me. We were all in good spirits. I think Betty felt as I did, as she was much more cheerful and like herself and talked to me quite naturally. Charles was in good spirits. I suppose he felt he was going to have his heart's desire at last. Even Pen seemed happy.

"Betty slipped upstairs after lunch to have a rest. I thought I'd go up after her and tell her that I had made up my mind to do what she wanted, then I thought perhaps I'd wait till Pen and Charles came in, then if Pen had refused Charles I'd tackle her right away, and if she hadn't I'd go to Betty and tell her that all was well. I went into the library, meaning to go through some papers and things. I emptied one drawer, the one I kept my revolver in, and I put the things on the table while I read an old letter. Then I suppose I was frightfully tired after my walk, and I fell fast asleep. When I woke up it was four o'clock. I couldn't see any sign of Betty or Pen, and I suddenly thought I'd go round and see Bob Deering. I hadn't seen him for some time and I felt I wanted to talk to someone. I didn't want to wake Betty up if she were still resting. If she had slept as badly as I had the night before, she needed her sleep.

"I strolled across to the Deerings. Bob was out but the old man was very decent, as he always is. I told him I was going to look out for a smaller house in the neighborhood and he was very interested and we went through the houses we knew—who had got them and all that sort of thing. Then we went and had tea with Lady Deering. Agnes and the old man went out and I stayed chatting with Lady Deering for a bit. She was rather sweet. She talked to me about her other son, Henry, the one who was killed. I had never known him very well, but Bob and I had been like brothers. She always talks in a vague inconsequent kind of way, not unlike Lupin, only more so, but as I got up to go she said, 'Make it up with Betty, Dick. I suppose she and your sister don't get on, but your wife should come first.'

"I was rather surprised and then I left. I suppose it was about a quarter to six. I know I looked at the clock and was surprised to see it was so late. I was impatient now to get home to hear what had happened between Pen and Charles and to tell Betty that I would do whatever she liked. I remember, now that you mention it, I did just see Baker scuttling across the churchyard. I stood for a minute or two watching the people going in, in case Betty should be among them.

"I saw Gladys Browne and she said, 'The mistress is minding baby.' Almost immediately after I heard a shot ring out from the direction of the Limes. I ran up the road and in at the side gate and made for the orchard.

"There was Pen slumped in her chair with Betty standing beside her wiping my revolver with her handkerchief. She looked up and saw me and she said, 'Penelope is dead! She is shot through the head.' I said, 'Who shot her?' and she said, 'She must have shot herself.' So I went and rang up the police."

"Yes, I think I see the whole thing," said Borden. "Your wife saw someone out of the window and in the distance thought it was you. She was in a nervous state, ready to imagine things, and when she found her sister-in-law shot she jumped to a conclusion which would have been impossible if she had been more herself, and the same with you. You must have been very far from normal to credit your wife with such an action."

"I have been an utter fool, but I knew I had left my gun lying on the table, and her face . . ."

"Naturally, if she thought it was you who were the murderer! But even if your wife had taken the gun from the table, would she have known how to load it?"

"Yes, that was the awful thing. One day she and my sister had been in the library and had asked me about loading it and I had shown them and I let them do it themselves. Of course, I was very wrong but they were interested and I never thought—but Betty was very clumsy, she might even have had an accident then."

"Yet you took it for granted that she had had no difficulty in loading it and shooting your sister with it, in spite of her clumsiness?"

"I don't know what I thought. I thought that it might have been an accident, that she had taken it out and threatened my sister and that it had gone off, but then why didn't she say so? She said she had murdered her, nothing about an accident. But of course she thought it was me all the time. We have both been utterly demented. My poor little Betty!"

CHAPTER 27

LUPIN was visiting Betty. She had only seen Borden for a few minutes that day and he had told her of Baker's evidence about Dick but not of his suspicions of Bob. Betty sat listlessly with a piece of knitting before her. Her once merry, rosy face was sunken and pale, and the shadows under her eyes were more marked than even Penelope's had ever been. The wardress, a good-hearted woman with a slightly rough manner, withdrew to a chair outside the door and though the door was left nominally ajar, she read her book without obtruding herself on them. "There you are, dear," she said. "Now you will be able to hear all about your lovely baby."

"Oh, Lupin, how is he?"

"Splendid," replied Lupin, "but of course he misses you. Gladys has been a perfect brick. Anyhow, you will soon be able to see for yourself, because Mr. Baker saw Dick a few minutes before six, so it can't have been him. And Dorothy swears it can't have been you and I know it wasn't me, so soon we will all be hotsy totsy again."

"Is that true about Dick?"

"Of course it is and even if he hadn't been seen, no one could possibly have been such a fool as to think such a thing about him except you, you turnip-top!"

"But he said he did it."

"So did you."

"I didn't know what to think. I saw him talking to Penelope in the garden and I wondered what they were saying. I thought, 'Perhaps she's telling him that she is engaged to Charles,' and then I thought, 'Suppose she isn't?' And I thought—oh, Lupin, it was so awful of me, but at the thought of her insisting on living with us and not marrying Charles after all and Dick and me always being at cross-purposes—I thought . . . I thought . . ."

"Well?"

"I wished she were dead, so in a way I am a murderer."

"You are the biggest fool I ever met! I remember quite well once, when I had forgotten to do my history prep, I thought how lovely it would be to hear that the history mistress had passed away in the night."

"Oh, dear, we are in a mess! I don't really think it was Dick. It was only just seeing him there and having seen him before and he looked awful and all those awful days he went on just as if he had a secret."

"He thought it was you, that's why."

"So he did and it wasn't really either of us. But, then, who could it have been?"

"I think you may have been mistaken in thinking it was Dick talking to her in the garden, because he seems to have been at tea at the Deerings and not come home until just before six. It is some way away and you just saw a man, and you took it for granted it was Dick."

Betty thought. "It looked like Dick," she said, "but it was only his back I saw and, as you say, it is a long way off. Oh!"

"What?"

"If only I hadn't wiped the fingerprints off, we would know who it was. But, of course, thinking they were Dick's, I wiped them off at once."

"*You* wiped off the fingerprints?" exclaimed Lupin.

"Naturally."

"Dick saw you with the gun in your hand wiping off the prints, so naturally he thought you had done it."

"It was the worst thing I could have done, I see that now."

"Never mind, just tell me the whole story as best you can, and see if we can think of anything. I wonder if it was Charles. He's got an alibi but alibis can usually be got round—at least, they can in books!"

"You know what a frightful time I had been having, how Pen announced to Dick that she would never marry but was going to live with us forever. I flew into a temper with Dick when be told me and went off to London the next morning. I see now I was silly. If I had been a little bit nice, Dick might have come to see my point of view. I don't know, though. He was mad about Penelope.

"Anyhow, I went to a friend and took Christopher, and I got a job typing in the mornings. I thought I would be quite independent but I wanted Dick all the time. And I made the excuse of needing some summer things to go down to the Limes for the weekend. I thought perhaps if I saw Dick I could get him to understand. I simply couldn't go on living with Penelope, he must realize that. It was all rather awkward, because if we left the Limes, Pen wouldn't be able to afford to live there. I saw Dick's difficulty when I thought it over but at the time I had been too angry to see reason.

"You see, Daddy had left everything equally between Dick and Penelope. Naturally he thought she would marry Charles. I am sure he knew all about that. I thought perhaps we might give Pen some of our money so she could stay on at the Limes. I suppose it was bad luck having to leave her own home. Dick had his salary from the works and I shouldn't have minded how poor we were if we were together. I could have gone on typing. I was full of plans but Dick was so cold to me, polite like a stranger. He couldn't forgive me for running away from him.

"Penelope was very sweet to me and I felt Dick was thinking, 'There now, how unreasonable of Betty not to be able to get on with Penelope when she's so sweet to her.' "

"I think you make Dick out a bigger fool than he is," remarked Lupin. "I think he has been realizing things for some time but did not quite know what to do. He doesn't think awfully quickly but his brain is all right."

"I know that," snapped Betty. "He is frightfully clever. As a matter of fact, they think the world of him at the works. They wanted him to go out and manage a factory in Canada but he didn't like to leave Daddy and Penelope." She paused.

"You've got to Penelope being very sweet," suggested Lupin.

"Yes, and after dinner when we were alone I tried appealing to her. I said, 'Pen, you have always been awfully nice and understanding—you do understand, don't you, about me wanting to have a home of my own?'

"And she said, 'Yes, dear, I think I understand you want somewhere you can call your own. I thought we might make a little flat for you so that you could feel quite independent, with your own bedroom and sitting room and bathroom and perhaps a little kitchen where you could try experiments, and we shall all knock on the door when we come to call on you.'

"As if I were a child being given a playroom to make toffee in! And we shall knock on the door! She and Dick, I suppose, living together while I was kept upstairs like a—like a—a—a—"

"Don't get excited or we will have your—er—nanny, or whoever it is, coming in."

"I could have murdered her then and there. I had been fond of her up till nearly the end. I *was* fond of her, but I saw red then. I said, 'Why can't you marry Charles and leave us alone?'

" 'Leave you alone! I don't want to interfere with you, dear, but I can never leave Dick alone. He could never get on without me. Dick and Dick's child, they are my life. I shall devote myself to them for what years I have left to me. I want nothing for myself.'

"I just shouted, 'You mean beast!' and ran out of the room, slamming the door. I met Alice and she was awfully nice. She put me to bed and gave me some aspirin but I didn't take it because I was hoping Dick might come. But he never did.

"The next morning Penelope greeted me as if nothing had happened, and we went to church together. I was so miserable I was afraid I was going to start crying every minute. And I felt so awful thinking of all my wicked thoughts and how I wished Penelope were dead.

"Then suddenly, I don't know exactly what moment it was, but suddenly I felt at peace. I felt that Dick did really love me and that things would come right after all and we went out into the sunshine and there was Charles! He had come over and he asked Penelope if he might stay to lunch and she looked pleased to see him and chaffed him about bringing his rations. I thought, 'There now, all that quarreling, all that rage for nothing. I should just have trusted. Penelope wasn't sure that Charles was coming back, so has said that about not marrying in case, but now she is pleased to see him and he will ask her to marry him and she will say yes and we shall all live happily ever after!'

"I think the same idea occurred to Dick, because he was quite cheerful at lunch, like himself again, and we all talked naturally. Then Charles and Penelope went for a walk. I was so tired I went straight up to bed and slept till about half past four. I had hardly slept at all the night before. Then I came down and there was no sign of anyone. I hoped Penelope and Charles might have come back from their walk engaged, but perhaps they were so happy they had lost count of time. I was so glad, I wanted Penelope to be happy even more than I wanted her to be dead.

"Dorothy brought me some tea into the drawing room and when I had had that, I went upstairs and sent my little nurse, Gladys Browne, home. She had been with Christopher all day. I noticed it was five o'clock when she left. I took him—naturally I should have taken him out but he had been out with Gladys all day and I felt rather tired still—so I played with him in the nursery till it was time to start putting him to bed.

"I was sitting by the window with him on my knee, powdering his toes, and I glanced out of the window and saw Dick and Penelope—at least, I thought it was Dick. I don't see who else it could have been—could it have been Charles? I don't think it was Charles. I wondered a bit about whether things were going to be all right after all, and I finished Christopher and played with him a bit and was just putting to put him into bed when I heard the shot.

"I went to the door and saw Dorothy, so I asked her to stay with him while I went down to see. I had an awful feeling of what had happened. Dick had been so queer lately. Suppose it had all got on his nerves and he had shot himself! There was no sign of him but Penelope was shot through the head and Dick's gun—I thought it was Dick's gun, we'd been playing with it quite a short time before—lay beside her. I picked it up and wiped it. No wonder he thought I'd done it, no wonder he looked like that," and she burst out crying. "It is all one frightful nightmare," she said.

"Anyhow," consoled Lupin, "you know now that Dick didn't do it and he knows that you didn't and I know I didn't, so that is three of us."

"Oh, it is a tremendous relief," sobbed Betty. "You are an angel, Lupin."

CHAPTER 28

THE CHIEF constable was with the inspector when Borden called at the police station. He had met him once or twice during the last few days and liked him.

"Well, Borden, this is a bad business," he said. "But it looks as if your fellow is out of it."

"Sir Henry came in this morning," put in the inspector, "and he said that he had just heard from his wife that Stevenson had stayed talking to her for some time after he had gone out."

"Did he, by Jove!" exclaimed Borden.

"He is a wonderful old gentleman," said the inspector. "It is a pity there are not more like him."

"I have known him all my life," said the chief constable, "and now I have got to accuse his son of murder."

"Sir Henry has had his suspicions all along," said Borden. "He certainly had something on his mind when I was talking to him yesterday."

"I would be ready to swear that he did not know about Stevenson's alibi until this morning," said the inspector.

"His wife may not have realized the importance, or, if she had done, it was difficult for her when her son was in danger. But she was evidently in great distress and told her husband, who came round here at once."

"Well, I've learned a little," said Borden. "I saw Stevenson and told him his wife was not under suspicion, and he told me the true story."

"What he calls the true story," corrected the inspector.

"He's a decent young fellow, too. It is a rotten affair. I wish we had called in Scotland Yard," said the chief constable. "No disrespect to you, Inspector, but it is unpleasant when one knows the people."

"Well, Stevenson says that when he appeared upon the scene his wife had the gun in her hand and was wiping off the fingerprints."

"That is suspicious."

"Yes," agreed Borden, "but suppose she looked out of the window and saw a man whom she thought was her husband with her sister-in-law, and within a few minutes heard a shot and found her dead. She may have jumped to the conclusion that it was her husband who had shot her and tried to remove the marks. And there is just one point I am afraid I must make. When I first went into the cell and saw Stevenson from the back, I thought for a moment it was Deering."

"They are the same build," agreed the inspector.

"I can't believe either of those decent young men could have murdered a woman," put in the chief constable,

"Of course," said the inspector, "if it is true that Mrs. Stevenson wiped the gun, we still have the possibility of suicide."

"I thought of that," said Borden.

"That is what it must have been," said the chief constable.

"But for what reason?" asked the inspector. "We have been through all her papers and there is nothing to give one any clue."

"Bob Deering on his own admission seems to have been the last person to see her alive. He ought to be able to tell us something, if he would!"

"He says that he asked the lady to marry him," said the inspector.

"That wouldn't make her shoot herself," complained the chief constable.

"According to Colonel Graeme, he had also asked her to marry him that afternoon. For a lady of thirty-nine to receive two offers on the same day would cheer her up rather than not, I should have thought," said the inspector.

"You mean," said Borden, "she would not be feeling that depression that women get when they approach middle age, thinking that no one wants them any more?"

"The two Stevensons are the only people who really had any motive, as far as I can see," said the chief constable, "and they are both out of it, according to the times. Why should Deering kill her—I mean, you don't kill someone just because they refuse to marry you—at least, I never did."

"There must be more to it than we know," said the inspector.

"What about Dorothy's young man, Horace West?" asked Borden.

"He is all right," replied the inspector. "Left on the 2:10 bus, arrived at Barnen Bridge at 3:20, went to his mother and was with her until six, caught the 6:30 bus home and arrived at 7:40. Recognized by both conductors, the constable on point duty at Barnen Bridge, vouched for by his mother, aunt, uncle, brother, brother's young lady and brother's friend."

"At present," said Borden, "you have Bob Deering, seen by Dorothy and her aunt at about 5:40 in the garden. Miss Stevenson seen by Dorothy at about 5:45, and the shot fired at about six. The presumption is, I suppose, that Deering was lying in wait for Miss Stevenson in the garden and shot her when she came out.

"But that leaves two questions. One, when did he get hold of Stevenson's gun? and two, why was Miss Stevenson looking 'so queer' when Dorothy saw her? She did not know then that she was going to be murdered."

"It is difficult to decide how much of that story is true," said the inspector. "It is extraordinary the things people think they have seen after a murder. I think I will have a word or two with the girl's aunt."

"What about Mrs. Stevenson? What is her story?" asked the chief constable.

"Her story is that she ran out into the garden and shot her sister-in-law and was just wiping her fingerprints off the gun when her husband arrived. Have you managed to get anything further?" the inspector asked Borden.

"No, but Lady Lupin was visiting her this afternoon, and she may have something for us."

"I doubt that she can help us much—a very pretty young woman and kindhearted, I'm sure, but not much of a headpiece," said the chief constable.

"There is more to her than you think," said Borden. "Look here, would you come round to the Limes this evening and have a talk with her and with Mrs. Dashwood?"

The chief constable shrugged his shoulders. "As you like," he said. "Mrs. Dashwood is a sensible woman but I doubt if anyone can do much. I am afraid things point to Bob Deering. Poor Henry!"

"It looks like it," agreed Borden. "He was besotted about Miss Stevenson and killed her, rather than let her marry Colonel Graeme. It is a very unusual case but it might be so."

CHAPTER 29

LUPIN could not remember ever having been so tired in her life. Standing in fish queues, running a Sunday school treat, or billeting evacuees was nothing to this. She greeted Mrs. Dashwood with, "It's all right, it wasn't them," then remained silent while she drank some sherry and smoked a cigarette.

"Betty wiped the gun with her handkerchief," she announced, as Alice handed her the soup.

"Then it was suicide," said Mrs. Dashwood.

"It was either suicide or else it was some stranger who did it," replied Lupin. "Perhaps it was a homicidal maniac, as Mr. Roberts suggested. Betty saw someone talking to Penelope and she thought it was Dick, so when she heard the shot, first of all she thought that he had shot himself and then she thought that he had shot Pen, so she wiped off the prints. If only she had left them on we would know by now what had happened."

As they were settling down in the sitting room after dinner, Mr. Borden was announced. "I have got some news for you," he said.

"Don't go, Alice," said Lupin. "You are in this with us."

"It looks very much as if it were Bob Deering," said the detective. "He admits that he was with her between five and six o'clock, though he never came forward to say so. When I first saw young Stevenson this afternoon I thought it was Bob Deering until he looked up. They are extraordinarily alike in build. It is quite possible that from an upstairs window Mrs. Stevenson might have mistaken one man for the other."

"But why should he kill her?" asked Lupin.

"Jealousy, I suppose. What the French call a *crime passionnel.* He admits that he asked her to marry him. I suppose she told him that she was going to marry this Graeme fellow, and he saw red and shot her."

"But Colonel Graeme says she refused him."

"That's true—she may have been egging him on, though, or she may have been one of these cold women who just enjoy playing with men. Whatever it was, it looks rather as if she went too far with young Deering."

Lupin leaped to her feet, dropping her coffee cup as she did so. "I have got an idea," she said. "I don't often get one, so I must make the most of it. I think you are very nearly right but not quite," and she rushed from the room and, picking up a coat on the way, was soon in the street hurrying in the direction of the hall.

On arrival she rang the bell and asked for Mrs. Deering, who came to her in the little room into which she had been shown.

"I am so sorry to butt in like this," she said. "I do hope that you had finished dinner but as I told Mr. Borden, I don't often get brainwaves and I can't afford to waste them. I have got a sort of idea that I am on the right track. It was Mr. Borden who put me there but he is a bit off the mark. Could you possibly persuade Bob to see me for five minutes?"

"I suppose you think that he murdered Penelope," replied Agnes. "The parents obviously think so. The whole world seems to have gone mad."

"Haven't they? There is hardly anyone in this village who isn't suspecting their nearest and dearest of murder. But I am not suspecting Bob. For one thing, he is not my nearest and dearest, though of course I like him very much. Still, I simply must have a few moments alone with him, if you don't mind."

"Why should I mind?" Agnes asked, and she withdrew, to return shortly followed by Bob, who had on his face that sulky expression which Lupin had learned to expect from all her companions during the last few days. Agnes left them together.

"Bob, I am practically certain that Penelope committed suicide, and that you alone can help me prove it. I know you don't want to, but you might think of Dick and Betty."

"I thought it was all right about them," said Bob. "Dick was with Mum at a quarter to six, so he couldn't have got back and done it in the time, and they tell me that the maid swears Betty couldn't have done it either."

"Well, now they think it's you," said Lupin, feeling it was no time to be tactful, "and even if you don't mind being hung yourself you might think of your father and mother and Harry and all that sort of thing."

"But it has been proved that it wasn't suicide. There were no fingerprints on the gun."

"Betty wiped them off."

"Betty?"

"Yes, she saw someone out of the window and thought it was Dick, so she took it for granted that he had killed Penelope and wiped the gun, thinking they would find his fingerprints on it."

"It may have been me that she saw out of the window."

"Yes, I think it probably was but I don't believe you killed Penelope. I believe she committed suicide and I think I know why. But only you really know, so I have come to you."

"If Dick and Betty are cleared there is no need for me to speak."

"Don't be a fool, I tell you. Do you want to kill your father and mother? You must say what happened during that last interview, surely you see that?"

"I should have tried to save Dick, naturally, but I could not see how my evidence would have helped, because it was proved that it wasn't suicide."

"Now it's unproved again. One never knows what is going to happen next in this case. Dick and Betty may get suspected again, anything may happen. But do let us put all the cards on the table."

"If Penelope committed suicide, I murdered her."

"You mean you said or did something that caused her to take her life?"

Bob nodded, then buried his face in his hands. Lupin felt terribly sorry for him. After all, there were some things a man couldn't say about a woman but it must have been he who had dealt the final blow to Penelope's self-respect.

"It is ghastly," said Lupin. "I can quite understand that you don't want to talk about it. If it could be kept dark we would all help you but it can't—you must see that yourself. Somehow during the time that you were with her you said something or did something that made her lose her faith in herself—that is the only thing that would make her kill herself, and that is what I think happened."

"Then I am the murderer!"

Lupin waited patiently She lit a cigarette and looked at a picture of Highland cattle over the mantelpiece.

"I'd always adored Penelope," began Bob, in a husky voice. "I thought at one time she was going to marry my brother, and I was terribly disappointed when she didn't. Of course I was only a brat at the time and I didn't understand about it at all, but I had always envied Dick having such a sister, so when I thought she was going to be mine, too, it seemed too good to be true. And so it was.

"But still, she was always awfully good to me and as I grew up I still thought she was the most wonderful woman in the world. I made up my mind I should never get married because I would never meet anyone like her. I knew that she had given up the idea of marrying herself, because she wanted to devote her life to her brother and her father, and I looked on her as a saint. She wasn't only the most beautiful woman in the world, she was the most wonderful character, too.

"I saw Colonel Graeme at Mr. Stevenson's funeral. I had heard about him and I don't think I was at all jealous. I was just glad that she was going to be happy at last and I hoped that he was worthy of her.

"I heard a bit about Betty and Dick having quarreled. I never knew quite what had happened. Mother and Agnes talked about it a bit, but Mother is always very vague and Agnes isn't a talker. There seemed to be some idea that Betty had gone away because she didn't want Penelope to live with them. I couldn't understand it, because for one thing surely there was nothing left now to prevent Penelope marrying Graeme and having a home of her own. And in any case, she and Betty had always been such great friends that I shouldn't have been surprised if they had all decided to live together.

"I had always liked Betty awfully, but I got the idea that she must be behaving pretty rottenly. Surely it was no time to quarrel with Penelope, when she was so miserable at the death of her father. I saw her one day and she looked so sad I felt furious with Betty. And poor old Dick, too—he looked terribly down in the mouth. Then on Sunday—that Sunday—I saw Betty in church and I was shocked at the change in her. She had always been such a jolly little thing and now she looked absolutely wretched and years older. What had happened to change her?

"I went out for a walk that afternoon through the woods and I was just turning into a clearing when I heard voices and there were Penelope and Colonel Graeme. I was afraid they would see me and I leaped behind an oak tree. I guessed that he had brought her there to ask her to marry him. There was no reason now why she shouldn't be happy and I really was most frightfully bucked about it all. I don't mean that I have ever been one of those noble self-denying sort of chaps you read about but, you see, I don't think I had ever exactly been in love with Penelope. I mean I admired her more than anyone else in the world but I didn't really want to marry her myself."

"That's what I thought," said Lupin.

Bob had been pale but now he turned a bright red. "Good heavens!" he exclaimed. "I am sorry," he added lamely.

"Go on."

"Well, as I was saying, I really felt most awfully happy about it all, though I know it sounds a bit soft. But I thought of how Penelope had loved this fellow all this time and how she had given him up so as to devote herself to her father and now her father didn't need her any more and she had the satisfaction of knowing that she had been wonderful to him right up to the end and now she was going to be happy at last. Well, that is how it struck me.

"It was deuced awkward crouching behind that blooming oak with my hands over my ears and I had just shifted my position a bit when I heard a strange voice scream, 'Get out of here. I never want to see you again.' Without thinking I peered out and there was Penelope—but I shouldn't have recognized her as Penelope if I hadn't known it was, any more than I should have recognized her voice. I just caught a glimpse of Graeme and his face…"

Bob paused and passed his silk handkerchief over his forehead. "Phew," he said, "if ever a man looked like death he did. He legged it through the trees and I sank back behind the old oak. I felt as if I'd been sandbagged. I don't know how long I was there and when I looked out again Penelope had disappeared. I walked home. My thoughts were in a whirl, I couldn't forget Graeme's face, and I remembered Betty's face that morning, and then I thought of Penelope's face, mad with rage, and I realized that she wasn't a saint after all, and that probably she had done something to hurt Betty as she had done to Graeme.

"Oh, I didn't know what to think! I slunk into the house. I didn't feel like facing the family. I thought I'd go straight to the dining room and get myself a stiff drink. As I was passing the telephone the bell rang and I answered it mechanically, never guessing—"

"Was it Penelope?"

"Yes, she said she must see me at once, that it was urgent."

"I tried to make an excuse, then I felt that I must see her. Perhaps I had imagined what had happened in the wood, perhaps she wanted me to go after Charles—oh, I don't know. I was a fool, but I went."

"Was she in the garden when you got there?"

"Yes, in the orchard in a deck chair. She was looking just like herself. What I thought I had seen in the wood must have been a dream! She looked very pale, very fragile. She was sweet to me and started talking about what old friends we were, and then—then—"

"She asked you to marry her?"

"However did you know?"

"I guessed."

Bob buried his face in his hands. "She couldn't really have wanted to marry me. She had quarreled with Charles, and she only wanted to marry me to spite him. I thought of her as she had looked in the wood and—oh, I don't know, everything was in a muddle. The old Penelope had faded away, if you know what I mean. She would never have asked someone to marry her. I really don't know what I said or did, but she looked, she looked—"

"Angry?"

"No, more surprised. But she can't really have killed herself because I didn't want to marry her."

Lupin looked at Bob with tenderness and said, "That was just the last straw. She had quarreled with Charles, and he had told her what he really thought of her. He loved her, you know, but he always saw through her. He knew she wasn't really unselfish but he loved her just the same, only she wanted to be thought perfect. It wasn't really love she wanted but blind worship, and I suppose she thought she would get it from you. But you are not to blame, you couldn't possibly have married her."

"I don't know. Naturally I never guessed. Then I heard she was dead and I thought it was suicide, but even then I didn't think it could be because of me. I thought she had gone a bit dotty, that when I saw her in the wood and she looked so queer that was what it was—and then her asking me to marry her! It was all of a piece. Then there was the inquest and it came out about the fingerprints and that it couldn't have been suicide. I didn't know what to think. I thought of Graeme, of course, especially as he had disappeared. But it didn't seem like him to come sneaking back to shoot her. If he had strangled her in the wood it wouldn't have been so queer.

"But things looked awfully bad for Dick—I mean I knew things had been a bit strained, what with Betty and—well, after seeing Penelope in the wood I realized that perhaps it wasn't all Betty's fault. I don't know really what I thought, but I couldn't see how I could help Dick or naturally I would have said something. As it was I thought the least said the soonest mended, but I suppose the parents thought I'd done it. I'd been out all that afternoon and never told them where I had been and then I was pretty wretched about everything. I felt guilty and I expect I looked guilty. Anyway, I can never tell the police the whole story. How can I?"

"It is the only thing to be done. Look here, will you come and tell Mr. Borden? I left him at the Limes with Mrs. Dashwood. He was saying that he was afraid it was you who murdered Penelope, then suddenly everything jumped into place in my brain, if you can call it a brain. He is awfully decent and he will advise us."

When Bob and Lupin arrived at the Limes they found that the chief constable was sitting with Mrs. Dashwood and Mr. Borden. Lupin's manner was quieter than usual. "Bob has something he wants to say," she said. "But I think he would rather tell it to one person alone."

The chief constable had known Bob since he was a boy. "May we go into the library?" he asked Mrs. Dashwood, and the two left the room.

"You were right about it being Bob with Penelope," Lupin said to Mr. Borden, "and about his being the cause of her death in a way. But he did not ask her to marry him. She asked him to marry her."

The other two gazed at her in astonishment. She went on. "He had always adored her in a boyish sort of way and that was what she wanted. She did not want love in the ordinary human way. She wanted to be thought perfect, and Charles Graeme, who loved her, did not think her perfect.

Unfortunately, Bob was in the wood when she was having her quarrel with Charles, and for once he saw the real Penelope and it appalled him. In any case, I don't think be ever wanted to marry her.

"But she asked Bob to marry her and he refused. And she fell down from her pedestal. It must have been a terrible shock. That was when Dorothy saw her in the library. She must have gone to get the revolver and she did not look at all like herself.

"Penelope could not go on living once she had fallen from her pedestal, and that is why she died."

THE END

If you enjoyed this Lady Lupin mystery by Joan Coggin, the first two books in the series, *Who Killed the Curate?* (0-915230-44-5, $14.00) and *The Mystery at Orchard House* (0-915230-54-2, $14.95), are now available. The fourth and final Lupin mystery, *Dancing with Death* (0-9152130-62-3, $14.95), is due out in December 2003. Rue Morgue Press books are available wherever books are sold. A catalog of our current publications follows this page.

About The Rue Morgue Press

The Rue Morgue vintage mystery line is designed to bring back into print those books that were favorites of readers between the turn of the century and the 1960s. The editors welcome suggests for reprints. To receive our catalog or make suggestions, write The Rue Morgue Press, P.O. Box 4119, Boulder, Colorado (1-800-699-6214). The Rue Morgue Press tries to keep all of its titles in print, though some books may go temporarily out of print for up to six months.

Catalog of Rue Morgue Press titles November 2003

Titles are listed by author. All books are quality trade paperbacks measuring 9 by 6 inches, usually with full-color covers and printed on paper designed not to yellow or deteriorate. These are permanent books.

Joanna Cannan. The books by this English writer are among our most popular titles. Modern reviewers favorably compared our two Cannan reprints with the best books of the Golden Age of detective fiction. "Worthy of being discussed in the same breath with an Agatha Christie or a Josephine Tey."—Sally Fellows, *Mystery News.* "First-rate Golden Age detection with a likeable detective, a complex and believable murderer, and a level of style and craft that bears comparison with Sayers, Allingham, and Marsh."—Jon L. Breen, *Ellery Queen's Mystery Magazine*. Set in the late 1930s in a village that was a fictionalized version of Oxfordshire, both titles feature young Scotland Yard inspector Guy Northeast. *They Rang Up the Police* (0-915230-27-5, $14.00) and *Death at The Dog* (0-915230-23-2, $14.00).

Glyn Carr. The author is really Showell Styles, one of the foremost English mountain climbers of his era as well as one of that sport's most celebrated historians. Carr turned to crime fiction when he realized that mountains provided a ideal setting for committing murders. The 15 books featuring Shakespearean actor Abercrombie "Filthy" Lewker are set on peaks scattered around the globe, although the author returned again and again to his favorite climbs in Wales, where his first mystery, published in 1951, *Death on Milestone Buttress* (0-915230-29-1, $14.00), is set. Lewker is a marvelous Falstaffian character whose exploits have been praised by such discerning critics as Jacques Barzun and Wendell Hertig Taylor in *A Catalogue of Crime.*

Torrey Chanslor. *Our First Murder* (0-915230-50-X, $14.95). When a headless corpse is discovered in a Manhattan theatrical lodging house, who better to call in than the Beagle sisters? Sixty-five-year-old Amanda employs good old East Biddicut common sense to run the agency, while her younger sister Lutie prowls the streets and nightclubs of 1940 Manhattan looking for clues. It's their first murder case since inheriting the Beagle Private Detective Agency from their older brother, but you'd never know the sisters had spent all of their lives knitting and tending to their garden in a small, sleepy upstate New York town. Lutie is a real charmer, who learned her craft by reading scores of lurid detective novels borrowed from the East Biddicut Circulating Library. With her younger cousin Marthy in tow, Lutie is totally at ease as she questions suspects and orders vintage champagne. Of course, if trouble pops up, there's always that pearl-handled revolver tucked away in her purse. *Our First Murder* is a charming hybrid of the private eye, traditional, and cozy mystery, written in 1940 by a woman who earned two Caldecott nominations for her illustrations of children's books. *Our Second Murder* will be published early in 2004.

Clyde B. Clason. Clason has been praised not only for his elaborate plots and skillful use of the locked room gambit but also for his scholarship. He may be one of the few mystery authors—and no doubt the first—to provide a full bibliography of his sources. *The Man from Tibet* (0-915230-17-8, $14.00) is one of his best (selected in 2001 in *The History of Mystery* as one of the 25 great amateur detective novels of all time) and highly recommended by the dean of locked room mystery scholars, Robert Adey, as "highly original." It's also one of the first popular novels to make use of Tibetan culture. *Murder Gone Minoan* (0-915230-60-7, $14.95) is set on a channel island off the coast of Southern California where a Greek department store magnate has recreated a Minoan palace.

Joan Coggin. *Who Killed the Curate?* Meet Lady Lupin Lorrimer Hastings, the young, lovely, scatterbrained and kindhearted daughter of an earl, now the newlywed wife of the vicar of St. Marks Parish in Glanville, Sussex. When it comes to matters clerical, she literally doesn't know Jews from Jesuits and she's hopelessly at sea at meetings of the Mothers' Union, Girl Guides, or Temperance Society ,but she's determined to make husband Andrew proud of her—or, at least, not to embarrass him too badly. So when Andrew's curate is poisoned, Lady Lupin enlists the help of her old society pals, Duds and Tommy Lethbridge, as well as Andrew's nephew, a British secret service agent, to get at the truth. Lupin refuses to believe Diana Lloyd, the 38-year-old author of children's and detective stories, could have done the deed, and casts her net out over the other parishioners. All the suspects seem so nice, much more so than the victim, and Lupin announces she'll help the killer escape if only he or she confesses. Set at Christmas 1937 and first published in England in 1944, this is the first American appearance of *Who Killed the Curate?* "Marvelous."—*Deadly Pleasures.* "A complete delight."—*Reviewing the Evidence.* (0-915230-44-5, $14.00). The comic antics continue unabated in *The Mystery at Orchard House* (0-915230-54-2, $14.95), *Penelope Passes or Why Did She Die?* (0-915230-61-5, $14.95), and *Dancing with Death* (0-915230-62-3, $14.95, December 2003).

Manning Coles. The two English writers who collaborated as Coles are best known for those witty spy novels featuring Tommy Hambledon, but they also wrote four delightful—and funny—ghost novels. *The Far Traveller* (0-915230-35-6, $14.00) is a stand-alone novel in which a film company unknowingly hires the ghost of a long-dead German graf to play himself in a movie. "I laughed until I hurt. I liked it so much, I went back to page 1 and read it a second time."—Peggy Itzen, *Cozies, Capers & Crimes*. The other three books feature two cousins, one English, one American, and their spectral pet monkey who got a little drunk and tried to stop—futilely and fatally—a German advance outside a small French village during the 1870 Franco-Prussian War. Flash forward to the 1950s where this comic trio of friendly ghosts rematerialize to aid relatives in danger in *Brief Candles* (0-915230-24-0, 156 pages, $14.00), *Happy Returns* (0-915230-31-3, $14.00) and *Come and Go* (0-915230-34-8, $14.00).

Norbert Davis. There have been a lot of dogs in mystery fiction, from Baynard Kendrick's guide dog to Virginia Lanier's bloodhounds, but there's never been one quite like Carstairs. Doan, a short, chubby Los Angeles private eye, won Carstairs in a crap game, but there never is any question as to who the boss is in this relationship. Carstairs isn't just any Great Dane. He is so big that Doan figures he really ought to be considered another species. He scorns baby talk and belly rubs—unless administered by a pretty girl—and growls whenever Doan has a drink. His full name is Dougal's Laird Carstairs and as a sleuth he rarely barks up the wrong tree. He's down in Mexico with Doan, ostensibly to convince a missing fugitive that he would do well to stay put, in *The Mouse in the Mountain* (0-915230-41-0, $14.00), first published in 1943 and followed by two other Doan and Carstairs novels. A staff pick at The Sleuth of Baker Street in Toronto, Murder by the Book in Houston and The Poisoned Pen in Scottsdale. Four star review in *Romantic Times*. "A laugh a minute romp...hilarious dialogue and descriptions...utterly engaging, downright fun read...fetch this one! Highly recommended."—Michele A. Reed, *I Love a Mystery.* "Deft, charming...unique...one of my top ten all time favorite novels."—Ed Gorman, *Mystery Scene*. The second book, *Sally's in the Alley* (0-915230-46-1, $14.00), was equally well-received. *Publishers Weekly*: "Norbert Davis committed suicide in 1949, but his incomparable crime-fighting duo, Doan, the tippling private eye, and Carstairs, the huge and preternaturally clever Great Dane, march on in a re-release of the 1943 *Sally's in the Alley*. Doan's on a government-sponsored mission to find an ore deposit in the Mojave Desert...in an old-fashioned romp that matches its bloody crimes with belly laughs." The editor of *Mystery Scene* chimed in: "I love Craig Rice. Davis is her equal." "The funniest P.I. novel ever written."—*The Drood Review*. The raves continued for final book in the trilogy, *Oh, Murderer Mine* (0-915230-57-7, $14.00). "He touches the hardboiled markers but manages to run amok in a genre known for confinement. . .This book is just plain funny."—Ed Lin, *Forbes.com*.

Elizabeth Dean. In Emma Marsh Dean created one of the first independent female sleuths in the genre. Written in the screwball style of the 1930s, the Marsh books were described in a review in *Deadly Pleasures* by award-winning mystery writer Sujata Massey as a series that "froths over with the same effervescent humor as the best Hepburn-Grant films." *Murder is a Serious Business* (0-915230-28-3, $14.95), it's set in a Boston antique store just as the Great Depression is drawing to a close. *Murder a Mile High* (0-915230-39-9, $14.00), moves to the Central City Opera House in the Colorado mountains, where Emma has been summoned by am old chum, the opera's reigning diva. Emma not only has to find a murderer, she may also have to catch a Nazi spy. "Fascinating."—*Romantic Times.*

Constance & Gwenyth Little. These two Australian-born sisters from New Jersey have developed almost a cult following among mystery readers. Critic Diane Plumley, writing in *Dastardly Deeds*, called their 21 mysteries "celluloid comedy written on paper." Each book, published between 1938 and 1953, was a stand-alone, but there was no mistaking a Little heroine. She hated housework, wasn't averse to a little gold-digging (so long as she called the shots), and couldn't help antagonizing cops and potential beaux. The Rue Morgue Press intends to reprint all of their books. Currently available: *The Black Thumb* (0-915230-48-8, $14.00), *The Black Coat* (0-915230-40-2, $14.00), *Black Corridors* (0-915230-33-X, $14.00), *The Black Gloves* (0-915230-20-8, $14.00), *Black-Headed Pins* (0-915230-25-9, $14.00), *The Black Honeymoon* (0-915230-21-6, $14.00), *The Black Paw* (0-915230-37-2, $14.00), *The Black Stocking* (0-915230-30-5, $14.00), *Great Black Kanba* (0-915230-22-4, $14.00), *The Grey Mist Murders* (0-915230-26-7, $14.00), *The Black Eye* (0-915230-45-3,$14.00), *The Black Shrouds* (0-915230-52-6, $14.00), and *The Black Rustle* (0-915230-58-5, $14.00).

Marlys Millhiser. Our only non-vintage mystery, *The Mirror* (0-915230-15-1, $17.95) is our all-time bestselling book, now in a seventh printing. How could you not be intrigued by a novel in which "you find the main character marrying her own grandfather and giving birth to her own mother," as one reviewer put it of this supernatural, time-travel (sort of) piece of wonderful make-believe set both in the mountains above Boulder, Colorado, at the turn of the century and in the city itself in 1978. Internet book services list scores of rave reviews from readers who often call it the "best book I've ever read."

James Norman. The marvelously titled *Murder, Chop Chop* (0-915230-16-X, $13.00) is a wonderful example of the eccentric detective novel. "The book has the butter-wouldn't-melt-in-his-mouth cool of Rick in *Casablanca*."—*The Rocky Mountain News*. "Amuses the reader no end."—*Mystery News*. "This long out-of-print masterpiece is intricately plotted, full of eccentric characters and very humorous indeed. Highly recommended."—*Mysteries by Mail*. Meet Gimiendo Hernandez Quinto, a gigantic Mexican who once rode with Pancho Villa and who now trains *guerrilleros* for the Nationalist Chinese government when he isn't solving murders. At his side is a beautiful Eurasian known as Mountain of Virtue, a woman as dangerous to men as she is irresistible. First published in 1942.

Sheila Pim. *Ellery Queen's Mystery Magazine* said of these wonderful Irish village mysteries that Pim "depicts with style and humor everyday life." *Booklist* said they were in "the best tradition of Agatha Christie." Beekeeper Edward Gildea uses his knowledge of bees and plants to good use in *A Hive of Suspects* (0-915230-38-0, $14.00). *Creeping Venom* (0-915230-42-9, $14.00) blends politics and religion into a deadly mixture. *A Brush with Death* (0-915230-49-6, $14.00) grafts a clever art scam onto the stem of a gardening mystery.

Craig Rice. *Home Sweet Homicide*. This marvelously funny and utterly charming tale (set in 1942 and first published in 1944) of three children who "help" their widowed mystery writer mother solve a real-life murder and nab a handsome cop boyfriend along the way made just about every list of the best mysteries for the first half of the 20th century, including the Haycraft-Queen Cornerstone list (probably the most prestigious honor roll in the history of crime fiction), James Sandoe's *Reader's Guide to Crime,* and Melvyn Barnes' *Murder in Print.* Rice was of course best known for her screwball mystery comedies featuring Chicago criminal attorney John J. Malone. *Home Sweet Homicide* is a delightful cozy mystery partially based on Rice's own home life. Rice, the first mystery writer to appear on the cover of *Time*, died in 1957 at the age of 49. 0-915230-53-4, $14.95

Charlotte Murray Russell. Spinster sleuth Jane Amanda Edwards tangles with a murderer and Nazi spies in *The Message of the Mute Dog* (0-915230-43-7, $14.00), a culinary cozy set just before Pearl Harbor. "Perhaps the mother of today's cozy."—*The Mystery Reader.*

Sarsfield, Maureen. These two mysteries featuring Inspector Lane Parry of Scotland Yard are among our most popular books. Both are set in Sussex. *Murder at Shots Hall* (0-915230-55-8, $14.95) features Flikka Ashley, a thirtyish sculptor with a past she would prefer remain hidden. It was originally published as *Green December Fills the Graveyard* in 1945. Parry is back in Sussex, trapped by a blizzard at a country hotel where a war hero has been pushed out of a window to his death in *Murder at Beechlands* (0-915230-56-9, $14.95). First published in 1948 in England as *A Party for None* and in the U.S. as *A Party for Lawty.* The owner of Houston's Murder by the Book called these two books the best publications from The Rue Morgue Press.

Juanita Sheridan. Sheridan was one of the most colorful figures in the history of detective fiction, as you can see from the introduction to *The Chinese Chop* (0-915230-32-1, 155 pages, $14.00). Her books are equally colorful, as well as examples of how mysteries with female protagonists began changing after World War II. The postwar housing crunch finds Janice Cameron, newly arrived in New York City from Hawaii, without a place to live until she answers an ad for a roommate. It turns out the advertiser is an acquaintance from Hawaii, Lily Wu. First published in 1949, this ground-breaking book was the first of four to feature Lily and be told by her Watson, Janice, a first-time novelist. "Highly recommended."—*I Love a Mystery.* "Puts to lie the common misconception that strong, self-reliant, non-spinster-or-comic sleuths didn't appear on the scene until the 1970s."—*Ellery Queen's Mystery Magazine.* The first book in the series to be set in Hawaii is *The Kahuna Killer* (0-915230-47-X, $14.00). " Originally published five decades ago (though it doesn't feel like it), this detective story featuring charming Chinese sleuth Lily Wu has the friends and foster sisters investigating mysterious events—blood on an ancient altar, pagan rites, and the appearance of a kahuna (a witch doctor)—and the death of a sultry hula girl in 1950s Oahu."—*Publishers Weekly.* Third in the series is *The Mamo Murders* (0915230-51-8, $14.00), set on a Maui cattle ranch. The final book in the quartet, *The Waikiki Widow* (0-915230-59-3, $14.00) is set in Honolulu tea industry.